## ON EARTH—

Janna Brill and Mama Maxwell find themselves up against the most challenging case of their law enforcement career, as they follow the trail of the corpse kidnappers and discover a secret that could change the power balance of the world.

## IN SPACE—

Brill and Maxwell stumble into a technological maze of trouble and treachery, as they battle a faceless opponent in a desperate attempt to discover the truth surrounding the Spider— before its creators can weave a web not even the united forces of Earth can hope to unravel.

# SPIDER PLAY

## LEE KILLOUGH

**POPULAR LIBRARY**

An Imprint of Warner Books, Inc.

A Warner Communications Company

POPULAR LIBRARY EDITION

Copyright © 1986 by Lee Killough
All rights reserved

Popular Library® and Questar® are registered trademarks of
Warner Books, Inc.

Cover art by Michael Herring

Popular Library books are published by
Warner Books, Inc.
666 Fifth Avenue
New York, N.Y. 10103

W A Warner Communications Company

Printed in the United States of America

First Printing: July, 1986

10  9  8  7  6  5  4  3  2  1

For Pat, my best critic and cheerleader, and for one of my favorite real-life leos, Bob Dickerson.

# PROLOGUE

The device bore little physical resemblance to a real spider. The long, flat, mechanical body on the monitor screen looked more like some gigantic centipede as it crawled in a spiral path around a suspended cylindrical frame, an embryo centipede trying to avoid entanglement in its umbilical cord. Laboratory lights reflected dully off matte-surfaced plastic and ceramic. It acted like a spider, though. Dark strands flowed out behind the body, strands that wove together into a continuous sheet, clothing the framework in midnight. The watcher before the monitor stood with arms folded, fascinated.

It obviously fascinated the coverall-clad technicians around it too. They circled the construct, holding on to the frame's guy wires for stability as they made notes on their clipboards and chattered back and forth. One young woman reached down to run exploratory fingers over the spider's produce, leaving her pen drifting in the air beside her, but smoothly retrieved it before the air currents carried it out of reach. None of them looked toward the camera. Naturally. The watcher grinned. None of them knew it was there.

"You aren't the only spinner of webs here," the watcher whispered at the spider on the monitor. "Only, mine are bigger than yours. Soon the whole solar system will feel the effects of them."

And the watcher carefully deactivated the secret camera, returning the monitor to normal surveillance before floating off to tend the newest strand of that web.

# CHAPTER
# ONE

<u>**Wednesday, January 24. 10:00:00 hours.**</u>

The web grew across the corner of the Shawnee County Police Department's Crimes Against Persons squad room. Picking her way delicately along the strands already laid, the spider added more filaments, filling in the pattern of gray gossamer stretching from the newscanner control box on the shelf above the caff urn up to the screen hanging on the wall, broadcasting its images of the world to oblivious leos—law enforcement officers. The spider's work had not escaped notice, however.

Sergeant Mahlon Maxwell, better known as "Mama" by his colleagues, said dreamily, "Isn't it exquisite?"

Staring from the web to her partner, Sergeant Janna Brill hissed in exasperation. "*This* is why you've been standing here for ten minutes while I worked alone on reports?"

And to think she had been concerned about him when she realized how long he had been gone and looked around from the dictyper to see him standing in a trance with his hand on the tap of the caff urn. He looked like a statue . . . or rather, she had reflected, some impressionistic representation of a human sculpted in dutch chocolate and drawn out to grotesquely lanky proportions surpassing even her own sinewy-lean hundred and eighty-three centimeters. She frowned. Lately he had been unusually quiet and distant. What was wrong . . . woman trouble again, or could he be flashing back? She had never seen Mama use recreational drugs, not even those accepted by the most conservative leos, but perhaps there had been something used beyond safe limits in the past?

"Mama?" She pitched her voice to carry above the din of buzzing phones and overlapping conversations between investigators and citizens in varying stages of irritation or anxiety.

He did not appear to hear. The pattern of light reflection did not change on his egg-bald scalp. No fold shifted in the fluorescent red-and-orange jumpsuit. Janna pushed away from the row of dictypers to hurry across the room. "Mama!" She touched his shoulder.

He finally moved, pushing his glasses up his nose. "Look, bibi." He pointed out the spiderweb.

All Janna's concern evaporated with his remark on the aesthetic value of the spider's creation. Exquisite? she thought. *He* would look exquisite . . . on the floor with the soles of her thigh boots in his face.

How could she ever have forgotten that her partner was brainbent, wickers, totally over the brainbow? Twice before he had made investigator and twice before had been busted back to uniform; between he had used his night-school law degree to defend other officers against disciplinary actions and had been shuffled through every division in the county for such infamous escapades as switching his duty weapon for an old-fashioned, forbidden firearm and managing to lock himself and a female partner in the back of their patrol unit when they climbed in for a game of Grope and Tumble.

"Mahlon Sumner Maxwell," she hissed, "being partners means we share the work of this job, in case you've forgotten, and that includes *all* of it, including the paperwork, not just 'the thrill of the chase.'"

His eyes rolled. "You've certainly gotten bitchy since Sid married the man of his dreams and moved out."

A spasm of guilt momentarily overwhelmed her anger. Had she? Well, maybe, but damn it, she and the assistant medical examiner had cohabed for nearly six years and been like sisters. The apartment felt desolate without his warmth and humor . . . without someone who cared whether she came home or not.

Then anger hissed back through her. "I'm going to be even bitchier if I have to keep talking at that damn dictyper alone. While we've got this little piece of the arctic"—she waved toward the swirl of white beyond the window slits—"keeping Topeka's deeks off the street for a change, let's make the most of it, huh? You can admire nature on your own time!" She reached out to brush away the web.

A chocolate hand caught her wrist. "Hey, bibi, she's not doing any harm, just looking for a place out of the cold, like everyone with sense."

"Except them." Janna nodded toward the newscanner screen, where Pennsylvania's Governor John Granville Hershey wore a presidential hopeful's smile amid the drifts of New Hampshire.

"Everyone with sense, I said."

Janna had to grin.

"President Lipp's African policy is a disaster," Hershey's resonant voice said, "totally failing to recognize that we are no longer dealing with a tribal mentality. The Union of African Nations represents a unity beyond even nationalism, and without delicate handling the UAN could become to the export of African resources what OPEC was to Mideast oil in the last century."

Mama straightened the containers of stirrers and sugar and cream substitutes into an even line beside the urn, then pushed his glasses up his nose, grimacing. "Much as I hate to agree with any politician, he's right. According to the *Wall Street Journal*, eighty-three percent of the mining companies on the African continent are owned by a single corporation, Uwezo— which means 'power' in Swahili—and its officers are high officials in a dozen different African governments."

Surprise wiped away the last of Janna's irritation. When

did Mama find the time for the *Wall Street Journal*? He must watch the *Journal* channel of his newscanner while he ate breakfast and prepared for bed.

"It's nice that some of us have slack time," a voice said behind Janna.

She swore silently as she recognized the voice, Pass-the-Word Morello, the squad clerk. Was he looking for an idle investigator to hand a new assignment to? Why had she ever left the dictyper? "It isn't slack time," she said, turning to look down at him. "It's just a caff break. We still have a mountain of reports to finish."

Morello's foxy face twisted into a smirk. "Crimes Against Property is still out on the street accumulating report material though. Not all of the criminal element is huddling inside by heaters."

Suddenly Janna understood the smirk and the gleam in Morello's eyes. He had a story he was dying to tell. Sometimes she wondered what Morello's home life was like. Word was he and his wife lived with his wife's mother and two sisters. Did he talk so much here in compensation for not being able to put a word in, or was home one endless, ecstatic gossip session, with a chance to repeat and embellish all the stories from here for a whole circle of listeners?

"All right, I'll bite. What's Crimes Against Property involved in?" she asked.

Morello grinned. "A hearse hijacking."

Mama spun away from the spider and the half-frozen, but determined, smiles of the candidates on the newscanner. "What!"

The foxy grin broadened. "Driven by Ms. Beta Nafsinger from the Nafsinger Mortuary. You've probably seen their TV ads."

Janna had. A family business, the smoothly solemn man sitting amid his circle of five solemn daughters with Greek-alphabet names.

"Nafsinger was on South Topeka Avenue yesterday morning, and while she was floating at idle for a light, four members of a street gang jerked open the door, pushed her out, and sailed off with the hearse."

Mama glanced toward the window slit and pushed his glasses up his nose, frowning. "In this weather? Which gang?"

"They wore stars painted around their eyes."

That would be the Orions, then, though South Topeka Avenue was a bit out of their Oakland territory. Which concerned Janna less than the sudden white-rimmed gleam of Mama's eyes. That look always preceded a wild leap over the brainbow. Thank god the hijacked hearse belonged to Crimes Against Property and not this squad. "Interesting. You let us know how the case comes out."

Morello smirked again. "You tell me. Lieutenant Vradel wants to see you in his office."

Janna glared at him. "Damn you, Morello. How can this hearse possibly have anything to do with Crimes Against Persons?"

Morello shrugged, grinning.

Hissing, Janna turned away and stalked across the room toward Hari Vradel's office.

The burly squad commander had company. Lieutenant Dominic Applegate from Crimes Against Property sat in one of the chairs by the desk, with two of his investigators leaning against the wall behind him, Galen Quist and Teda "Teddybear" Roos. The nickname came from that blue-eyed, freckled, cuddly look, though Lowell Danner from Juvenile reported that Roos could rip a man's head off if she wanted. Rumor was that she and her partner spent all their time together, on and off duty, but not counting coup. According to Pass-the-Word Morello, they had tried sleeping together but found each other such poor lovers that they stuck to what they really wanted to do, anyway: tinker with Quist's motorcycle.

Applegate and the two investigators stared as she and Mama came in.

It was a reaction Janna had grown used to. People not

around Mama all the time tended to be restartled at every meeting by his taste in clothes and by his gleaming scalp, which, except for the lack of paint or tattoos, made him look more like a tripper who had blundered down the hall from Narcotics than a leo. Everyone else in the room had chosen a more conservative appearance, jumpsuits or tabard-over-bodysuit combinations in subdued checks and diagonal stripes. The men sported mustaches, and the whole group wore full heads of hair curled in the tight mop used so often by leos meeting the requirement for hair that would not interfere with their vision. The style had become known as a "lion's mane." On top of everything else, there was Janna's smoky blondness to contrast with Mama's darkness.

"You know Sergeant Brill and Sergeant Maxwell, don't you?" Vradel asked his visitors.

"Oh, yes." Applegate's grimace at Mama indicated he knew Janna's partner far better than he wanted to. "Still looking at the world through windows, I see."

Mama smiled easily. "I still can't tolerate contact lenses."

"Both Brill and Maxwell have experience with the Oakland area and its gangs," Vradel said. "Brill, Maxwell . . . Lieutenant Applegate would like our help locating the Orions who jacked the hearse yesterday. I'm assuming that with Morello outside you're already aware what hearse." He leaned across the desk to hand them a report form, then picked up a pencil and began sketching idly on his blotter. "That's the stolen vehicle report filed by the victim."

Janna read through it quickly with Mama breathing down her neck. The report went into details of the appearance and conversation of the three males and one female who had taken the hearse, but that only confirmed their identity as Orions and told her nothing new. "Why is Crimes Against Persons being brought into this? The driver wasn't hurt." The tone of Nafsinger's statement indicated more outrage than pain.

Mama took the report from her and laid it on the corner of the desk, meticulously lining the pages up parallel to and at equal distances from both sides of the corner. "Maybe it has to do with who else was in the hearse, bibi."

Oh, god, no, she thought with an inward groan, but a quick glance at Vradel found the squad commander nodding. The outline of a space shuttle grew under the point of his pencil. "Perhaps you ought to explain, Dom."

Applegate picked up his report from the desk. "Nafsinger states she was on her way back from Forbes Field, but what she forgot in her zeal to remember exactly what her assailants looked like was that she had been to Forbes to collect a body—the corpse of one John Paul Chenoweth, an employee of the Lanour–Tenning Corporation—from their space platform. He died Saturday when his pressure suit ripped while working on construction of an addition to the station. His body was to be left at the Nafsinger Mortuary until his family made more formal arrangements for it."

Janna lifted a brow. "I take it this particular information comes from sources other than Ms. Nafsinger, then."

Applegate tugged at the drooping ends of his handlebar mustache. Behind him, Quist and Roos exchanged glances and grinned. "The information comes from Mr. Leonard Fontana, director of the Lanour platform. Mr. Fontana apparently feels very serious about his responsibility to Lanour's employees, living and dead. He called the mortuary from the platform this morning to see if the Chenoweth family had contacted them yet."

"And he wasn't at all happy to find Chenoweth had . . . gone astray," Roos murmured.

Applegate pretended not to hear. "After talking to the mortuary, Fontana made a second call . . . to *our* director, and Paget called me. He suggested we make this a multisquad investigation." He frowned toward Mama. "I really don't expect to accomplish any more than Quist and Roos could alone, but it'll look like a good-faith effort to the brass and Lanour."

The face Vradel was sketching developed a scowl, but he

said only, "Oh, I think we can do better than that, Dom. Four pairs of legs always cover more ground than two."

Mama murmured in Janna's ear, "I didn't know Lanour carried this much clout way out here in Kansas."

"I still don't understand why we should be excited." She glanced from Applegate to Vradel. "The Orions will dump the hearse as soon as they've had their fun, and Nafsinger will have it and the body back, though the hearse will probably be stripped." They all ought to know that.

"They hadn't abandoned it by evening as far as we can tell," Quist said sourly.

Vradel laid down the pencil to chew on a corner of his mustache. "If it's in a snowbank, we might not find it until this junk melts, which could be late March the way the weather bureau is talking." He paused. "Some kinds of heat don't warm up a winter at all."

A glint in his eyes, like sunlight shining on ice, told Janna that he would have said something quite different if they had been alone, like, "Stop arguing and go wrap those Orions. Find that body!" But he would not chew on them in front of visiting troops any more than he would openly criticize a fellow lieutenant's snide crack in the earshot of subordinate officers.

Janna did not wait for stronger phrasing. Digging into the sleeve pocket of her jumpsuit for vending tokens, she tossed a couple into the cup on the corner of Vradel's desk and headed out the door with Mama. Like everyone in the squad, she rarely paid attention to the newscanner and could not even remember where it came from, whether it had been a gift, abandoned, or recovered stolen property "forgotten" to be turned into the property room, but along with everyone else she contributed tokens Vradel could redeem for credit to pay Newservices, Inc., for the subscription.

Quist and Roos followed her out of Vradel's office.

Outside, the scanner was still covering presidential candidates. Senator Scott Early frowned gravely into the camera.

"Part of this nation's metal shortage must be attributed to the colonial movement. How can we who choose to remain loyal to Earth rather than abandon her in her difficulties to flee to the stars possibly build a fleet to mine the asteroids when the colonists take so much metal with them in the form of tractors, choppers, and ships' hulls? It should be the sacred duty of the next president to institute a moratorium on colony ship-building until such time as the people of this nation have enough metal from asteroid or sea-bottom mining that we need no longer depend on African resources."

Mama's eyes gleamed. "Bibi, this hearse—" he began.

Janna tried to head him off. "Just what kind of trouble did you have with Applegate?"

Roos said, "The lieutenant told us that when he was a uniformed sergeant in the Gage division, Maxwell put static-adhesive plastic over the solar receptors on his patrol car." She grinned wickedly. "He didn't say so, but I got the impression that what really popped him was cursing and kicking the car for ten or fifteen minutes before it occurred to him to switch to battery power."

Janna grinned, too, but Mama protested indignantly. "*I* didn't do it!" His expression went thoughtful. "But that explains some things. I didn't think he would stay so mad about the shotgun."

"Shotgun?" Quist said.

Mama nodded. "I happened to trigger my shotgun in the course of checking it one time. Unfortunately, being in the watch car, it blew a hole in the roof and took off part of the light rail. The sound startled my partner so much, she ran the car into a power pole and wrecked it. We happened to be going rather fast at the time, chasing some deeks who'd just boosted a jewelry store." Mama pushed his glasses up his nose. "But this hearse . . . it's damn strange, a street gang joyriding in this weather. It's even stranger that they'd take a *hearse*, though. I'd expect them to go after something more like a Vulcan or a Cheetah." He shook his head. "Something's wrong here. The whole thing smells. It stinks clear to the orbit of the Lanour platform."

Janna had to agree that the Orions were not behaving very characteristically, but the orbit she was worried about was the one Mama seemed about to go into . . . dragging her with him.

# CHAPTER
# TWO

<u>**Wednesday, January 24. 10:30:00 hours.**</u>

"God, I hate going out in this shit again." The garage gave Quist's voice a hollow boom. "Sometimes I wonder why I ever became a leo."

"You wanted a legal way to race a Harley down city streets." Roos lifted her brows at Janna and Mama. "Well, how shall we divide Oakland?"

"What did you cover yesterday?" Janna asked.

"Nafsinger said that bibi called one of the jons 'Pluto,' so we went looking for Kiel Jerrett."

Janna nodded. Jerrett being the Orion leader and Pluto his street name.

"We checked his girlfriend's apartment, and then his mother's place. We checked Orion hangouts. No Pluto. No Orion at all."

"They all crawled down their roach holes," Quist growled.

Roos did not look at him. "So, suggestions, anyone?"

"I say check the salvage yards," Quist said. "In case Jerrett is selling the parts from the hearse."

Mama pursed his lips. "He's not light-witted enough to do that. Let's hit all the obvious places again. He may figure you won't be back. And I'd go for the bibi first." He grinned. "Weather like this, if I weren't working, I'd be warding off the cold with shared bodily warmth."

Roos glanced inquiringly at her partner.

He frowned. "I don't know about all of us going to one place. We'll have a better chance if we spread out and hit all his holes at once."

"The trouble with Jerrett isn't finding him; it's _keeping_ the slippery deek," Mama said.

Quist considered, then nodded. "Sunny Kriegh lives at 520 North Twiss."

They headed for their cars, both Datsun–Ford Monitors like all the others in the row, though Mama had somehow managed to locate and gain assignment of a prussian-red vehicle among the collection of tans, blues, and greens. Quist and Roos eyed the car with envy as Janna and Mama slid into it and across the spreading airfoil skirt that gave the car a shape some department wit had dubbed "bullet on the half shell."

"See you in Oakland," Roos said.

One thing about floatcars, Janna reflected as the Monitor lifted off its parking rollers and sailed up the garage ramp onto Van Buren, they did not have to wait for snowplows to clear the streets after a winter storm. The air cushions created by the fans just carried them over the drifts.

Once out of the dim garage, Mama switched from batteries to direct sun power and turned south toward Sixth Avenue, grimacing as the car bucked in the wind.

Janna switched on the car radio and tapped her button radio as she plugged it into her left ear. "Indian Thirty, Capitol. We're activating."

"I have your Twenty on the board, Indian Thirty," the dispatcher's flat voice replied in stereo from the car radio and ear button.

Janna also keyed in the Oakland division frequency before settling back in her seat. She and Mama might lose track of each other in a chase or canvassing Oakland, but if they ran into trouble, the transponders in the car and the ear buttons that broadcasted their locations to Dispatch's board would let help find them fast. The transponders would locate them even when they did not care to be found.

The voices of dispatchers from both divisions murmured in her ear, sometimes overlapping. Because of the duplex system, however, she could not hear the officers' replies.

"Beta Oakland Twelve, see the woman Galaxy Lane, the brown house." After a pause the dispatcher continued, "Brown house is all the description she gave. Check the area. She said she would be there waiting."

Mama turned the car onto Sixth Avenue, heading east past the downtown area and over I-70 into Oakland. Twentieth-century buildings of age-darkened brick with old-fashioned rectangular windows stood between newer structures of buff-colored native sandstone with windows of the energy-efficient slit design in one-, two-, and three-slit groupings. But even the oldest buildings' roofs sported a row of the honeycomb-looking solar panels made up of the solar conversion cells Mr. Edward Lamar Simon had perfected forty years ago, turning light into a truly efficient energy source.

Mama said, "You miss Sid, don't you?"

Janna grimaced. For all the times her partner seemed totally oblivious to everyone beyond himself, other times he read her very well indeed. She did not feel like baring her soul to him, however. "What about you? What's your problem these days?"

"Alpha Oakland Eighteen, report your Twenty. Your transponders do not register on the board. Do you have a malfunction I should report to the supervisor?" After a pause the dispatcher continued, "Disregard last signal. You're now activated."

Mama chuckled. "Isn't it amazing how fast a 'malfunctioning' transponder is cured with a threat to notify the supervisor?"

So he did not want to talk, either. Janna sucked in her lower lip wryly. Maybe both of them were due for a chat with Schnauzer Venn, the department tick tech.

In Oakland the streets looked untouched since the last snowfall. A few cars sat with only their airfoil skirts covered, but mounds marked where other cars with no garage to protect them had been incapacitated by the bitter cold earlier in the month. They now sat buried, waiting for a thaw before their owners made another try at starting them, if even warm weather would help. The tanglewood yards and turn-of-the-century houses bore testimony to oppressive poverty . . . roofs sagging, plastic panel siding warped and cracked. Under the snow the cars were probably sagging and rusting too.

Back in the early part of the century some city council had tried to fight back at the Oakland decline by putting up module town houses along North Twiss. Once the staggered rows with their slit windows and angular roofs topped with panels of Simon cells must have looked stylish. Now, however, many of the solar panels were cracked. Seams between the modules gaped, many of the window slits had been boarded up, and wood-grained plastic railings on second-floor balconies sagged, broken. The spray-on plastic siding hung peeling in long, faded strips that rustled in the wind like dead leaves. Not even the alpine charm of the snow and icicles could hide the sad ugliness.

Mama parked the Monitor behind Quist and Roos near the end of the block, well away from 520's window slits. Climbing out, the four of them conferred with backs turned to the sting of the north wind. "Who goes to the door?"

"Since you and Quist came yesterday, why don't one of you knock today?" Janna said. "The other can go around to the back door." She turned enough to eye the row of balconies stretching down the length of the building. "Mama and I will cover the ends."

Behind his glasses, Mama's eyes regarded her with reproach. "Do we draw straws to see who takes the north side?"

Janna grinned. "Let the Oakland dispatcher decide. If the next call is for an even-number car, the north end is yours, partner."

And the voice of the Oakland dispatcher promptly murmured in her ear, "Beta Oakland Eleven, see the woman, 202 South Lime, the apartment in back. A co-wife is refusing to vacate after cancellation of the marriage contract."

"Damn!"

Janna trudged north well ahead of Roos, huddling deep in her jacket, hands jammed into her pockets. One problem with not plowing streets was that it left nowhere clear to walk when the residents felt unmoved to shovel their walks. She waded through knee-deep snow all the way up the block and across the lawn area to the end of the building, circling wide so her tracks would not be immediately obvious to someone on the end balcony. Around the corner, she stood shivering, keeping the hood pulled closed around her face. The wind leaked in through the opening to sting her nose and cheeks, anyway.

"Beta Oakland Three, your 10-28 is on a 2072 Volkswagen Moth, registered to an Erica Friesen-Yager and Dara Yager-Friesen of 1715 Downs Road."

Oh, to be back on patrol right now, snug in the warmth of a watch car, Janna thought with longing, or anywhere but here with cold seeping through the soles of her boots. She stamped her feet, swearing silently. How long did it take Roos to knock on the door, anyway? If something did not happen soon, she would freeze solid. The department swatbots searched buildings and defused bombs. One ought to be programmed to wait in snowdrifts with a microfilament-mesh net for throwing over rabbiting fugitives.

"Alpha Oakland Twenty, contact management, Drug World, Belmont Mall, reference individual attempting to obtain heroin with an expired addict card."

Then around the front of the building someone swore, and feet thudded on a balcony floor. A split second later Mama's voice shouted, "Police! Stop!"

Janna peeked around the corner. She could not see who was on the balconies, but Mama plowed through the drifts

in front of the building, gun in hand, the long, thin barrel of
the needler aimed upward.

Janna jerked back out of sight. It was easy to imagine what
had happened. Jerrett, thinking to leave the apartment by
climbing from balcony to balcony along the route that Janna
had anticipated, had been headed toward the south end when
either something made him suspicious or Mama looked around
the corner at the wrong moment. Jerrett had reversed and was
now coming in her direction.

The thud of leaping feet and the plop of snow and icicles
knocked from railings marked his progress. Janna forgot the
cold in a fiery wash of adrenaline. Was he armed? She felt
inside the top of her thigh boot for the gun she had holstered
there.

Snow fell just around the corner, followed by the drop of
something heavier, then a figure hurtled past her, a male with
his face and depilated head covered with bright colors. A
bare chest showed under his half-opened jacket.

Janna raised the needler. "Freeze, Pluto."

Awareness of the snowball came an instant too late. His
arm swung, and the handful of snow he must have scooped
up along the way struck her square in the face.

Instinctive reflexes snapped her eyes shut just in time to
protect them, but training sent her diving blind toward the
last location in which she had seen Jerrett. The slick synthetic
of his jacket slid from under her hands. She grabbed at it,
throwing her arms around the form, and her momentum carried both of them down to land rolling in the snow. Jerrett
writhed. An arm jerked. With another surge of adrenaline,
Janna heard the hissing *snick* of a switchblade opening. She
used their roll to carry him under her, pinning his knife arm,
then released her grip with her arms and jackknifed to land
with knees between his shoulder blades and in the small of
his back and the muzzle of the Starke against his neck.

"Relax, jon." She wiped her eyes clear.

"Or you'll shoot me full of percurare and leave me paralyzed here in the snow to catch pneumonia?" He snorted. "That's the only way you can hang on to me, isn't it, puss?"

Mama waded up to them. "Are you so sure she's carrying percurare? We've had explosive needles okayed as ammunition now too."

If only, Janna reflected wistfully, but Jerrett went very still and craned his neck around to peer up at her and the needler, his eyes white-rimmed in the center of four-pointed scarlet stars. "Explosive needles? You're off your tick."

"No, no," Mama said. "*I'm* the one who's off my tick. She's just a mean bitch of a she-lion." As Janna backed off Jerrett and hauled him to his feet by the collar of his jacket, Mama patted him down and took not only the knife but also a spool of fine wire he found in one jacket pocket.

Microfilament! Anger flared in Janna. Strung across an opening where someone would hit it, say a leo on a chase, the wire could cut legs, or a throat, to the bone before its victim realized what was happening. Her previous partner had been blinded by microfilament. She hated it and anyone who used it. Her finger tightened on the Starke's trigger with longing to put a few too many needles into Jerrett and leave him suffocating with his chest muscles paralyzed.

Mama's eyes flashed, too, but he said nothing, just stepped back, pocketed the wire, and began cleaning his nails with the knife. He looked nonchalant, though his hands must have been freezing. "That's a nice jacket, Pluto. One of the new no-weight, superinsulating mountaineering/ski models, isn't it? I wish I were underprivileged so the government would give me coupons for clothes like that."

"Or did you pay for it with the profits from moonlight requisitioning?" Janna snapped.

"I don't know what the hell you're talking about, puss." The chatter of Jerrett's teeth spoiled the sneer, though.

"Stripped parts and, in particular, parts stripped from a hearse."

"You ain't making any sense at all." A shiver racked his

body. "It must be the temperature . . . you know, like lizards and snakes slow down in the cold? Maybe if we go inside, your brains will warm up and start working again."

"Why, thank you," Mama said. "See, bibi, I told you he'd be a gracious host. Lead the way, Mr. Jerrett."

Quist met them at the door. Behind him lay a living room furnished with tip-over occasional table/chairs and molded-foam easy chairs covered in fake fur. Roos sat on a scarlet couch with a young woman whose face and head—depilated except for a long blond horsetail on top—carried the same colorful star designs as Jerrett's. Sullen eyes, with red stars surrounded by wide borders of yellow, then blue, watched the investigators. The painted-on fit of Kriegh's canary body-suit left little of her anatomy to the imagination, but it was not transparent enough to tell whether her torso also carried the planet and comet tattoos the open jacket revealed on Jerrett's chest.

"Tell us what you've done with the hearse, Jerrett," Quist said.

Jerrett's lip curled. "You got frostbite of the brain too? I don't know nothin' about any hearse."

"Who has the frostbite?" Janna said. Reaching inside her jacket, she tapped on the microcorder in the breast pocket of her jumpsuit. "Yesterday morning, Tuesday, January twenty-third, your people jacked a hearse, license number RSN 405, on South Topeka Avenue. The driver described you exactly and heard your fem friend call you by name. You're lion meat, Jerrett."

Jerrett flung up his garish head. "Not me, leo. I was here all day, wasn't I, star?" he asked Kriegh.

"All day, Pluto." She glared defiantly at the leos.

"Maybe I did hear something yesterday about a hearse, but what would I be doing jacking anything in this weather? I like my fun in the sun, and . . . a hearse? Shit, I got a whole lot better taste than that. If I take a car, I want something top dink, like a Vulcan or a Jaguar. I don't go downstreet."

Mama sent Janna a didn't-I-tell-you smirk.

"Someone else took the hearse and just wants me blamed for it."

"Why?" Roos demanded. "Who?"

Jerrett shrugged. "Anyone. Everyone envies the Orions."

"It can't be the Bolos," Quist said. "They couldn't paint over their faces heavy enough to cover up their rivet and steel-plate tattoos."

"It couldn't be the Simbas or Samurais, either," Janna said. "The jackers were Caucasian."

"Check the Toros," Kriegh said. "Wearing paint, the taco squad could almost pass as human."

Jerrett smirked. "That's good, star. I'll have to remember that. Did you ever think it might be the Pirates? South Topeka runs through their turf. But how should I know who might have done it? You're the great detectives. It's your job to track down criminals and find who's trying to frame innocent citizens."

"Innocent," Quist snorted. "We'll see how innocent you are. Put on a shirt and let's go downtown where some people can look at you."

Jerrett frowned. "I want a lawyer."

"Sure," Janna said, "though I don't know why. We aren't arresting you. Aren't you just being a good citizen and proving your innocence by assisting us with our inquiries?"

He smiled thinly. "Oh, of course, puss . . . but I want counsel."

A public defender met them in the Crimes Against Persons squad room at headquarters, a new woman Janna had never met before. She looked like all the others, though, with a savior-to-mankind gleam in her eyes and a conservative lavender paisley tabard and bodysuit she had probably spent a week or two of salary credit on because she wanted to look like a lawyer someone paid for. Frowning, she fussed around the squad room overseeing the painting of the clerks and

investigators drafted for the show-up. "You may not have
formally arrested my client, but that doesn't absolve you from
the responsibility of following procedure."

Roos looked up from the phone where she sat calling Beta
Nafsinger and bared her teeth in a wolfish grin. "Oh, we'll
follow procedure, counselor . . . to the letter."

Across the squadroom the newscanner murmured and flickered, and for a moment her attention was caught by the word
_sligh_. Janna turned to watch a debate on the proposed state
bill to make Identation mandatory. "Of course this is a free
state in a free country," a legislator was saying, "but can we
really give credence to the claim of these Undocumented
persons we call 'slighs' that Identation restricts their freedom?
Doesn't it endanger the freedom of us all, instead? We have
proven examples that a large number of them turn to criminal
activity to survive, and when they commit crimes, they are
untraceable and untrackable. Worse, by their lack of Identation, the honest among them are being robbed of necessities
all civiiized people should share, like good education by
licensed teachers, sufficient food, medical care, and decent
housing. For their own good and for the protection of all
Kansans, every citizen _must_ become Idented."

Janna turned away in disgust. Self-righteous bastard. Slighs
were brainbent, of course; they had to be to prefer their
bartering, scraping existence to Documented life, where the
Social Care and Identification Banking Card insured everything one needed and, as a credit card, also bought almost
anything else desired. Most slighs in her experience were not
criminals, only quiet people desperately playing invisible to
escape notice. Why legislate against their life-style, especially
when almost every other had been legitimized?

Watching the clerks and investigators make themselves up
to look like Orions, Mama shook his head. "It's a waste of
time. Nafsinger won't be able to put the nod on Jerrett."

Janna frowned. "You don't mean you actually _believe_ the
deek when he says he wasn't responsible for the hearse?"

"The crime and the time just don't match him, bibi."

"Oh, come on. He got cabin fever and went looking for a new thrill. It certainly doesn't figure that someone would jack the hearse to make trouble for the Orions, because it wouldn't make trouble, not worth mentioning. Not even if the hearse is stripped. Jerrett can handle a GTA sentence with his hands tied. The prison in Hutchinson is practically a second home to him."

"No," Mama agreed, "it doesn't figure."

"So Jerrett has to be guilty."

She expected him to argue, but Mama just pushed his glasses up his nose, regarded her thoughtfully through them for a moment, then turned away. His silence left her itching with sudden disquiet. Could he be right? But . . . if Jerrett were not involved in taking the hearse and body after all, and nothing would be gained by framing the Orions for it, then what the hell was going on?

# CHAPTER
# THREE

<u>**Wednesday, January 24. 13:00:00 hours.**</u>

When she and her father arrived at headquarters, Beta
Nafsinger bore, in person, little resemblance to herself as she
appeared in the TV commercial. Janna found herself shaking
hands with a strapping young woman who looked like she
should be on a farm tossing hay bales instead of corpses.
Janna liked her on sight. Mama, Quist and other investigators
around the Crimes Against Persons squadroom also eyed her
appreciatively. Cornflower-blue eyes snapped with fierce satisfaction in the middle of a painted butterfly spreading blue-
and-gold wings across her face.

"So you caught the sons of bitches. Good work. Where
are the bloody bastards?"

Janna liked her even better.

"Beta, please. Your language." But a crinkle of William
Nafsinger's eyes and a twitch at the corner of his mouth belied
his protest. Then the inner laughter vanished as he looked
past his daughter to Roos and Quist. "Have you found Mr.
Chenoweth?"

Janna winced inwardly. Mama studied his nails.

Roos gave both Nafsingers a bland smile. "Not just yet,
I'm afraid. Will you come this way, please?" She led the way
out of the squad room and down the corridor toward the show-
up room.

William Nafsinger sighed. "Leonard Fontana called me

from the Lanour platform again this morning. He's very concerned."

They circled around three officers—two in the tight gray, red-sidestriped uniform jumpsuits and the third plainclothed—scowling at a thin, pale woman with the vacant expression of a tripper and a flower-tattooed scalp.

Beta Nafsinger eyed the pilgrim disapprovingly. "We're concerned too. Mr. Fontana entrusted us with Mr. Chenoweth, and we don't like betraying that trust."

Quist said, "Identification of these people we're about to show you may convince them to be more cooperative."

Roos pushed open the show-up room door. Beta Nafsinger glanced curiously at the public defender already in the room waiting for them, but when no introductions were offered, she took a chair facing the screen wall and sat poised on the edge of it.

Expectancy became dismay, however, as Quist tapped the activation switch on the controls by the door and the wall screen lighted to reveal a line of four men and four women standing before a wall marked in height graduations. "They all look alike!"

Jerrett and Kriegh did almost vanish among the others, especially with everyone wearing jackets and hiding both hair and bare scalps under stocking caps like those Beta Nafsinger described the jackers as wearing. The public defender smirked at the results of her fussing.

Nafsinger's father touched her arm. "Just relax and look them all over. Take your time. There are bound to be differences between them. Remember your trick of reading a deck of cards by minute differences on the backs?"

Nafsinger sent him a grateful smile.

Watching the affection between father and daughter, Janna felt a sudden sharp pang of homesickness for her own father. She ought to call him tonight. It might make the apartment bearable.

Beta Nafsinger leaned forward again, studying the line of

men and women on the screen as manipulation of the controls focused on each in turn and filled the screen with them from the waist up. "I don't know. They look like the people who pulled me out of the hearse, but . . . I just don't know. Something's wrong."

The public defender's smirk broadened.

"Wrong?" Roos frowned.

Quist smiled tautly. "Look closer." The view on the screen started to shift. "What about the jon wearing—"

The public defender snapped, "Officer Quist, that's leading the witness! Just pull back and let her see everyone."

Scowling, Quist snapped the screen back to the original view.

Nafsinger bit her lip. "When the bastard the girl called Pluto started pushing me out of the hearse, I quit fighting and concentrated on memorizing what they looked like so I could give a good description and identify them, but maybe I didn't look close enough." She sighed with a note of distress. "I don't recognize any of these people."

Her father patted her hand.

Mama moved to the chair beside her and gave her what Janna recognized as his reassuring smile. "You said something about them is wrong. Can you tell us what?"

"Well . . ." Nafsinger stared hard at the four men and four women, grimacing with the effort of concentration. "They look . . . neater. Take that one." She pointed at Jerrett's image. "His jacket looks new. The gang members I saw wore older clothes. Pluto's jacket had patches."

"Patches." Mama glanced toward Janna.

She swore silently. Jerrett might have worn another jacket yesterday, but she doubted it; at least not a patched one. A gang leader did not have to dress like a fashion plate or someone from a castlerow section of town, but he had to look as though he knew how to obtain from life what he wanted.

Mama smiled encouragingly. "That's good. Go on. Anything else?"

Nafsinger's forehead furrowed more deeply. "Yes, but I can't quite—" She broke off, closing her eyes for a minute. "Oh, I know . . . the stars." Her eyes reopened, wide with relief. "The stars aren't painted the same."

"What do you mean?" Quist tapped the controls. The eye of one clerk expanded to fill the entire screen.

"The people I saw had red stars around their eyes like these people, but the borders were blue, then yellow on the outside."

Janna sat bolt upright. The wrong color sequence!

"You say the stars were painted?" Mama leaned toward Nafsinger. "You're sure they weren't tattoos?"

Nafsinger thought, then nodded. "The girl's anyway. The star point above her left eye was smeared."

She had looked close, all right, Janna reflected, a *hell* of a lot closer than most victims or witnesses ever thought or managed to.

The public defender stood up. "I don't see any further need for detaining my clients, do you?"

Quist punched the screen off and spoke into a speaker. "Turn them loose, Ed."

They filed out of the show-up room.

Mama caught Janna's eye. "I guess we'd better get back on the street and start asking who could profit by masquerading as Orions." He sounded infuriatingly close to an I-told-you-so.

"Isn't looking for the people first the long way around?" Beta Nafsinger asked. "Wouldn't the hearse be easier to find?"

Roos's smile froze into the professional politeness used toward an outsider. "I know it would seem so, ma'am, but our county-wide bulletin on it hasn't found anything so far. It may be hidden somewhere."

"You mean the bastards who took it want it for something, like to use in a robbery?"

A bolt of shock jolted Janna. That was something she had not considered. She swore silently. It just might be the answer.

Someone taking it for a purpose like that would want to lay down a false trail that would send them hunting the wrong quarry.

"There's another possibility we might consider too," Mama said. "Can either of you think of someone with a grudge against members of your family personally or professionally? The theft and the way it was done could be a strike at you."

Father and daughter stared. "A grudge!" Beta snorted. "That's ridiculous."

Her father shook his head. "Not ridiculous, but unlikely, I think. I'm sure I'm not universally loved, but I don't know of any outright enemies. We work hard to insure client satisfaction. Our clientele also comes from the Gage area and better parts of Highland Park, a class of people who complain to the Better Business Bureau, or sue, when they're unhappy."

"What about competitors?" Quist asked.

Shock became amusement. Janna thought Beta struggled not to laugh aloud. Her father sent her a reproachful glance. "A mortuary war . . . rivals stealing each other's equipment, sabotaging funeral arrangements? Come now, Officer Quist. Besides, I can't imagine any of my immediate competitors knowing enough about street gangs to imitate one so closely. I'm sorry we couldn't help, but call again if you need us, and please, you'll let us know the moment you locate Mr. Chenoweth, won't you?"

Father and daughter walked away down the corridor.

From the other direction, behind the investigators, came the group from the broadcast room, sighing in relief as they pulled off caps and shrugged out of jackets. Jerrett swaggered up, grinning. "See, I told you I was innocent. You're lucky we don't sue your badges off for false arrest and mental anguish. Then maybe you'd learn not to harass innocent citizens."

Jerrett would look good bouncing off the corridor wall, Janna reflected grimly, but she remained motionless while the Orion leader and his girlfriend strutted off down the corridor with the public defender.

Quist wore a stony mask, she noticed, and while Roos kept smiling her teddy-bear grin, a killer light glittered in her eyes. Being wrong hurt more some times than others.

After a minute Janna looked around at the others with a wry smile. "How shall we divide up Oakland?"

Janna and Mama drew the area north of Seward Avenue. Driving down the long stretch of drifts and shabby buildings, she grimaced. Some aspects of police work had not changed since officers were called cops. Legwork was one of them . . . exhausting, tedious, time-consuming. And today, when even the word *north* made her shiver— The thought broke off as a snarl in her gut reminded Janna that noon had passed some time ago. "How about lunch before we split up?" she asked Mama.

"Ten four!"

The Oakland division station sat on Seward. She parked in the visitors' lot where the snow had blown off to only ankle deep. Waving greetings to the officers in an incoming car, they waded to the café across the street.

Her ear button murmured: "Alpha Cap Ten, stalled vehicle 10-47 Kansas and Tenth Avenues. Semi down with two rear quarter fans seized up."

Seward looked like a street out of history. Janna doubted it had changed much at all in the past century. No one had added new buildings, and the only attempts at modernization were Simon cell panels on the roofs while windows that were not show windows had been bricked up into a series of slits or replaced with glass brick. The effort failed to look anything but shabby, especially with so many of the storefronts and solar panels marred by graffiti—gang names and challenges, profanities, telephone numbers with symbols which, to the knowing, meant unlicensed drug dealers and prostitutes— and the holo images faded or flickering.

Lazaro Wu, owner of Las Comidas Café, managed better than most businessmen along this street. His building remained clean of graffiti, though hints of color remaining in depressions on the age-darkened brick, the glass brick of his window, and the panels on the roof testified that the neatness came only at the price of effort.

The interior smelled of generations of hamburgers and french fries mixed with the odors of sweat, wet boots, and uniforms that lingered after the leos who had previously crowded its counter and booths at noon. Not a leo was in sight in it now, nor waitresses, only Lazaro Wu, sitting at the register frowning over the screen of his briefcase computer.

Glancing up at them, he yelled, "Carita!"

An hispanic girl hurried out of the back to take their order, then vanished again.

On the small wall screen above the register, a newscanner commentator analyzed the latest stock market quotations. The name Lanour caught Janna's ear, and she looked up to see a down symbol by the Lanour–Tenning quotation but caught only the last part of the commentator's remark: ". . . that the expected proxy fight may drive stock prices even lower."

She lifted a brow. "It sounds like our company has more troubles than an accidental death on the job."

Mama shrugged. "I have a hard time working up sympathy for multinationals." He paused. "We ought to do something tonight. The Kansas City Opera is at the Civic Center for a week, and this evening's performance is *Madame Butterfly*. Want to go?"

"To an opera?" Janna grimaced. That sounded no better than going home. "Besides, I have to work all day with you. Isn't that punishment enough?"

He sighed. "Bibi, there's more to life than—" he broke off, scowling. "The bastards!"

She blinked. "What?"

He pointed at the newscanner.

The screen showed a group of sign-carrying picketers. A

voice-over was saying, ". . . at the Tellus Technics offices around the world by families of its space-station employees protesting the rumored decision that the corporation will shut down the station later this year. A Tellus spokesman denied—"

"Lied through his teeth is more like it," Mama spat.

Janna frowned. "What makes you so sure?"

"I saw an interview with Tellus's new general manager. He thinks space development is a waste of time. You watch; he'll shut down that platform. No matter that the medical research there is turning out the best new allergy medications in the world—do you know I can actually pet cats now?— and that they're close to the greatest discovery of the century, a drug that keeps bone from losing calcium!"

Any moment now he would jump on the table and start shouting. Janna said hurriedly, "What were you saying about how my life should be more than this job?"

Mama blinked with the blankness of disorientation. "What? Oh. Yes . . . you have to do something more than work, work out at the gym, and take criminal justice classes toward Investigator III. Broaden your horizons. I had to put a wrap strap on you to get you to the ballet with me, but didn't you end up enjoying it?"

She nodded reluctantly.

"Then give opera a chance. If a semester in UMKC's theater arts curriculum can teach a Western Kansas rube like me to appreciate it, a city girl should take to it right away."

"Why don't you take Lia?"

He hesitated a moment too long before answering. "She's busy tonight."

Janna straightened. So it was woman trouble after all . . . again. And here she thought he had finally found a stable relationship in his current cohab. Maybe his apartment was becoming as desolate as hers. She regarded him with sympathy. "Okay, I'll—"

A stream of shrill Spanish rose in the kitchen. Something crashed.

Wu stiffened. "What the hell's going on out there!" he yelled, then glanced at Janna and Mama. "Leo's, would you mind having a look?"

They headed for the kitchen door. It was only fair, quid pro quo, for tolerating the leos' discharge of job tension that erupted as rowdiness at feeding time.

In the kitchen the waitress, Carita, stood with her back to a stainless-steel table spitting at two hispanic youths planted in front of her while a third in a greasy apron fried hamburgers on an old-fashioned grill, ignoring the commotion. The two wore scarlet jackets with black bulls charging across their backs. Their long hair had been pulled into bullfighters' pigtails at the napes of their necks.

"You ought to be nice to real people, sweet thing," one was saying in Spanish as Janna pushed open the door.

"Real people?" Carita spat at them. "You're cockroaches!"

The second one clucked mockingly. "That's not nice, little pig. What if we tell old Chopsticks you're being rude to customers? You'll lose your job. Or maybe we'll just tell Human Services that he hires slighs that he can pay off in food instead of paying standard wages to real people he has to file all that paperwork on."

Janna kicked aside a pot on the floor. "What do you know, Mama. Toros. And I thought we might have trouble finding some. These cucarachas friends of yours, Julio?" she asked the cook. "You know the Department of Health requires a certain standard of hygiene in the kitchen of a public restaurant. Does Mr. Wu know how dirty you're letting his get?"

The Toros turned languidly. "It was clean until you came in, leo."

At Janna's shoulder Mama said, "Let's sit down out front and talk about that."

The two tensed, and the cook's hand twitched, as though to reach for the long knife on the nearby chopping block. Janna balanced on her toes and let her hand drop down by the top of her boot, adrenaline rushing hot and cold through her.

Then the Toros shrugged and smiled mockingly. "I guess we got some time we can spare you, leo. You buying the caff?"

Mama followed them out.

Breathing again, Janna remained to eye the cook and ask the waitress, "Will you be all right?" She would never have taken the girl for a sligh, not with that kind of outward show of anger.

Carita tossed her head, eyes smoldering. "I am, will be, and would have been! You didn't need to interfere. They would have quit sooner or later, or I would have made them lose interest."

The first part of the sentence sounded like a sligh, but not the second, nor did the hard glitter in her eyes match a sligh. It was the kind of look that in Janna's experience went with thinking of ways to get even.

"You know there are people in the legislature right now trying to characterize Unidenteds as dangerous people."

Carita grimaced. "I saw that toad on the scanner. His turn will come, too. We're not about to let anyone number and file us."

These slighs were going to ruin their own cause yet. Totally wickers, all of them. "Be careful how you avoid it," Janna suggested, for all the good it would do, and left the kitchen.

"Beta Oakland Nine, 1832 Division, the apartment in back. Check on a Caroline Bellman. Carephone advises she does not answer today, and she is extremely elderly."

"Orions?" one of the Toros was saying as Janna sat down at the table. He laughed. "Hell, leo, who don't wish the Orions trouble? That Pluto is one arrogant bastard. We gonna mash him one of these days."

"But who hates them in particular?" Mama asked. "Who might pretend to be Orions to make trouble?"

"Hey." The second Toro leaned forward. "Is this about that

hearse-jacking?" He grinned broadly. "Far star. But, hey, maybe it isn't anyone outside the Orions. Could be internal, a power play, someone who wants Pluto caged so he can take over."

"What's the color sequence around the Orions' eyes?" Janna asked.

The Toros blinked. "Colors? Red over their eyes, of course, then . . . blue and yellow? No, yellow, *then* blue." They grinned. "What prize do we win?"

Mama gave them a thin smile. "You don't have to come downtown. Where's Ladino?"

Their eyes slid away. They shrugged. "Who can say? The jefe is like smoke, like la sombra, a shadow."

"Well, you let the smoke know we want a call from him."

"Ciertamente." They pushed away from the table in a loud scrape of chairs and swaggered out of the café. "Adios, gatitos,"

Janna frowned after them. "If Toros pulled that masquerade, I don't think those two know about it."

"No," Mama agreed. "They'd be gloating." He pushed his glasses up his nose. "I don't think any of the gangs did it. Nafsinger's idea of stealing it for a robbery has a better feel. It would explain why we haven't found the hearse, either. When we finish eating, you go west and I'll head east. Let's tap for rumors."

"Beta Oakland Fifteen, traffic assistance, East Sixth and Golden, woman in the intersection exhibiting seizure-type behavior. Complainant is a physician and suggests possible trick intoxication."

Janna grimaced in disgust. The public was so stupid! With all the legal drugs on the market, they still wanted the forbidden ones like trick and trilight, the killers. Maybe the government should legalize everything so natural selection would weed out the mental defectives.

\* \* \*

Slogging west on Seward proved not only cold and tedious but fruitless. Everywhere she asked, stores and bars both, no one could suggest what gang might have tried to hang a grand theft auto charge on the Orions. No one had heard any rumors of impending breakings or boostings that might involve the use of a hearse.

Like most of the bars, Le Play sat almost empty at this time of day, its stale air still relatively free of smoke and drug fumes. At the back of the room ran a holo of Porphyry, the hot new jivaqueme band, playing one of the songs from its current album. The music reached Janna almost subliminally, its rhythm and call to dance reverberating in her bones. A few girls and boys—a purely honorary term since some looked almost middle-aged—from the rooms upstairs sat wrapped in robes at one of the back tables, drinking tea while they played poker for vending tokens. They eyed Janna as she approached the table, but since they were safely ensconced in a licensed, medically inspected house, they smiled and offered her a chair.

"What can we do for you, leo?"

Nothing, it turned out. They could only shake their heads when she asked her questions. "Sorry, we haven't heard of anything in the chute."

"Maybe you should ask Quicks—" one of the boys began, and broke off with a yelp. Glaring at the girl next to him, he reached under the table to rub at his leg.

"Quicksilver?" The sligh teacher. Janna knew little about his background, even less than a Documented could learn about most slighs, but his appearance suggested he came of mixed blood—caucasian, afro, amerind, with possibly some oriental breeding as well—and he had once told her that he had managed to educate himself by haunting public libraries and reading tirelessly. He had also perfected the art of invisibility. The Toros might call their chief smoke and shadow, but Quicksilver really *was*, conducting his school everywhere, always on the move, successfully keeping ahead of the raids that would wrap him for teaching without a license and force idention of his sligh students. And, in the course of it, he often managed to see and hear a great deal about things of interest to the police. "Is he holding school up in the gambling rooms here today?"

"Tongue," the girl hissed at the boy.

"If Quicksilver is here, would you ask him to come down?" Janna said. "I assure you I've never helped a raid on his school. I used to warn him when I knew they were coming. Just ask him."

They eyed her skeptically, but after a minute one of the boys stood and padded out the back of the room. Janna sat back in her chair, careful to keep her hands away from her ear button.

A short time later the boy came back. He gave her a twitchy smile. "Sorry. He's gone. I guess school let out when we weren't looking."

Janna stiffened and stared at him narrow-eyed. "Gone?"

The boy met her eyes. "You're welcome to look if you want."

That meant Quicksilver *was* gone. She stood. "Thank you for the help." Running a thumb down the pressclose of her jacket front, she stalked out of the bar.

"I don't like this," she told Mama when they re-joined an hour later and climbed into the car. "It isn't like him. Quicksilver hasn't cut cloud on me in years."

"He knows something and doesn't want to talk about it." Mama's eyes gleamed behind his glasses. "It must be something big, too, to frighten him like this. Didn't I tell you this case smells? Now all we have to figure out is what it could be. Powerful criminals? The government?"

Janna rolled her eyes. Oh, god, here they went, right into orbit. "No," she hissed. "We're not speculating. I repeat, *not* guessing, and most *certainly* not dreaming up blue-sky theories that take us on flying carpets to Never-Never-Land. There's some simple explanation for Quicksilver's behavior.

I've used up my credit with him, maybe. What we *do* do is follow the book . . . gather evidence, examine it, and come to a conclusion."

Mama regarded her unperturbed. "We'll never solve it that way, bibi."

His smug sureness goaded her. "Personally, I don't care if we *ever* solve it," she snapped. "All I want to do is *clear* it and get back to real police work . . . murders and assaults."

"Reports," he said.

*Lord, don't let me kill him here with the Oakland division for witnesses.* "Shall we just go back to headquarters?" she said through gritted teeth.

"Alpha Cap Five, will you 10-9 your last signal? Was that license number RSN 405?"

Janna sat upright. The Nafsinger hearse! She tapped her ear button. "Indian Thirty Central. Stolen vehicle RSN 405 is my case. Where has Alpha Cap Five found it?"

"Indian Thirty, Alpha Cap Five reports vehicle abandoned in the Topeka Cemetery. Advises vehicle vandalized and . . ." The dispatcher hesitated before continuing "Contents, likewise."

Contents vandalized? The careful phrasing sent cold crawling up Janna's spine. She met Mama's eyes and found his mouth thinning into a grim line.

"Kick it, bibi. I think we'd better get right over there."

# CHAPTER
# FOUR

## Wednesday, January 24. 15:45:00 hours.

The word *vandalism* hardly did credit to the hearse's damage, even viewing it a good fifteen meters back from where the vehicle sat at the end of a trail of scraped and awry early- and middle-twentieth-century headstones, its front end butting into a tall gray obelisk. Doors hung open and wrenched almost off their tracks. The access covers had been ripped from the top of the airfoil skirt, windows smashed, and curtains torn down. Comments on what could be done with a corpse by someone depraved enough spread across the paint with a metallic brightness that suggested they had been written using a tube of acid paste. The vandals had even reached up on the roof to smash the solar receptors. All Janna could see for certain of the interior, however, was the outline of a shape sprawled on the floor beside an overturned stretcher.

She eyed the snow between the hearse and the drive, a pristine expanse with no recent footprints and only slight depressions left where the snow had blown into those made yesterday. Nothing must disturb it until the Forensics team recorded everything. "May I borrow your hand scanner for a look at the body?"

One of the watch-car team handed her the scanner. She held it up to her eyes. With the light-enhanced mode switched on, the hearse's interior sprang into sharp visibility. Their vandals had overlooked nothing . . . smashing the instrument panel and slicing the side and ceiling lining to ribbons. Ribbons just about described the body too. Janna's gut lurched. It was as though the vandals had gone into a frenzy, slashing over and over through the face and throat, chest and abdomen. Rage boiled up in her. How could any human mutilate another like that, even a dead man?

"At least we can quit worrying about the hearse being used for a robbery," Quist said.

"A cemetery." Roos grinned. "What an appropriate place to dump it. How did you happen to find it?" she asked the team from Alpha Cap Five.

"You can see the top half of the obelisk from California. We noticed it was tilted and came in to see why."

Janna thrust the scanner at Mama, who peered through it, then gave Quist and Roos their turns.

"Christ." Roos grimaced. "If Fontana was upset at his employee being lost, he's going to love learning that all the family has left to bury is cube steak." She sighed. "I wonder, though. Can we be certain the jackers did this? It's possible they dumped the hearse and someone else came along and worked it over."

Mama pushed his glasses up his nose. "Whoever it was didn't waste much time, if each of those depressions used to be a track. There aren't that many. It looks like the vandals walked around once, smashing as they went . . . very efficient and businesslike, not like someone on a rampage at all."

A chill slid down Janna's spine. Businesslike. Watching the glitter of Mama's eyes behind his glasses, she remembered his speculation about government involvement.

"Here comes Forensics," Quist said.

The van swung in through the south entrance, where tombstones gave way to flat markers and the cemetery became a rolling lawn. The van's paint matched the watch cars, white over black with a broad stripe of reflective red separating the two colors. As it hummed up the drive the noise of its fans triggered sound-activated holos set in some of the markers, so that for a few moments as the van passed, monuments rose out of the snow, castles and mausoleums and singing angel choruses. Above one grave the image of a nude young woman danced dreamily in the iridescent coils of a huge snake. Its timer had a long setting. The image lingered after the others had faded, turning above the snow until the Forensics van swung around an island occupied by a small, freestanding mausoleum, a real one, and settled on its parking rollers.

Side and rear doors slid open. Technicians bundled like arctic explorers swung out and began unloading their equipment: 2D holo cameras; the video scanner and fingerprint detector's laser generator.

"Can't you people stick to finding bodies in nice weather?" one tech complained. "This isn't the optimal temperature for all these electronics."

Janna wiggled numbing toes. "Hard card."

Mama said, "I don't suppose there's any way to use all these fancy electronics to blow out the tracks so we can see what's at the bottom."

Another tech eyed the snow briefly and shook her head. "Not when the two layers are this much alike." She checked the connections between the generator, fiber-optic cable, and the minivid camera with its monitor and video recorder.

"Then we'll be depending on you to find some useful prints with that elf-lip," Quist said.

The tech winced. "It's LVIP, officer. Laser Video Intensified Print system." But she said it in the weary tone of someone used to her words making no impression. Hoisting the generator/recorder pack on her back, she trudged off toward the hearse.

"Oh my god. Poor Mr. and Mrs. Kiorpes, and Mr. Durning and Miss Lowe!"

Janna turned to find a small, stocky man in a grease-stained jacket staring at the hearse in horror. Hair as orange as a carrot and as curly as steel wool stuck out from under a stocking cap.

"What? Who are you talking about?" she asked.

"Them." The little main pointed at the obelisk and the headstones wrenched from their places by the hearse's passage.

"Who are you?" Roos asked. "How did you get past the police line?"

He drew himself up. "I'm Albert Tenpennies, the caretaker. You're going to move all that, aren't you, not just keep on walking around over the top of the Kiorpes' sons?"

Roos leaned close to Janna. "I think Mr. Tenpennies only has seven or eight left."

Quist frowned at Tenpennies. "Do you live on the grounds?"

"In the stone house by the cemetery office back on the west side."

"But you didn't see this hearse drive in here yesterday?"

Pale eyes sparked. The carroty hair seemed to bush sideways even more. "I would have come up if I had, wouldn't I? Especially since there were no burials scheduled."

"You don't check the cemetery every day?"

Tenpennies stiffened. "I try to. I'm the only person who cares about some of these graves. Yesterday, though, I had to spend the whole day in the equipment barn working on the backhoe. Didn't any of your cars patrol through here?"

Now the watch-car team stiffened.

Touché, Janna thought, biting back a grin. She nodded at Tenpennies. "Thank you very much for your help. We'll be out of here as soon as possible."

"Without causing any more damage for me to repair, I hope. Think about the poor people you're walking over." Tenpennies stalked off.

The investigators and watch-car team rolled their eyes.

Bob Welliever, the Forensics team supervisor, beckoned to the four investigators. "Can you help us look for the access covers and side mirrors that were torn off? They might have useful prints on them."

"You mean you want *us* to paw around on the Kiorpes family too?" Roos said. "That's disgusting."

"And cold," Janna added.

Welliever grinned. "Pretend you're a kid gathering material for a snow fort."

Pretend she was sitting beside a warm fire, Janna reflected ten minutes later as she waded in a careful spiral out from the hearse, feeling with her feet and gloved hands for any foreign object under the snow.

A gust of wind lifted the top layer of snow, sending a chilly spray of it into her face and across her tracks.

Pretend she was not courting frostbite and pneumonia.

"Beta Oakland Nineteen, request you go to Sunrise Court off Croco Road. Fire department responding to alarm and requires traffic assistance."

But there were worse places to be today. At least she was not a firefighter with all that water coming back in her face as ice and turning the ground into a skating rink

Her ankle knocked against something. Digging it out, she found only a flower vase full of mummified stems. But five minutes later the snow yielded one of the access covers. The camera techs photographed its position in relation to the hearse before letting Janna deliver it to the fingerprint tech for scanning.

Under the green light of the argon laser several series of loops and arches fluoresced and were duly photographed by the minivid camera and recorded on tape.

"I don't know if they'll do you any good, though," the tech said. "See the smears across those two? Marks like them are all over the hearse on doors and this access cover, where you'd expect the vandals to have touched it. Made by gloves, probably. It looks like your vandals weren't cooperative enough to run around bare-handed."

Which meant that the clear prints probably belonged to no

one useful, just the Nafsingers and their employees. Janna sighed and returned to wading through the snow.

The searching and scanning continued until the hearse had been completely covered and all its missing pieces found. By that time the sun had set. Forensics packed up in fading twilight and left the cemetery, following the Medical Examiner's wagon that had come for the body and the department flatbed that hauled the hearse to the police garage where it could be examined more thoroughly and in greater comfort.

"They're going back to heat," Roos said. "I think I hate them."

Janna refused to think about it. Shoving frozen hands into her pockets, she shrugged. "No need. When our bodies reach the ambient temperature, which should be any second now, we'll stop feeling the cold. If you two take the houses west of the cemtery, Mama and I will check those across the street north and east."

"Beta Cap Twenty-one, 10-98 crowd at 17th and Western. Religious protest blocking entrance to Fantecstacy Palace."

Janna decided that she hated canvassing houses more than she did bars. At least she could go inside the latter. No one invited her into these underground and berm houses, new and better cared for than houses farther north in Oakland. The occupants just stood in the doorways with heat and tantalizing cooking odors ebbing past them as they shook their heads and said no, they had noticed no one in the Topeka Cemetery yesterday, neither people nor vehicles, including hearses.

"I didn't even see anyone in Mount Auburn," a man in one of the berm houses added, pointing past the earth sloping up to his eaves toward the little cemetery lying across California Avenue from its larger counterpart.

Then one elderly woman just north of Mount Auburn said, "Why, yes, I saw a hearse."

The temperature suddenly became unimportant. Janna reached into her jacket to tap on her microcorder. "What can you tell me about it?"

"Not very much, I'm afraid." The woman hugged herself and backed farther into the glass-brick foyer of the underground house. "It drove in across the street about eleven o'clock and had no procession. I don't know when it left."

Eleven o'clock. The "Orions" had pushed Beta Nafsinger out of the hearse at ten forty-five. They must have driven straight here afterward. They had definitely not taken the hearse for joyriding, then. So why *had* they taken it, and who were they? "A hearse without a procession didn't strike you as odd?"

The woman shook her head. "I've seen it before." She sighed. "It's tragic, isn't it, that people can die alone and be buried without anyone noticing or mourning them?"

The eddy of heat from the foyer made the air at Janna's back feel all the colder. She tightened her jaw to keep her teeth from chattering. "Yes, ma'am. Did you happen to notice anyone on foot around the cemetery at that time? Or do you remember what the driver of the hearse looked like?"

The old woman shook her head.

Thanking the woman, Janna tapped off her microcorder and left, jogging to warm up.

No one beyond the old woman had seen anything, either, and after leaving the last house she headed with relief back for the car. The very marrow of her bones must have frozen by now. She barely felt her feet as she dashed across California just ahead of a semi . . . and narrowly missed being hit by a Chrysler Elf beyond the truck because she slowed down, not seeing the little runabout coming through the snow kicked up by the semi's thundering fans.

Adrenaline produced a fast thaw, she discovered. Still, she was glad to see Mama already in the car and the engine running. Scrambling in, she held both hands and feet down by the heat vent.

"Bless you. Have any luck?"

He shook his head. "What about you?"

She played him the old woman's statement.

Mama straightened, eyes glittering behind his glasses. "Fifteen minutes from jacking to cemetery, and the next day we find the hearse vandalized. It's like the jackers stole it just to tear apart. Didn't I tell you this case smells, bibi?"

"I wonder if Quist and Roos learned anything useful." Their car was gone. Janna tapped her ear button. "Indian Thirty Central, what's Indian Twelve's Twenty?"

"Indian Twelve is deactivated," the dispatcher replied. "I believe they were going 10-19."

"Then let's head for lion country too," Janna told Mama.

Back at headquarters they headed upstairs for Crimes Against Property. Compared to its daytime activity, the squad room seemed deserted. A couple of investigators sat at the dictypers and another talked on the phone, scowling into its screen. Three more lounged near the caff urn. Quist and Roos stood in the doorway of Lieutenant Applegate's office watching the evening commander talk on the phone. Seeing them, Roos left the doorway and crossed the room to her desk, where she sat down on one corner and grinned at them.

"Lieutenant Yost is on the phone to Director Paget and guess what? Because of the mutilation, Paget is giving the case to Crimes Against Persons." Her grin broadened. "It's all yours with my blessing, dear children."

Mama pushed his glasses up his nose. Behind them his eyes gleamed.

Janna could not share his relish. This did not look like the kind of case where solutions came easily. "Shit." She dropped into a chair. "Give us everything you have, then. What did you learn from the people in the houses behind the cemetery?"

"Nada. However—Maxwell, don't houseclean *my* desk!"

Mama pulled back from the stack of forms and printout he had picked up and started to tap into a neat stack.

Roos eyed him a moment, as though to reassure herself that he would not attempt another violation of her territory, then continued, "I do have this." She produced a card from a sleeve pocket. "The telephone number for Mr. William Nafsinger. You can call and let him know his property and client have been recovered."

Janna took the card with a grimace. "May your children divorce you and your spouse cancel your marriage contract renewal in favor of a dog and a flock of sheep."

Roos grinned.

"Want me to call, bibi?"

Janna held on to the card. "Why don't you see if Vradel is still here and give him a quick oral report?" She punched the Nafsinger number.

A young female face answered the phone, another from the TV commercial. She called, "Dad!" when Janna identified herself.

The view on the screen slipped sideways as the girl swiveled the screen, giving Janna a blurred view of what looked like a moon crater...until she realized it was a three-wall TV tuned to a cineround program on the moon colony. Then William Nafsinger's face filled the screen, his forehead furrowed with hope. "Thank you, Omega. Sergeant Brill, isn't it? Have you found Mr. Chenoweth?"

"Yes, and the hearse."

The furrowed forehead smoothed instantly. Nafsinger beamed. "That's wonderful. Where may I come after them?"

Janna took a breath. "I'm afraid we'll have to keep both for a bit yet. They're evidence in a felony and need to be examined for associative evidence." She hesitated. Should she tell him about the vandalism?

"Keep them? For how long? I'll be calling Mr. Fontana and I'm sure he'll want to know."

From behind the phone screen Roos grimaced.

Janna put on her blandest mask. "I'm afraid I can't give you a definite answer just now. There was . . . some damage, and . . ." Why not tell him? He would see for himself sooner or later. "When the vandals took a knife to the interior, I'm afraid they didn't bother to differentiate between—"

"Vandals?" Nafsinger interrupted on a rising tone. "Knife? Oh, my god."

Suddenly a crowd of daughters surrounded Nafsinger against a background of mining robots boring tunnels through moon rock, all talking at once and staring in consternation at the screen. Beta's voice rose above the others. "This is unbelievable! Nothing like it has ever happened to one of our clients before. It's outrageous. Poor Mrs. Chenoweth. Do you have any estimation at all of when we can proceed with the funeral arrangements?"

Janna gave her an apologetic smile. "The Medical Examiner will examine the body in the next few days to assess and document the damage. After he's finished, we—" Their stricken faces brought a surge of sympathy. "I have a friend who is an assistant M.E.," she said on impulse. "I'll check with the night attendant to see what the schedule is like. My friend might be able to do the autopsy tomorrow."

Punching the morgue on the internal line minutes later, though, she wondered if Sid would appreciate being volunteered.

The attendant who answered the phone had blue hair and painted wings sweeping up his forehead from his eyebrows. "What's Dr. Chesney's schedule like tomorrow?" Janna asked him.

"We're running slack right now. He has just two indigents, both probably hypothermia deaths."

"Then will you see if you can schedule him for the body that came in from the Topeka Cemetery this evening?"

The winged brows rose toward the blue hair. "Why? Kolb's doing the PM now."

"*Now*?" Janna sat bolt upright. And Sandor Kolb, the chief Medical Examiner himself? This Leon Fontana, or the Lanour Corporation, must have even more influence than she thought. Punching off, she scrambled for the door. "When Mama comes back, point him toward the morgue."

The section of headquarters that Forensics and the Medical

Examiner shared lay almost at the opposite end from the investigations squad rooms on the city block covered by headquarters. Janna ran most of the way through the maze of corridors, however, even taking the stairs down to the morgue in the basement instead of waiting for an elevator.

The blue-haired attendant looked up in astonishment as she came pounding through. "Can I help you, Officer?"

A newscanner sat on the desk behind the counter, its screen out of sight but the sound clearly audible, tuned to an interview program. "I'd like to ask the distinguished senator from Kansas why the Humanitarian Party has joined the Libertarians in their opposition to Senator Early's colonial moratorium proposal. Surely this is a strange coalition, or doesn't the senator consider that it benefits the greater good to conserve our resources?"

Janna waved the attendant back to his chair. "I know the way in."

The corridor led past the lucite-sided shaft where corpses on gurneys could be lifted to the viewing room on the floor above and past the prep rooms and banks of storage drawers to the autopsy room at the far end with its long row of troughlike plastic tables. The sound of Senator Barbara Landon Kassebaum-Martin's thoughtful voice followed her. "Certainly it's important to conserve resources, but while my esteemed colleague in the Democratic Party foments panic over mere metal, what we're losing—and to the space stations and the Moon and Mars as well as emigration—is the most vital resource of all, one that cannot be held by force ... people. Space and the stars are stripping us of men and women with technical skills, the very backbone of our work force and economy. What we need is not a moratorium on colonization but a program to persuade these people that Earth still offers a good life. Let's stop strangling their personal liberty with laws intended—and failing—to identify and enfranchise the underprivileged portion of our society. Let's lift the crushing tax burden that our compassion has removed from the poor but political favoritism continues allowing the rich to evade."

As always, Janna had the feeling of having walked into a dreamworld in the morgue. Instead of the gleam of stainless steel that microfiche books and TV still used to characterize medical settings, these surfaces all had soft, matte finishes of pale blue—tile floor, walls, plastic countertops and cooler fronts, and autopsy tables—fading into one another so that she seemed to walk through foggy twilight.

Even the dead man's ashen gray flesh faded into invisibility on the autopsy table. By comparison, Sandor Kolb's rust jumpsuit became a blaze of color, a baggy, wrinkled blaze of color he might have been wearing and sleeping in for a week. He didn't wear mask or gown, just gloves with his sleeves rolled above his elbows. A tangle of gray hair stuck stiffly out from his head, almost touching the minivid camera hanging just above him like a bizarre third eye, its sensors letting it match each turn and tilt of the M.E.'s head.

Janna circled the table to stand beside the attendant assisting Kolb. "I can't believe Paget made him come back at night to do this," she whispered.

The attendant rolled her eyes. "He didn't come back. He was still here from today, asleep on one of the tables. He woke up when the body came in and said we ought to get to work."

"There's no use in putting it off," Kolb said. He peered across the table. The minivid lens stared at Janna and the attendant, too, recording Kolb's interest in them for posterity along with the rest of the autopsy. "You didn't think I heard you, did you? Here, Arrivillga, put these specimens in formalin." As the attendant dropped the slices of internal organs into a container of liquid, he leaned back over the body. The camera tilted downward. "I may be a little absentminded about minor details, but I'm not deaf, nor off my tick. Contrary to popular opinion, I do remember that I'm married, and where home is; it's just that there's so much to do here.

And if I sleep on an autopsy table once in a while, it's only because the High Muckies put my office way up on the fourth floor and I don't dare sleep on the gurneys. The one time I made that mistake, Blue Hair out there came by so toxic on fantasy dust, he couldn't hear me snoring and thought I was a new delivery, so he tagged me and shoved me in a storage drawer. A nasty piece of business, this." He patted the dead forehead, almost the only unmarked piece of flesh on the body. "Vicious. He didn't die of it, though. He's been dead for, oh, three or four days. See how the eyes are sunken? No remaining trace of rigor, either." He wiggled the jaw. "Not much putrefaction, though."

"He died Saturday on the Lanour platform and was probably in cold storage waiting for a shuttle to bring him down," Janna said.

"Platform? Ah, that explains how he died of decompression. See the petechia all over the skin? That means little hemorrhages. It's from rupturing capillaries. Petechia in the mucosa of the trachea, too, and ruptured alveoli in the lungs." He gestured toward a lung lying on the cutting board at the head of the table, sliced like a loaf of bread. "All consistent with decompression. What happened to him?"

"An accident with his pressure suit, I'm told."

"Accident." Kolb sounded vaguely disappointed. "Then it's the mutilation he's here for?"

"Yes, sir. We need it documented."

Janna stood watching while Kolb probed the seemingly hundreds of slashes, muttering up at the minivid as he worked. After a while she wondered why she stayed. It was not as though this autopsy would give them information vital to solving the crime. She had work waiting upstairs, too, crime scene and field interview reports to make out. But a vague disquiet held her, an echoing memory of Mama's suspicions, and after a while Mama himself slipped into the room to join her.

"Anything you can tell us about who did it, Doc?" Mama

asked. "Is he left- or right-handed? What kind of blade did he use?"

Kolb glanced up. "Left-handed. The blade was a long, thin one. Most interesting is his inconsistency, though. Outwardly the mutilation looks uniformly vicious, but actually, most of the cuts are shallow, except for a few across the abdomen in the upper left and right quadrants and across the throat. In the throat both the trachea and esophagus have been completely severed here and here, and the trachea severed and the esophagus slightly cut in this third—" He broke off, leaning down close to the body's throat.

"What is it?" Janna asked.

Instead of answering, the Medical Examiner ran an exploratory finger along the edge of the severed tissues. "Fiberoptic."

A long cable of fiberoptic material fed down from the ceiling, followed by a cardboard-thin monitor. Kolb slid the lens into the corpse's neck and frowned at the image on the monitor for several minutes before ordering, "Retract."

Cable and monitor disappeared into the ceiling. Kolb dissected out a length of what Janna took to be esophagus. Slitting it lengthwise, he spread it open and held it up closer to the light, angling it first one way, then the other. "Arrivillga, let's look at this under the microscope."

Putting the tissue on a slide and examining it all took time, during which Kolb offered no explanations, just muttered under his breath, leaving the two investigators raising their brows at each other in an agony of curiosity.

Finally Janna could stand it no longer. "Dr. Kolb, what are you looking at?"

Kolb continued to stare into the microscope. "Abrasions. I happened to notice a roughness to one end of a neck wound that could not have been produced with a knife. There was tearing rather than severing of the tissue. Now I find abrasions in the esophagus." He straightened and turned. "But these are abrasions with no leucocytic activity in the area as there would be if the trauma occurred during life."

Janna heard Mama's intake of breath behind her. "Are you saying something was shoved down his throat after he died?"

"That would not be inconsistent with these findings."

Cold crawled through Janna. Something shoved down his throat, something no longer there after the vandalism and mutilation. She looked around at Mama, who said nothing, just pushed his glasses up his nose and stared past her at the corpse.

She followed his gaze. Oh, god, she hated this, but it fit. It explained. It reverberated in her bones with rightness. Now the time and crime made sense. The rest, the Orions and vandalism, were all just a masquerade to hide the fact that the jackers had been after the body, or rather, what was *in* the body.

"Did you talk to Vradel?" she asked.

"No. He'd gone home."

"I think maybe we'd better call him."

# CHAPTER
# FIVE

**Wednesday, January 24. 20:00:00 hours.**

"Smuggling? Isn't that nice," Vradel said, grinning at Janna and Mama from the screen of their phone in Crimes Against Persons. His mustache twitched with happiness. "We can dump this on the federal boys. I'll call Customs first thing in the morning."

"What!" Mama swiveled the screen around to face him. "Who's told us we have to give the case up?"

Vradel scowled. "Good god, Maxwell. Wrap the paranoia. *No* one has ordered us to give up the case; it's just what we have to do. With smuggling involved it becomes a federal matter."

"The hell with that! You know the federal boys. Give the case to them and it may never be solved, and we'll never know if it is or is not. What if these people start doing to live people what they did to Chenoweth's body?"

The angled view Janna had left on the screen thinned Vradel to a sliver not much thicker than the screen. The sliver's mustache twitched again. "Maxwell, don't try pushing my serve-and-protect buttons. We can't keep the case and that's that. The perpetrators are probably long gone from our jurisdiction, anyway."

"Maybe not. How could outsiders know enough about the Orions to call someone by Jerrett's name?"

Vradel hesitated before answering, then it was with a question. "What's the matter, Maxwell? Why do you really want this case so much?"

Mama leaned toward the screen. "I worry when I see people behaving cold-bloodedly. I worry about what they might do next. There's all kinds of research on the corporate platforms, some because it's too deadly to work with down here."

Vradel sucked one end of his mustache into his mouth and chewed on it. "You make a grim case, but are you sure you're not blowing the matter out of proportion simply because you hate having a puzzle taken away from you before it's solved? If there's espionage involved, it's probably just the industrial variety."

"*Just!*" Mama yelped. "Lieutenant, we're not talking about a new dress design or a car-body improvement. We don't have any *idea* what could have come down from the platform and what effect it might have in the wrong hands."

Vradel sighed. "How do you feel about the case, Brill?"

What could she say? The treatment of the corpse enraged her as much as it did Mama, but . . . She swiveled the screen to face her again. "Isn't that immaterial, sir? Protocol is very clear on jurisdiction regarding smuggling across the national border, which includes from platforms and the Moon and Mars colonies."

Mama sent her a look of reproach, but Vradel nodded. "You see, Maxwell? We have regulations, and when we follow them, our part of the world runs a trifle smoother. I think we'd be in over our heads with smuggling, anyway. Have a good evening, both of you. I'll see you in the morning."

The screen went dark.

Mama slapped it face down and whirled angrily on her. "By-the-Book Brill."

"Shut up, Mama." She was exhausted. She wanted to go home yet hated to. Maybe talking to her father would help. He would be one person glad to hear that she had survived another day.

"Sometimes I think that clearing cases really is all you care about, not solving them," he persisted.

Janna sighed. How in god's name had he managed to be on the force for fourteen years and still maintain this rookie idealism? "Right now all I care about is going home."

"Do you care about Chenoweth, bibi? How can we be sure the smuggler just used his corpse? He, or she, could have arranged for it to be available."

The man was hopeless! "Space platforms are out of our jurisdiction too," she snapped.

He grinned. "At least you recognize that murder is a possibility."

To keep from assaulting him, she buried herself in finishing the reports she had been working on that morning, dictating as fast as possible and stubbornly ignoring all suggestions for improved phrasing the dictyper's polite voice offered. Then, with her share of the stack finished, she marched out.

Exhaustion sank into depression in the stretch of street between the bus stop and the steps leading up the side of the twentieth-century stone house where she leased the second floor; no Sid to welcome her, to scrub her back while she bathed, to trade off accounts of the jokes and horrors of the day while they provided shoulders for each other to cry on.

Dropping into the molded-foam easy chair beside the phone, she punched her father's number in Wichita.

But no one answered. No one answered Sid's number, either.

Around her the empty silence of the apartment reverberated like thunder. Janna slapped down the phone screen, snatched up her jacket, and headed back for the door.

The leos who took their second and unofficial debriefing in the Lion's Den on the ground floor of the sandstone, slit-windowed New Hotel Jayhawk down the street from headquarters had thinned from the crush of late afternoon by ten o'clock. Stayers and the addition of a few civilians, however, kept the bar crowded hip to hip. The noise level also remained high, surely audible in the bordello upstairs—the New Hotel Jayhawk had *never* been a hotel, despite the sign and holographic jayhawk on the roof—and spoiling the concentration of Fleur Vientos's boys and girls. If anyone but leos had been responsible for it, the Tactical Squad would have been called in with riot gear.

With the double doors hissing closed behind her, Janna surveyed the pandemonium and nodded in satisfaction. People and noise were just what she wanted, enough distraction that she could forget everything in the real world.

She shouldered toward the bar through the crowd and through smoke and drug fumes so thick that the holo of the band Heylen's Comet playing inaudibly above the scrap of dance floor had lost all color, fading to monochromatic blues. Bumping into a she-lion still in uniform, Janna mouthed an apology, then belatedly realized that the knee boots and skin-tight gray jumpsuit had been painted on bare skin. The girl was a lion buff, here to be around leos, possibly hoping to count coup on one. Another lion buff danced on a tabletop, nude except for a g-string and tattoos: "Be safe tonight; sleep with a leo"; "Take me to TaSq"; "I welcome assaults with friendly weapons."

Behind the bar, Vernon Tuckwiller, the owner, bellowed, "Tea as usual tonight, Brill?"

She never failed to marvel at his ability to make himself heard without visible effort. That voice and his bulldozer body must have struck fear into the hearts of countless deeks as Tuck came crashing through their doors back in his Vice Squad days. Janna eyed the cabinet behind the bar dispensing recreational drugs but decided against any of them. The trouble with chemical boosts was that one always had to come down afterward. "A Black Hole and vending tokens!" she shouted back.

His brows skipped. "Alcohol?"

"And strong!" To hell with her intolerance for it. The hell if she fell asleep in the middle of the game. She wanted to be unconscious.

Tuck mixed the drink and held out his hand for her Scib Card. The Card went into the register; she stared into the retinal reading plate, and when the r.r. blinked confirmation of her retinal pattern, she signed the screen. Moments later the register bleeped verification of her signature, too, and returned the Card. With her bank balance now smaller by the price of one drink, Janna held the tall glass high above her head and worked her way back to the bank of holo games.

Scraps of conversation reached her out of the cacophony, war stories and bitching, acid comments on the presidential candidates, debate on the Identation Bill in the legislature and on the suggested colonization moratorium. Opinion seemed for the former, against the latter: Let those who felt so sure they knew how to set up the perfect society do it on some other world.

Only the Deathrace game remained open, but Janna did not mind. Running down civilians suited her mood just fine. She gulped a mouthful of the Black Hole, amber on top, evilly undulating reddish-black on the bottom. With the liquor spreading fire through her, she dropped a token into the slot.

A holographic town sprang up on the board, complete with streets, houses, and people working at everyday tasks. Her car floated down the incoming highway, a blood-red Mercedes Vulcan. Janna stabbed the start button. Sailing into town, she started by running down a pair of joggers and a man walking his dog, followed by a woman with a baby stroller. A second child with the stroller-woman saved herself by dropping flat on the ground, and an old woman on a motorized wheelchair escaped the Vulcan through a narrow space between two buildings, but Janna made up for the points lost by quick wheelwork that netted her all the contestants in a bicycle race.

By now the village had been alerted. A tank rolled out of the police station looking for her. She whipped the Vulcan down an alley, however, then through a footpath underpass in a park, which not only netted her ten more points for another jogger but eluded a vigilante civilian with a bazooka. Grinning, she spun the Vulcan in a one-eighty turn to sixty-one two leos chasing her on motorcycles.

Then the grin faded and Janna swore. Motorcycles. Quist and Roos. The hearse and body. The outside world came crashing in on her.

Her hands tightened on the game control buttons. Damn. Why had both her father and Sid chosen this evening to go out?

She ran the holo Vulcan after the children playing in a school yard.

A teacher swept up one child and dashed for the safety of a doorway. Janna sent the Vulcan after them. Suddenly the teacher set the child down and whirled, pulling an old-fashioned shooter from her belt, a .45 autoloader, and fired.

"Shit!" Janna hauled desperately at the joystick.

But she was too late. The Vulcan's windshield shattered. The car went from a veer into a roll and exploded in flame against the wall of the school. The holo dissolved.

Janna's fist crashed down on the empty board.

"You break it, you better have the Card to pay for it before you leave tonight, leo!" Tuck bellowed from the bar.

"You still lasted longer than I usually do," a male voice said behind her.

Lion buff, she thought, and whirled to disembowel him with some scathing comment. But the man looked familiar, even aside from that indefinable something in expression and carriage that marked him as a leo. Instead of sarcasm, she gave him a polite nod.

"Are you thawed out from this afternoon yet?" he asked.

Thawed out. *That* was why she knew him. "You're Alpha Cap Five."

He smiled wryly. "Dale Talavera, actually."

He had, Janna realized suddenly, a nice set of shoulders

and fine, dark eyes she had to look *up* into. She smiled back. "Janna Brill. Would you like to make a contest of it?" She jerked her head toward the Deathrace board. "My token."

He shook his head. "Thanks, but I've seen you play before, and you have this habit of suckering your opponent into a position where the defensive forces wipe him out while you escape. How about something less tempting to your killer instincts?" He pointed to the holo of the band.

Why not? After gulping the rest of her drink, she followed him through the crowd toward the dance floor.

The size of the floor left no room for self-indulgence or acrobatics; nothing, actually, but standing close to one's partner beneath the holo and swaying in place. As the alcohol lightened her head and the melody of an old Elric Corbin ballad rewritten into jivaqueme rhythm flowed into her bones, she and Talavera moved even closer. On the next song they wrapped their arms around each other.

Now this was what she really needed, Janna reflected, fitting herself to the length of Talavera's body. This chased the echo of the apartment much better than a dozen Black Holes or a high score at Deathrace. He felt lean and hard and smelled pleasantly of spicy cologne and department-issue shower soap. His breath tickled her ear as he sang along with the music.

"What are you planning to do the rest of the night?" she asked.

"Sleep somewhere warm. What about you?"

His body heat soaked into her through her jumpsuit. She dug nails into his shoulders. "Where do you live?"

"Tecumseh division."

Way out on the east side of the county? "I'm on Mulvane just north of the WSU campus."

His hands slid down her back, pulling her hips hard against his. "My car is in the garage across the street."

They left without waiting for the song to end.

\* \* \*

The landing at the top of the outside steps was freezing, and the sonic lock on her door seemed to take forever to yield to the combination of tones produced by her palm-sized keypad, but eventually it clicked and the door swung open. Janna did not bother with the lights, just kicked the door closed and started peeling Talavera out of his coat and jumpsuit to the accompanying rip of pressclose seams. He returned the favor. "The bedroom is straight down the hall," she said against his mouth.

But instead of following her tug, Talavera froze. Janna felt him tense, even his breathing halting. At almost the same moment alarms shrieked in her too. Someone else was in the room. She felt the presence, heard breathing.

It came from behind her.

Janna dropped, rolling off to her left. Her ears told her Talavera had gone in the other direction to the safety of the kitchen doorway, a greater dark in the darkness. Silently cursing the entangling loose ends of the jumpsuit, she came up behind the end of the couch, reaching for the .38 Magnum shooter cached under the backrest cushion.

A dark shape filled the easy chair, vaguely silhouetted against the window behind. She aimed for the middle. "Don't move, jon; don't even breathe unless you're interested in a cardiac transplant."

"It's just me, bibi."

Relief flooded her, followed by cold fury. "Turn on the light," she snapped, and when he had touched on the table lamp, she glared at him over the sights of the shooter. "How the hell did you get in here, Maxwell?"

He pulled a sonic keypad out of his pocket. "I've had musical training, remember. I have an ear for tones and I've been home with you before. A little experimentation told me that *one* on your keypad is the same as *three* on mine. You know, you really are paranoid, bibi, programming the lock so you not only have to simultaneously punch in your birthdate and swearing-in date, but also repeat the sequence twice.

I about froze my nuts out there transposing the combination to my keypad."

"Hard card," she snapped. "You have to the count of five to get the hell out. One."

He grimaced. "Bibi. I have to talk to you."

"I said sail. Two."

He frowned at the shooter. "It's important."

"Three."

In the doorway of the kitchen, Talavera slid his arms back into his jumpsuit and pressed the front closed. "Maybe you ought to listen to him."

He had a shooter, too, she noticed. Interesting how off-duty weapons remained the old-fashioned firearms the public had officially taken away from them.

"I've listened to him too often. Four!" She thumbed back the shooter's hammer.

"Jan, I've just talked to Leonard Fontana on the Lanour platform," Mama said hastily.

Shock choked her. "Oh, god!" She released the hammer. "For once, I hope to hell you're imagining things, partner."

He held up a microcassette. "I taped the conversation."

She opened her mouth, closed it again when she could think of nothing to say, and pulled her jumpsuit back on. At least she did not have to deal with this half naked.

Talavera eyed both of them. "Do you want me to leave?"

"We could use a referee," Mama said.

"But that would also make me a witness . . . and I think the less I know about this, the better." He picked up his coat. "Maybe we can try again sometime, Jan."

The door closed behind him.

Janna glared at Mama. "You're going to interrupt my personal life one too many times, Maxwell."

Mama pushed his glasses up his nose. "Hit-and-run sex is no kind of relationship. You need—"

"I need you to tell me about this call to Fontana!"

Mama pulled off his glasses and pressed the heels of his hands against his eyes. "Oh, yes . . . Fontana."

Janna arched her brows. "What's the matter? Do you admit that this time you may have gone too far?"

His hands came down. "Fontana isn't god. Why shouldn't I talk to anyone I want who's connected with one of our cases?"

"Except it won't be our case much longer, and I wonder if the brass would appreciate you cutting them out of the communication chain." She sighed. "May I ask why you did it?"

"Well . . ." He sighed in turn. "I was there at the station finishing up my half of the reports, and I got to thinking about Fontana's big concern over the body. I thought, what if—but maybe you should see this before I tell you what I thought."

He turned to the phone and, flipping up the screen, traded his microcassette for the one already in the side of the phone.

"You called from *headquarters*?" She stared at him in horror. "Where every word is now on tape in Communications and any one of the brass can personally witness what you've done?"

He put his glasses back on, settling them in place with painstaking care. "That's where this recording came from, off their master."

She groaned and dropped onto the couch. Wickers. Totally off his tick and right over the brainbow. "I'll bet Fontana really appreciated being called in the middle of the night."

"He was still in his office. I think their schedule must be different from ours."

The screen remained blank the first couple of minutes as the telephone system connected to the satellites that relayed on to the Lanour platform, then flashed with a succession of faces representing the platform communications hierarchy, until finally the image became that of a trim man with a look of experience and authority, but almost no lines on his face and a full head of dark hair untouched by gray. Eyes as amber as a wolf's stared out of the screen above a polite smile.

"Good morning, Sergeant Maxwell. I'm Leonard Fontana. My secretary tells me you're with the Shawnee County Crimes Against Persons squad and in charge of the investigation regarding John Paul Chenoweth?" He spoke with a faint drawl.

Mama's face did not appear on the screen, but the tape recorded his voice, which was crisply professional. "Yes, sir. I thought you'd want to know that we've found Mr. Chenoweth's body."

The smile vanished. A hard gleam made his eyes look even more lupine. "I know. I spoke to the Nafsinger Mortuary not long ago. From here, where Earth looks so peaceful and beautiful, it's difficult to believe that there are people who can be so wantonly destructive. Will it help to find the gang members who did it if I arrange a reward?"

"We now doubt that any street gang was involved, sir." Briefly Mama told him about the autopsy and the conclusions drawn from it.

"Watch his face, bibi," Mama whispered.

The planes of the face congealed. "Smuggling? That's impossible, Sergeant."

"But isn't the platform a research facility? Some of that research must be of interest to other parties."

Fontana smiled again, but instead of reflecting humor, the gesture slammed a mask over his face. The drawl thickened. "Oh, I reckon competitors Like DuPont, Astrodyne, and Mitsubishi have a yen now and then to look into our labs. Just like I wouldn't mind knowing what's going on in theirs. We don't mistreat corpses to satisfy that impulse, though. We're not working with state secrets, after all, just products we're considering manufacturing, consumer goods."

Janna frowned. Did he really expect them to believe that?

"Can you think of anything at all that someone might be interested in stealing from you?" Mama's voice asked.

"I didn't really expect him to answer," Mama said, "but I wanted his reaction."

The smile never flickered. "Sorry. I just can't think of a thing. But even if there is something, it couldn't have gone out in the body. Nothing leaves this platform, not packages or personnel, without a thorough examination, and believe me, Sergeant, in the hands of my security chief, that's a thoroughness that makes Fort Knox look like it has an open-door policy."

"You go to all that trouble when you have no valuable secrets?"

The grin broadened, never touching the hard shine of the wolf's eyes. "Between you and me, I reckon Geyer's a little overzealous." He paused, glancing at something or someone out of screen range, then focused back on the screen. "I wonder if your vandals had something to do with those— abrasions, you said?—in his throat. Anyone who would mutilate a corpse wouldn't stop at shoving something down its throat. Well, according to my chronometer, I'm keeping you up past your bedtime, so I'll let you go. I'd be interested in knowing when you catch the toads who did that to Chenoweth, though."

"Finding them might be easier if you could give us some idea who to look for," Mama said.

The amber eyes flickered. "Sergeant, I have no idea."

Mama punched the stop button. "Well, what do you think?"

Janna shrugged. "He evaded earlier questions, but I think he was telling the truth at the last. What did you want me to see?"

He pushed his glasses up his nose. "Why do you think he evaded?"

"Oh, come on." She hugged her knees. "Do you think he's going to talk about research on a call anyone might be listening to and that he can be sure we're recording? And in his place I wouldn't want to admit that anything could leak out, either. Lanour would not be pleased."

"Considering what's happening to the Tellus platform, failing security might kill Lanour's station, too, but maybe Fontana is concerned with more than his job. If security is that tight and something still leaked, someone very high up has to be involved."

She sat straighter. "You're thinking about Fontana?"

The glasses slid down his nose as he leaned forward to rewind the tape. He peered at her over the top of them. "He certainly has to be up on the list. All his concern about the body could be just a way of keeping track of what we're doing, to see if we've fallen for the masquerade."

"So you call him up and warn him we haven't."

For once, sarcasm did not just slide off. He winced. "It was a risk I had to take to see his reaction. The smuggler doesn't have to be Fontana, though. The chief of security would be in an even better position to punch a leak."

She nodded thoughtfully. "His zeal could be just a cover." She frowned. "I don't suppose we'll ever know."

Mama sat upright, eyes gleaming. "His Earthside contacts have to be local. It isn't midnight yet, and the clubs don't close until three. If we start flushing out our favorite Eyes and Ears, we might find those contacts and close this case before morning."

He tempted her. The anger she had felt in the cemetery hissed back through her again as she thought of the mutilated body and a knife slashing through the flesh, looking for ... something of commercial value. Her hand actually reached for her jacket before a jaw-cracking yawn brought her to her senses. She dropped the jacket and sighed. "Mama, we're not going to accomplish anything tonight, except give ourselves pneumonia and maybe get ourselves killed because we're working when we're tired. Why don't you go home before Lia starts to think you're putting two with a human woman and not just Lady Justice?"

The light in his eyes died. He pushed up out of the chair. "I wonder if she'd give a damn."

It sounded like the problems at home were serious. Curling up alone in bed a short time later, she wondered if that could be the reason for his obsession with this case, to bury himself in his work. And if that were true, could his feelings about it be trusted any longer? Perhaps it was just as well that they were handing it over to someone else.

# CHAPTER
# SIX

**Thursday, January 25. 7:15:00 hours.**

The temperature remained well below zero. A pewter sky and a scattering of flakes drifting past the squadroom window slits threatened more snow. There were only a handful of overnights, though, complaints passed on for investigation from the evening and morning shifts: a couple of rapes, several assaults, a possible abduction, and one homicide.

"Involving our old friend Wendell Twissman," Lieutenant Vradel said, looking around the squad room.

Janna raised her brows. His tone sounded solemn, but his mustache twitched above a mouth whose corners fought to stay straight.

Inspector Leah Calabrese grimaced. "Is he out of Lansing again already?"

"You know the compassion of the Adult Authority for the suffering caused by incarceration. As soon as he was out, Wendell apparently went after one of the witnesses against him. Found the man's wife instead and, according to her statement, tried to attack her in her car. She pulled a shooter out from under the seat and dropped Wendell in his muck-lucks. Cardarella and Kazakevicius, you follow up on it."

"Ten-four." Inspector Cardarella scribbled in her notebook. "Lieutenant, will silver be good enough for the medal or should I order gold?"

Raising his voice to be heard above the laughter and cheers,

Vradel went on briefing them on general department activity since the day before, including faces and activity to watch for, and finished handing out the overnights.

He gave Janna an aggravated rape of a parking lot attendant. "The couple who assaulted him, one male, one female, beat him pretty badly in the process. You and Maxwell can head over to St. Francis to talk to him as soon as we've handed Customs the Chenoweth body. And by the way," he added, looking around the squad room, "where is your other half?"

She made herself shrug. "Maybe the fans on his car froze. I'm sure he'll be here soon, or call."

Inwardly, however, she could not feel so confident. Her gut had been knotting and unknotting all during briefing, wondering where he was. Had he persisted in going looking for the jackers after he left her place instead of heading home? Behind her eyes ran visions of his body frozen under a snowdrift in some alley or vacant lot in Oakland.

Vradel eyed her with the skepticism of a commanding officer long used to partners covering for each other, but shrugged in turn. "Come on in my office while I call Customs."

Janna poured herself a cup of caff first. The spider sat waiting patiently at one edge of the web below the newscanner, she noticed. A newswoman murmured, "Port Bradbury on Mars and Port Diana on the Moon have announced an expansion of six hundred additional personnel each by this summer. NASA is taking applications now for people with technical training for Port Diana and with technical and agricultural expertise for Port Bradbury."

Janna picked a chair where she could see both the phone screen and the squad room door.

All the activity remained on the screen, however. After a succession of secretarial faces in the Federal Building, a round face with a drooping walrus mustache regarded Vradel soberly. "Smuggling from a space platform using a dead body?

There's nothing they won't try, is there? What's the contraband?"

"We don't know yet," Vradel said. "Lanour's platform director should have some idea, though, and I'm about to call him."

A mask dropped over Walrus's face. The hair rose on Janna's neck. The platform name meant something special to him. What? A glint in Vradel's eyes suggested he was asking himself the same question.

Walrus provided no answer, however, only toyed with a computer light pen. "You mean you haven't asked if anything is missing?"

"Not yet, but—what is it, Brill?"

Had she groaned aloud? Damn. She grimaced. "Well . . . we *have* talked to Fontana, and—"

"Just a moment, Agent Burwell," Vradel said, interrupting her. Punching off the phone sound, he tipped the screen face down and frowned narrow-eyed at Janna. "What do you mean, you've talked to Fontana? When? After you talked to me last night? After I told you the case was going to Customs?"

Janna resisted an urge to sink down in her chair. "Well . . . yes." Damn that Maxwell! Think fast, girl. "We thought we ought to pass on as much information as possible to Customs. But Fontana says there's nothing on the platform that anyone would find worth smuggling off, though he also says their security is hermetically perfect even if there *were* something valuable around."

Vradel stared at her for what seemed like an eternity, chewing on his mustache, icy glints in his eyes.

Janna swore bitterly and silently . . . at Mama and at herself. Why was she doing this? Why not admit the call had been his idea? "It's all on tape in Communications, sir."

Without a word Vradel flipped up the screen and punched the phone sound back on. "It seems there's been a conversation with the Lanour platform, after all. They're not sure what was taken."

Walrus's mustache performed a hula under his nose. "Do you mean you can't even be certain there's *been* smuggling?"

Vradel's smile froze. "Of course there's been smuggling. We have the abrasions in the dead man's esophagus proving something had been shoved down it."

"I hardly call that proof. It can't be impossible for those marks to have been made some other way, and even if something were put down the throat, it can be only supposition that it was contraband. Lieutenant, until it's established that there actually *has* been smuggling, and *what's* been smuggled, I don't see that this case falls within our jurisdiction."

Mama came through the squadroom door as the phone screen went dark, not exactly resplendent in the neon brightness of his chartreuse tabard and bodysuit, but certainly impossible to overlook.

"Maxwell!" Vradel bellowed.

Mama slouched across to the office and leaned against the side of the doorway, sighing. "I know I'm late. I'm sorry, sir."

Janna blinked. No song and dance, just an admission of fault and an apology? What had happened to him after leaving her last night? She peered more closely at him.

Vradel eyed him with the wariness of a bomb squad officer studying a strange package. "You missed hearing Customs decline the Chenoweth case. It's still yours."

Mama returned his gaze without expression. "Okay."

Janna stared. What! Was that all he had to say? He must be ill.

She felt sure of it when she told Mama about the call to Customs on the way down to the garage, and he shrugged indifferently. "We already know someone highly placed has to be involved. Why be surprised he's pulling strings at Customs as well as here? Well, what do you want to do about looking for the jackers?"

Now he was even asking for her ideas. Unbelievable. "Find

Quicksilver." The sligh's desire to avoid talking to her about the hearse was the only lead they had.

Finding him was a problem in itself, of course. He had not earned his reputation by being visible. This time of year, the number of places he could be holding his school became more restricted because he needed heat, but Janna did not waste energy checking the back rooms of stores or idle gambling rooms of clubs on the hope of stumbling across him. She made quick visits to businesses like Las Comidas, where she knew slighs worked. Leaving word with them that she needed to talk to Quicksilver, she headed for the hospital to visit the aggravated rape victim and wait for Quicksilver's call.

Mama came along, too . . . as animated and useful as a store window mannequin.

She took the victim's statement and called the description of his attackers in to Dispatch for countywide broadcast. She also called Records. The computer reported three possible matches for the male, five for the female, and one pair when the two lists were cross-referenced.

Listening to the sultry female voice, Janna reflected that maybe she should have made Mama call in. Sexy crooning in his ear might be therapeutic.

The "wanted" bulletin became much more specific.

By mid-afternoon the pair had been located and brought to headquarters. An order to look at their bank records found three transactions at locations and times in the vicinity of the assault. Janna interviewed the suspects in one of the interview rooms off Crimes Against Persons, standing so that in looking up at her, the hidden camera could record the dilation of their pupils in response to questioning. A recorder measured stress in their voices.

By sunset the victim had picked their pictures from a stack of photographs, under the watchful eye of the couple's attorney, and the couple was formally booked.

Quicksilver did not call.

They spent the evening sweeping through Oakland's clubs, catching up with known Eyes and Ears, keeping their own eyes and ears open for Quicksilver or his close associates. In vain. No one had heard anything about smuggling from the space platforms . . . and Quicksilver never appeared.

"It looks like he isn't going to come out," Mama said. It was his longest sentence of the day.

Janna fought the wind trying to kick the Monitor into the oncoming lane. Her jaw set. "Tomorrow I'll *make* him come out. The question is how do I make *you* come out?"

He blinked. "Me?"

She nodded grimly. "I'm not about to spend another day dragging around Mr. Catatonia. It's worse than hanging on a leash behind Brainbow Man. Do you want to talk, or do I sic the professional prying of Schnauzer Venn on you?"

At first she thought he was going to ignore the question, but then he sighed and shrugged. "There's no need for that, bibi. Lia and I just spent last night discussing our relationship and deciding to terminate it. I'm moving out as soon as I find a new place to live."

*They* had made a decision to end the cohabitation? From the mask pulled tight over Mama's expression, Janna suspected that Lia had made the decision and he had spent the night in a fruitless effort to change her mind. "I'm so sorry. Would you like to go by the Lion's Den for a drink?"

He shook his head. "Thanks, but I just want to find a bed for the night and forget the whole world."

God, he *was* feeling bad. Was he safe to leave alone? "Sid's bed is empty."

He blinked at her in astonishment and gratitude. "I—thanks, Jan. I really appreciate that."

She shrugged. "There's an ulterior motive. Riding home in your car saves me a miserably cold wait at the bus stop, and we can get an early start rounding up Quicksilver tomorrow. You just better not walk in your sleep."

"I go comatose," he promised. "I'm told I don't even snore." He paused. "Just how do you plan to round up Quicksilver?"

She smiled grimly. "By being a mean bitch of a she-lion and making avoiding me infinitely worse than talking to me."

# CHAPTER
# SEVEN

The oriental-hispanic sligh who called himself Amber smiled at Janna and Mama with a careful politeness that walked the edge of cringing anxiety. "Quicksilver? I heard you were looking for him, so I'm sure he has too. If he hasn't shown up, it must be because he isn't interested in seeing *you.*"

He switched on the chip setter in his hand and resumed planting micro price-and-antitheft telltales in the labels and sleeve ends of a rack of electric-hued jumpsuits. Janna glanced at Mama.

She crossed the stockroom to put an arm between Amber and the jumpsuits. "I don't give a damn what Quicksilver wants. He has information I need, and I will see him. Today."

The sligh looked up, body quivering with an obvious effort not to retreat from her. "Excuse me, but I need to mark these suits. I can't help you find Quicksilver. He's his own master. He does as he wishes. Sorry."

"Sorry?" Janna bared her teeth. "You're going to be a whole lot sorrier."

Fear and anger flashed in the dark eyes. He glanced toward the doorway, but Mama lounged there, cleaning his nails with the switchblade he had never bothered to return to Kiel Jerrett.

Janna moved closer to Amber until the tension in him told her she had violated his personal space, then decreased the distance between them still further and dropped her voice to a hiss. "For years I've declined to hunt you people. You're gutsy, if brainbent, to stick this hard by your principles. But you can all go to hell when your 'freedom' interferes with my job. I want Quicksilver, and I'm going to have him or you'll suffer for it, *you* personally, Amber. If I haven't heard from Quicksilver by noon, at one o'clock Human Services and IRS representatives are going to march into this store and request the records of tax and OHS withholding on all its employees. After paying the fines for failure to file proper withholding, I doubt the manager of Teddy's Togs will ever use sligh help again. I'll point HS and the IRS at enough other businesses in this city so that no owner or manager will dare hire slighs, either, and that will be the last of the inventory you're begrudged in payment for your labor. Then what will you barter for food, housing, and other necessities?"

Amber went ashen.

"You have until noon," she repeated for emphasis, and stalked out of the stockroom.

Mama followed. "Christ. When you turn mean, you don't hold back, bibi."

She grimaced at the admiration in his tone. "I feel like a toad. All these people need is someone else harassing them." She sighed heavily. "But come on, let's visit our next victim before I lose my stomach for it."

The wind had died today, and the sun shone in a flawless cobalt sky but without lessening the bitter cold. The blinding glare sent Janna groping for her aviator glasses while Mama's lenses darkened to black.

Mama started the Monitor's engine. "I don't know if this will help, but you might try remembering that Lanour–Tenning is a very big corporation that owns dozens of companies, some of them with Defense Department contracts, and all of their research that needs zero-gee—alloys and polymers and drugs—or has to be conducted in space because it's too toxic for an atmosphere, is probably done on that space platform. That includes the Defense Department work, Fontana's claims to the contrary. We *have* to know what left the platform in Paul Chenoweth. If you want, I'll play bad guy at the next stop."

She stopped brushing the snow from her knee boots to glance across at him and smile. Sometimes he was a very nice person. "Thanks, but everyone is used to your histrionics. If I do it, they'll take us seriously."

The thought of a Lanour-built time bomb ticking here on Earth added passion to the icy anger of half a dozen more repetitions of her act, and it helped mindset her for the most distasteful task of all, the pièce de résistance, raiding a school.

They headed the car for the Oakland division station where Janna explained her needs to Lieutenant Nevil Enserro of Juvenile division.

He leaned back in his chair, shaking his head and sighing. "I knew it would come to this. Brill, you've been working with this black rack too long. I can't haul down a school without booking the teacher and identing the kids."

She gave him her most persuasive smile. "You can if you don't bring them back here to school right away." The division's slang still kept the old identity of the station house even half a century after the churches' losing their tax-free status had forced the Sacred Heart Church to auction off the time-grimed brick school building with its worn concrete steps and empty statuary niches. "We'll hold the kids where we find them. If Quicksilver doesn't respond, we'll bring them in and follow normal procedure."

Enserro pursed his lips. "That's going to take us out in weather when we usually don't bother with schools, and tie up at least two teams all morning. What's in it for us?"

She raised her brows. "Our thanks for cooperation in resolving a major case, plus the satisfaction of knowing you're helping find a possibly dangerous object and return it to safekeeping. Also, we owe you a favor."

Lacing his fingers together behind his head, he leaned back

farther in his chair. "I don't think that's enough. How about if you, personally, owe me a favor?"

"Toad," Mama muttered behind her.

But Janna smiled sweetly. "Well, if we're talking personal favors, Lieutenant, wouldn't this about make us even for the time Wim Kiest and I played back the tape on the interview-room camera looking for footage on a breaker we'd strapped and—"

Enserro sat bolt upright. "That was a long time ago!"

"And unknown but to thee and me, since Wim and I thoughtfully erased the evidence. That earned us your undying gratitude, you said at the time." She batted her eyes at him.

The lieutenant's mouth set in a thin line. "Where's the school?"

Six of them conducted the raid: Janna, Mama, a team from Juvenile, and another from the plainjane squad, just enough to block the exits from the casino room of La Juerga. Sealed in, no one offered resistance, though the teacher, Plum Nguyen, looked up as Janna's plastic wrap strap circled her wrists, adhering to itself, and said, "Don't take the children. I'll go; I'm obviously guilty of teaching without a license, but they've done nothing, just tried to become educated the only way they can."

Janna led her out of the casino room and into the bar, where Tito Duarte, the owner, sat watching in smoldering silence. Both his eyes and Nguyen's widened in astonishment, however, when Janna pulled the little polarizer out of a thigh pocket and touched it to the wrist strap. The restraint fell away instantly.

"Maybe we won't have to take in the kids, or you, either." While she explained the price of that generosity, she reversed the polarizer, restoring the charge in the strap before carefully sliding it back into the thigh-seam pocket of her jumpsuit.

Nguyen snapped to her full height, about the middle of Janna's chest. "You intend to hold the children hostage? Bitch!"

"Blame Quicksilver. He cut cloud when he knows I've always played fair with him." Janna glanced at her wrist chrono. "It's ten-oh-five."

Nguyen stared from Janna back to the casino door where Mama and one of the janes slouched against the wall. After a minute she pulled on her coat and hurried out the front door.

La Juerga included Deathrace among its half dozen holo games. Janna dropped a vending token in the slot and played while she waited.

"How do you leos face your mirrors?" Duarte asked.

"Believe me, I'm the lesser of several evils." But if this did not bring in Quicksilver, or it turned out he knew nothing useful, that mirror might be giving her problems for a while.

Duarte punched on the newscanner hanging over the bar.

"... despite a proposed moratorium on colonization inspired by Senator Scott Early in a campaign speech earlier this week, colonial companies continue to be formed and seek shareholders. In Kearney, Nebraska, Matthias Mankiller announced the incorporation of the Dakota Company, open to those having half or more amerind blood, but with preference given to members of Sioux tribes."

Mama left the doorway to watch the game over Janna's shoulder. "What was that interview-room tape you and Enserro were talking about?"

"Let's just say it was a screwup worthy of you, partner." She crashed her car through a parade, claiming points on half the band, the parade marshal, and the marshal's horse. "But at least the time you locked yourself in the backseat of that watch car it was with your partner, not a superior officer's wife, and unlike Enserro, you didn't have a hidden camera or accidentally bump the activation button."

Nguyen reappeared shortly after eleven. "I couldn't find him. I don't have any idea where he is. Please, won't you let the children go, anyway? I'll stay as your hostage."

"You all stay." Janna kept her eyes on the game. She was still on her first token, though the points came slower now as the local population dwindled and she had to spend more time dodging the increasing power of the weapons carried by the survivors.

"But surely you can't expect me to be Quicksilver's keeper. No one has a right to control another's life. We are each autonomous."

"But unless we act in cooperation, we can't survive as a society," Mama said.

Acting in cooperation, the board characters finally trapped and destroyed her car. She started another game. Concentrating on it became increasingly hard, however, as the numbers on her wrist chrono advanced toward twelve noon. Nguyen and Duarte sat drinking tea and alternating between glares and anguished glances at the wall chrono above the bar.

The radio button murmured in Janna's ear. "Alpha Oakland Nineteen, render assistance to snatcher victim, Michigan and Sardou. Loss of food and housing coupons."

Mama sighed. "I don't think he's going to make it, bibi."

She ran the playing car in through the hedge around a garden café to smash a lean waiter between her bumper and the building wall. The waiter reminded her of Quicksilver. Janna bit her lip. Could she have miscalculated? She always thought he had become a teacher, scraping by on the little food and clothing the parents of his pupils could spare, because he cared about children and minds, but could hiding what he knew matter even more than the welfare of other slighs?

"If he doesn't come, are you really going to go through with the school strapping and calling HS and the IRS?"

She sighed. "If we don't, what happens the next time slighs don't want to talk to us?"

The populace wiped her out again. She gave it up and turned away, glancing at her wrist chrono. And wished she had not. It read eleven fifty-four. Damn Quicksilver. Her gut knotted.

"Maybe I could play good guy and forcibly take over the operation," Mama said.

"Except you haven't objected before. It'd look like the act it would be." Eleven fifty-five. "We'd better make our calls." Double damn the man!

"Make the calls, all right, Brill. Call off your goddam wolves!"

Janna whirled. Quicksilver stood in the doorway, as lean and sallow as ever, wrapped in a parka several sizes too large.

She kept a mask pulled tight over her relief, however. "You and the kids can go, Nguyen. Mama, would you please call the others and tell them the cavalry arrived in time?"

He headed for the phone, his grin a white blaze in the darkness of his face. Plum Nguyen hurried into the casino and reappeared with her students, leading them quickly through the bar and out the front door.

Janna beckoned to Quicksilver as the doors hissed closed behind the school. "Sit down. Want some tea?"

He dropped in the chair, eyes blazing. "What the hell are you trying to do to me? In one morning you've turned my friends into a lynch mob."

She regarded him coldly. "You wouldn't talk to me. Talk to me now."

His expression went blank. "How can I, Sergeant? I don't know anything."

After all this he was going to play *that* line? The people involved must be very dangerous indeed, or powerful. Then she cursed her own stupidity. No, of course not. How could she be so blind. Quicksilver feared no one, only *for* someone . . . slighs. But . . . how could slighs know anything about Lanour and industrial espionage?

She leaned back in her chair. "Some loyalties are danger-ous, Q. These are ticklish times for slighs with that Mandatory

Identation legislation in the Statehouse. Any sort of serious trouble could tip the balance toward passage."

Quicksilver regarded her steadily. "I'm aware of that."

"It's better to clean your house. Auto theft is a serious charge, not to mention the kind of attention bound to be given to what happened to the body afterward, but protecting these slighs will only make matters worse for all of you when these are caught . . . and eventually they will be, that I promise you. And I'll get back what they took out of that body."

"They didn't take anything." Quicksilver leaned toward her. "They didn't touch the body. They were shocked even to find it there. They're angry and light-witted but not vicious."

"Just criminal. They were willing to hire out to impersonate Orions and jack a hearse."

Quicksilver sighed. "Impersonating the Orions was their idea. They needed a disguise and picked one they hoped would also bring a little grief to some people who like to torment slighs. They never even thought of the jacking as criminal. Since no one was going to be hurt—they were just supposed to take the hearse and deliver it—it looked like a way to strike back at 'Real People.' And that's all they did, took the hearse and delivered it."

"We want them," Mama said behind Janna's shoulder.

Quicksilver frowned. "They won't come in to be strapped. Not even I could talk them into that."

Janna tilted her head back to look up at Mama. Catching his eye, she raised her brows. His chin dipped in reply.

Her gaze returned to Quicksilver. "They won't be strapped. We just want to talk to them, to find out what they know. Come on, Q., you know little fish aren't important. It's the people who hired them I want."

The sligh's lips pursed. "No prosecution of any kind? You promise?"

"Since they didn't hurt Ms. Nafsinger, if they talk, they walk."

Quicksilver stood up. "I'll call you about where to meet us."

Dispatch radioed them a telephone number about two o'clock at Stormont–Vail Hospital where they were interviewing the victim of a hit-and-run. By three they had parked the Monitor at the Oakland Mall and made themselves at home in The Magic Pan, sipping cups of hot chocolate. A few minutes later Quicksilver walked into the crepe shop.

None of the four with him could have been over twenty. Janna saw why they made convincing Orions. Even now they walked with the swagger of street gang members. Smoldering eyes met hers boldly as Quicksilver introduced them: a red-haired boy calling himself Titan, another boy named Mustang, a boy and girl named Havoc and Tempest, hispanic and so similar in appearance that they must be brother and sister. Was the arrogance bravado? Thinking back to the waitress at Las Comidas, Janna thought not, and she wondered in dismay if this could very well *be* a street gang, a new one, and a new breed of sligh. She had never before heard slighs use names like Tempest and Havoc.

"My god," Mama breathed next to her. "What are we creating?"

So he was thinking the same thing.

The four brought plastic pseudo-wicker chairs over from another table and sat down straddling the backs.

"Buy us some hot chocolate," Mustang said. "Our memories work best when we're thawed out."

"Food would help too. I'll take strawberry crepes," Tempest added.

Quicksilver frowned but Janna hesitated, torn between automatic hostility at the tone and a keen awareness that these four must have rarely, if ever, enjoyed such a treat. Why not, for once, let them indulge in one of the little extras that Documenteds took for granted? Only . . . they had demanded, not asked. "Don't push your luck, muchacha."

She did punch up more hot chocolate on the table's menu pad, though. A waitron looking like a meter-tall pillar slid up to the table minutes later with the order on its tray top. Mama handed the steaming mugs around.

"You're welcome," the waitron intoned, and glided away on invisible rollers.

Havoc glared after it. "We shouldn't touch anything where they use those things. They take away sligh jobs."

His companions nodded grimly, but once Quicksilver gulped his chocolate with a speed that burned Janna's throat to watch and left, pleading other business, one by one the young slighs casually picked up their mugs too.

Mama leaned back in his chair, eyeing all four. "Do you have a name for your ... group?"

Red-haired Titan smirked. "You mean, like a gang? No. Gangs are conformists. Like the whole damn world. Conformity is really what's behind this Identation shit, you know. Uncle's afraid of wild cards, anything that isn't analyzed, labeled, and—"

"Suppose you tell us about the people who hired you to jack the Nafsinger hearse," Janna interrupted. "Who were they?" Letting her hand drop out of sight under the table, she tapped on the microcorder in her thigh pocket.

The slighs exchanged glances but said nothing until Janna reminded them that their freedom depended on cooperation, then Havoc said sullenly, "There were two jons."

"Did they give you any names?" Mama asked.

They shook their heads.

"What did they look like?"

They shrugged. "Afroams."

"Try being more specific."

Tempest rolled her eyes. "One of them was about his color." She pointed at Mama. "The other one looked really black."

Janna nodded. "How tall were they? Fat? Thin?"

Havoc frowned in thought. "One was about a hundred sixty

or seventy centimeters, maybe. Kind of stocky. He was the chocolate one. His hair looked kinky and bushy."

Mustang nodded. "And the other one, the black one, who did most of the talking, was a rack, about like you two ... real short hair, very fuzzy, and he had a couple of scars here." He drew his fingers across his cheeks. "He had an accent of some kind."

"Jamaican," Titan said.

Tempest frowned. "I thought Jamaican had more singsong to it."

"How did they approach you?" Janna asked.

"They came up one night in the Buenas Noches," Mustang said. "Asked if they could buy us a beer. We'd been seeing them in there for a couple of nights, so we said sure. If they wanted to be so generous with their Card, who were we to refuse them?"

"What night was that?"

"Last Friday," Tempest said.

"The nineteenth, then." Mama pushed his glasses up his nose. "Go on. What did they say?"

"We sat around talking about things for a while, and they bought us another beer, then the tall one said he hated the way Uncle keeps claiming that everyone is free to live his own life-style but passes all kinds of laws that make it impossible to live decently without being Idented," Titan said.

Tempest's dark eyes smoldered. "The shorter one said that if he were us, he'd be so mad, he'd want to bomb the Statehouse or something. I told him that sounded like a good idea."

"So then the taller one got this big grin and said he had an idea," Havoc said. "He had someone he needed to get even with, and if one of us could drive and we wouldn't mind helping him, we could not only get back at the RPs, but they would give us a hundred credits each worth of gift certificates from stores of our choice."

"I know how to drive," Titan said, "so I said, what did he want us to do?"

"You never stopped to think that if he wanted to pay you, it must be illegal?" Janna asked.

His lip curled. "We're not light-witted, leo. Of course we knew, but he promised us no one had to be hurt. We could handle the driver any way we wanted as long as we didn't bring him along when we delivered the hearse to the Tonaka Cemetery."

"We said we'd do it, and we told him what stores we wanted the certificates from," Mustang said. "He said he'd let us know where and when to go after the hearse, and then they left."

"When did you see them again?" Mama asked.

"Monday night. They said the hearse would be coming north on Topeka Boulevard sometime after ten in the morning."

"It was colder than hell waiting for it too," Havoc said.

Janna raised her brows. "You're lucky it stopped for a light near you."

They snickered. "If it hadn't, Tempest was going to run out and throw herself down in front of it so the driver would think he'd run over her and stop."

"I thought calling Mustang 'Pluto' when we pushed the driver out was a nice touch." Tempest smiled smugly. "We hear you actually arrested him for a while."

"What happened when you took the hearse to the cemetery?" Mama asked.

"Nothing," Titan said. "They were waiting there. We climbed out; they handed over the gift certificates and climbed in; we left."

"You didn't see them drive off?"

"Nope. They told us to sail and waited while we did."

"Did you see any car that they might have come in?" Janna asked.

"Nope."

"What stores did the gift certificates come from, then?

We're not going to cancel them," she added as the faces of the four froze into stony masks.

Once they had reluctantly recited the list, there seemed to be nothing more to be learned. Janna tapped off the microcorder and stood up. "Thank you for your help."

Tempest drained the last drop of chocolate from her cup. "If you think we helped a lot, could we have another cup?"

The little-girl tone plucked at Janna. She glanced toward Mama. His forehead creased into furrows of solicitude. Janna dug into her breast pocket for her Card.

"I'll pay for ten credits worth of merchandise on my way out. Eat it up however you want."

In the car she grimaced. "I must be going wickers. The next time we meet that quad, I'll probably be throwing wrap straps on them."

"Them and how many other angry young slighs?" Mama shook his head. "That's another time bomb ticking away among us."

Janna shook her head, too, but she was thinking of the afroams. She did not like the thoughts. "You realize that although our Genghis Four were approached last Friday about jacking the hearse, Chenoweth's fatal accident didn't occur until the next day?"

"I noticed." He pushed his glasses up his nose. "It looks like our smuggler *did* arrange to have a body available."

Murder. Anger simmered in her. "Mama, let's find those deeks."

# CHAPTER
# EIGHT

**Friday, January 26. 16:00:00 hours.**

"Our jackers have expensive taste," Mama said.

"Impractical, though, if they want goods to barter with."

Just looking around the Granada Mall without ever stepping into any of the shops, Janna estimated the prices at half again what similar items brought elsewhere in Topeka. The mall, one of the new chain of Holimalls, catered to the Cards of passengers and crews passing through the sprawl of the Forbes Aerospace Center across Highway 75. The Holiday Inn stood at the center, a luxurious tower presiding over one square mile of flanking shops, restaurants, theaters, gardens, and sport and recreational facilities, all under one transparent, almost unnoticeable roof.

"I think they're more interested in things to *have*, bibi." Mama glanced around. "Have you ever been out here before?"

She shook her head. "Our Gang of Four seems to know it well enough, though. I suppose they've been riding out on the bus with transport tokens won by hustling pool and holo games."

Her ear button murmured. "Alpha Forbes Twenty, attempt to locate. A Mr. Samuel Benning. He should be driving a white-over-blue '78 Smith Sundowner, license number KWP 442. There is a family emergency; he needs to call home immediately."

"We should have asked them how to find this Supramodes shop," Mama said.

"Let's ask the mall."

Janna stopped at a computer terminal with a holo above it flashing DIRECTORY in all directions in glowing orange letters and typed in the shop name Tempest had given as one of those where the afroams bought gift certificates.

"Welcome to Granada Mall," a cheery female voice said. "It is a pleasure to help guide you. You will notice that each walkway is named. The names appear in the floor every twenty meters. To reach Supramodes, turn left at the next intersection onto Beta Lyrae and follow it to the red slidewalk. Ride the slidewalk across the mall to Copernicus." As the voice talked, a map appeared on the terminal screen and a line zigzagged across it, illustrating the vocal directions. The computer gave the directions twice, concluding with, "Should you have any further difficulty, please do not hesitate to consult me through another terminal. I am always at your service."

They found the slidewalk without difficulty, though Janna wondered if she would notice their exit when it came up. The walk ran through countless holographs that blocked her view of things on down the walk. Some were ads for shops in the mall . . . a room full of furniture to demonstrate Furniture Castle's wares, models posing in clothes obtainable at certain clothing shops, and one beautiful young woman advertising Bodie Nouveau's body-painting arts by wearing only an intricate floral pattern. Other holos danced words before Janna, reinforced by an audio reading . . . biblical quotes from a local religious organization and a public service announcement urging her to buy her narcotics from only licensed government-approved stores and dealers. "Bargain drugs can be fatal," the announcement said ominously.

But the Copernicus exit lay in a blessedly clear gap between holos. A voice with the solicitude of a worried mother called the name of the exit aloud too. From there they found Supramodes without difficulty, its entrance spreading wide across from the legal offices of Bliss, Hart, and Long, whose window sign announced bargain rates for one- and five-year marriage contracts for couples and groups of any sex.

A chime rang as they stepped into the shop. In the open center of the store a glittering crystalline-looking sculpture beneath spotlights waved vanes like spider's legs, scattering rainbows around them.

A tall, dark-haired woman in a clinging iridescent dress floated around the sculpture toward them. "May I help you?"

Five minutes later they stood in the office section of the back room talking to the manager, trying to convince her to call up her transaction records.

With one golden brow raised skeptically above eyes painted like ladybugs, and a hand held to breasts threatening to spill out of the neckline plunging to her waist, she looked from their badges and ID to Mama. Her expression clearly reflected her difficulty in picturing him as a police officer. "Do you have a bank authorization?"

"We don't need one, ma'am," Janna said patiently. "A bank authorization is required by law for examination of the financial transactions of a particular individual. To look through your shop's records, however, which are business, not personal, all we need is your permission."

The manager folded her arms, accentuating her cleavage. "I really don't see what a couple of gift certificates—"

"Every scrap of information becomes vital in light of the heinous nature of the crime we're investigating," Mama said solemnly, eyes on her cleavage.

The manager's brows skipped. "Heinous crime?"

He dragged his eyes up to her face with obvious effort. "Well, I'm not in a position to give out details because of certain public figures involved, but . . ." He edged closer to her. "Necrophilia is involved, and activities in a graveyard too disgusting to discuss in even a society as permissive as ours."

Janna winced inwardly at the outrageous lie, but the manager's eyes lighted. "Public figure? Necrophilia? Are you sure you can't say anything?"

Mama sighed in regret. "We have orders straight from the top. Which means we're under real pressure to produce evidence. Ms. Dorn, you could really be a big help to me in getting the brass and political High Muckies off our rears."

"Important politicians are involved in this?" The manager almost squealed. "Oh, well . . . let me see what I can do." She sat down at the terminal on one edge of the transparent acrylic oval of her desk and punched in a code. "Do you want everything back to last Friday?"

"Just Saturday, Sunday, and Monday will do."

More code, then she punched the print button. In minutes hard copy filled the catch basket.

"Use my office as long as you need to," the manager said. "I'll be on the floor if you have any questions." She paused. "Graveyard? How deliciously scandalous." The word rolled around in her mouth. Still savoring it, she left.

Saturday and Sunday had been busy days, they discovered. Dividing the printout, each went through half, line by line.

"Maybe I ought to start coming out here," Mama said. "They carry Giancarlo's line. He's just starting to attract notice, but I predict that in a few years he'll be a major fashion voice."

"He styles in fluorescent colors?" Janna asked without looking up.

Mama did not reply for a moment, then said, "You could do worse than shop here too. You're an attractive woman who could be really flash if you'd wear clothes with a little more excitement."

She snickered. "That's just what I need, fashion advice from a man who wears mauve and chartreuse together."

"At least it's individual and not—here it is, bibi! Sunday, January twenty-first, 3:37 P.M., one hundred-credit gift certificate, one fifty-credit certificate. The name is Charles

Emerson Andrews, and the bank is the Maritime Bank of Houston."

"Houston?" She leaned over to read the printout. "I suppose we should expect them to be from out of town." She pursed her lips. "They'll have been staying in a hotel, then." She grimaced. "More legwork."

They thanked the store manager on their way out. She smiled conspiratorially. "I'm always glad to help our public servants. The case sound terribly . . . depraved. Is it a Kansas political figure involved?"

Behind her, two clerks leaned forward, ears almost twitching. Obviously the manager had been passing on the lurid details.

Mama assumed a concerned face and shook his head. "A national figure, or he could be one if matters in New Hamp— I'm sorry, I'm talking too much."

"New Hampshire?" the manager whispered. "You mean it's one of the *presidential candidates*? Oren Travers? I've never liked that smile. You can't trust bible cultists. You just know that the minute they get into power, they're going to start legislating their beliefs into law. Or Senator Thayer? I'd love to see some dirt on him. Thanks to his trade protectionism bills, it's almost impossible to import those lovely African fabrics anymore. Or is someone else involved?"

Hissing, Janna grabbed the front of Mama's jacket and dragged him out of the shop. "Are you *really* brainbent? That's slander!"

"Not as defined by law, bibi. These are public figures, so there has to be a malicious intent proven, and I didn't come up with the name; the manager did."

She sighed. "Never mind. Shall we start looking for our deeks at the Inn and hope we get lucky?"

It was a hope in vain, of course. Although the desk clerk, and then the manager, responded to their badges more quickly than Supramodes' manager had, asking the hotel computer for a Charles Emerson Andrews registered sometime in the past two weeks brought only a polite "I'm sorry" from the computer.

"I wonder if we can be sure that Andrews rented the room," Mama said.

Janna considered. "The shorter man could have signed the register."

"Or they work for someone powerful enough to provide them with several identities."

The manager frowned. "That's impossible. The government checks the fingerprints and retinal patterns of all applicants against the files to make sure that person hasn't already been issued a Scib Card." He paused. "Unless the government itself is doing it."

"Or a foreign government," Mama said.

Watching the manager's eyes widen, Janna said hurriedly, "Don't be paranoid. It doesn't have to be that complicated and you know it. Our jons could have a joint account, programmed to accept any number of names. Let's ask for guests with Cards on Andrews's bank."

While Mama queried the computer Janna gave the manager descriptions of both men.

Those produced no results, either. "We serve hundreds of guests a week," one of the desk clerks complained when Janna carried the questioning to him. "How can I possibly remember one?"


## Saturday and Sunday, January 27 and 28.

The sentiment was shared by most of the desk clerks they interviewed over the next two days in the course of visiting every hotel and motel in the greater Topeka area. None remembered a pair of afroams of the description the four young slighs provided. Not even the distinctive feature of the scarred cheeks helped. Nor did the name of Charles Emerson An-

drews appear in any of the hotels' computer registration files.
A number of other Andrewses did, though none with Scib
Cards from the Maritime Bank of Houston. Each still had to
be checked, anyway, either with phone calls to the listed
address or through tracing car license numbers back to car
registrations and driver's licenses. None of them were the
afroams.

By Sunday evening Janna's eyes ached from squinting at
computer monitors and near indecipherable lettering on hard-
copy from worn printers in cheap hotels.

Leaving the last hotel, she swung across the Monitor's
airfoil skirt and dropped heavily into the passenger seat. Thanks
to having sat in the sun for the past hour, the car felt almost
warm. She slid the door closed against the frigid temperature
outside and laid her head back against the seat. "I'm beginning
to wonder what the hell we think we're doing. Those deeks
are long gone, maybe even out of the country."

Mama pushed his glasses up on his forehead and rubbed
his eyes. "Working is better than going home, isn't it? Even
if those two don't have something we may not want loose in
the world, they're our only lead to the killer on the platform."

That toad. Anger flared in Janna at the thought of his
destroying another human being just to provide himself with
a messenger for his contraband. Not that they could really
do anything about him. The platform was out of their jurisdiction. Still, it would give her satisfaction to hand the deek's
identity to Fontana. "Any suggestions where to go from here,
then?"

"Maybe they didn't stay locally."

She frowned. All that was left were the little towns in the
far south and far north edges of the county, where strangers
created attention and memory—surely not what their afroams
wanted—and places out-of-county. But the two had been at
the Buenas Noches every night for several nights and must
have spent some time prowling the city and the Oakland area

looking for just the right people to hire for the jacking. So they could not have stayed very far out of the county.

"You're thinking Lawrence?" she asked.

"It's just half an hour down the road."

## Monday, January 29, 8:30:00 hours.

Mama made it to Lawrence in fifteen minutes the next morning.

Janna tightened her seatbelt as the snowy countryside blurred past the car. "You'd haul down any civilian you caught going this speed."

"Sure." He grinned. "For them it's illegal. For us it's a fringe benefit."

Their ear buttons could not pick up the highway patrol band, but Janna set the car radio for the frequency and listened with one ear, hoping the Monitor stayed on the road. The snow cover left the trees and rolling hills around them so uniformly white that contour and detail had vanished. Except for the fans of the big trailer trucks keeping the roadbed blown clear, it would have been easy for the car to miss a turn and end up wedged in a fence or between trees.

But the car was still sailing and in a single piece when Mama skimmed down the east Lawrence ramp off I-70. As always when she visited Lawrence, Janna wondered why someone had chosen the one mountain in Kansas to put a university on. Anywhere on campus always seemed up from everywhere else. The University of Kansas hill with its sprawl of classroom buildings and towering dormitories dominated the skyline of the town.

They stopped at police headquarters to explain their presence to the Lawrence leos and talk a Records clerk into printing out a list of local hotels and motels. Then they began making the rounds.

*      *      *

The results were about the same as in Topeka. The name Andrews turned up on several registers, and even one Charles Andrews, though with the middle name of William; but none of the Andrewses banked in Houston. Still, Janna wrote down all the information to check out once they were back in Topeka. Their descriptions met shaking heads everywhere.

"No one of that description has stayed here in the past two weeks."

"I don't remember any black man with scars on his cheeks."

"Officer, I can't possibly remember everyone who checks in here."

Then, in the records office of the Konza Motel, a geodetic-dome of bronze-colored glass, a name leapt out of the screen at Janna: Maritime Bank of Houston. The name with it was Milton Lowell, not Andrews, but the room had been a double, two beds, two persons, occupied from Tuesday, January sixteenth, to the morning of Tuesday, January twenty-third. Electricity lifted the hair all over her body. They left the day of the jacking!

"Mama!"

"I see it. It looks like you were right; they've got a joint account." He scribbled down the accompanying information. "Hamilton Lowell and friend William Solomon, 1902 Runaway Scrape Court, Richmond, Texas. That's a Missouri tag on his car, though."

"Ten to one it's a rental."

They headed out for the desk.

The two-sided newscanner screen on the counter carried an interview with the lead guitarist of Crosswhen, competing with a blaring advertisement for halucinogens on the wall-size TV screen across the lobby. Janna lifted a brow at the musician's thick accent. After a century, bands were still Britain's number-one export.

Mama showed the desk clerk the registration information. "Do you remember these men?"

The clerk, a dapper oriental, frowned. "In 151 until Tuesday? I don't think—"

"Two black men," Janna prompted, "a smaller one who was very dark, and a taller, lean one the same color as my partner, with scars across his cheeks?" She crossed her fingers.

"Oh, them. What did they do, violate someone's copyright?" The clerk snickered.

Janna blinked, nonplussed. "What?"

"They were here for the seminar on Patent, Trademarks, and Copyright being held at the Law School."

"They told you that?" Mama asked.

The clerk shook his head. "I heard them talking to each other about it when they checked in. They looked like lawyers . . . zigzag pinstripe and green paisley jumpsuits."

"The room record says they didn't make any calls from their room, but did they receive any?" Janna asked. They would have to have been contacted about when to expect Chenoweth's body.

"We don't keep records of incoming calls."

Mama raised a brow at her. "If they called out, they probably used a public phone."

And no doubt called collect, sparing themselves the use of their Cards and the attendant record of that use and the number called. Janna grimaced. "Do you think it's worth trying to talk the Lawrence PD into scanning the room for prints for us?"

Mama switched the raised brow to the clerk. "Is 151 occupied now?"

"It's on its second set of occupants since Mr. Lowell and Mr. Solomon left."

"Not a chance of a snowflake on Venus, bibi."

For the sake of thoroughness they stopped at the university, but, of course, no one named Charles Andrews, William Solomon, or even Hamilton Lowell had been registered for the legal seminar.

Driving back to Topeka, Mama said, "These jons are careful, finding a motel near the university instead of just off the Interstate, checking to see what was going on on campus so they could use it for cover."

"I wonder how much that's going to make this name and address worth."

A computer query to Missouri's DMV in Jefferson City brought no surprises. The license number of the car the two men drove was registered to Heartland Car Rentals at Kansas City International Airport. For grins they tried calling Heartland but found it had closed its desk for the evening by that time. Another computer query, this one to Texas, came back with a notice that the Austin computer was down and could not provide information until morning.

Janna swore. "We send people to the stars and they still can't make computers that give you what you need when you need it. If we were in hot pursuit with every second counting, we'd be left wrapping nothing but air."

Mama shrugged. "Bureaucracy never changes."

## Tuesday, January 30. 10:30:00 hours.

Not that the driver's license information on Hamilton Lowell proved worth waiting for when it finally arrived from Austin in the middle of the next morning: Born 01/14/23, one hundred seventy-nine centimeters, seventy-seven kilos, brown hair, gray eyes. The license picture showed a middle-aged caucasian male with thinning hair but a luxuriant bush of muttonchop whiskers. Obviously not one of the jons in question.

Janna spat in disgust and complained to Vradel, "So we still know nothing except that our jons also have connections that find them valid driver's license names and addresses."

"And keep their credit at the Maritime Bank of Houston." He handed her an authorization to request a bank check on account number 10-009-682419. "You want and need this, I believe. May it give you answers, because Fontana's been calling Paget almost every day, and it would be nice to have something positive to report when Paget asks *me* how we're doing."

She nodded grimly.

MB of H proved stuffy but polite. As soon as their telscriber spit out a copy of the authorization, the bank official assigned to them, a sleek Ms. De Allende, called up the account's records.

"The name on the account is Wofford Ceramics," De Allende informed them.

Janna exchanged frowns with Mama. Ceramics might well be something Lanour was experimenting with, but could they be worth murder to smuggle? "It's a business account? Who's authorized to draw on it?"

De Allende glanced off to the side, presumably toward her computer monitor. "That varies, Sergeant. Wofford maintains the account to provide noncitizen personnel with a local credit source while they're in this country."

Mama kicked Janna's ankle and grinned. She winced. Noncitizen personnel. The tall, scarred jon had had an accent. Scars! She sat upright, suddenly remembering a Nigerian boy she had known in college, and the scarring across his face that he had proudly explained was traditional and proclaimed his tribal affiliation. Damn! Why had she not thought of that sooner? "Do you have a record of the current or recent Card holders?"

"I'm afraid not. Wofford has a code that gives them access to their account in the computer, and they file new signatures and retinal patterns themselves."

"Is that a usual practice at the bank?" Janna asked.

Ms. De Allende sat fractionally straighter. "On request we will tailor accounts to meet very specialized needs. In this case, of course, Wofford has been required to release the bank from any liability should that code fall into other hands and fraudulent use be made of it." She paused, then said, "The account is fifteen years old. How much of its records do you need?"

Janna checked her desk calendar. "From January ninth to the present should be sufficient."

"Our computer will send them to yours immediately. If we can be of further help, please do not hesitate to call on us again."

They headed down to Records as soon as they punched off. The printout sat waiting for them when they arrived.

"I don't know what I expect to learn from it, though," Janna said.

"That they left the country Wednesday afternoon, maybe," Mama replied. "Look." He showed her the last page. "No transactions since then."

Janna's fist came down on the Records counter. "Damn! They're gone, and the whatever has gone with them. We don't know who they are or where in the world they are." She chewed her lower lip. "I wonder what Wofford Ceramics makes and, since they have foreign personnel, where their branch offices are."

"Some of my buddies from law school have gone into corporate work. I'll give a few of them a call."

Her father's voice and his face on her phone screen warmed the apartment that evening. Janna met his smile. "So this year you really think you'll do it?"

"Cat says I'd better, because she's been listening to me go on for the last nine years about preferring to make jewelry full-time to designing for Boeing, and if I don't stop talking and *act*, she won't renew when our marriage contract is up."

"Good for her!"

He rolled his eyes. Janna saw herself in the gesture. "You're all in league to push me out of the Boeing nest. You know, I ran into your mother the other day, and in the course of an actual civil conversation with her, she expressed the same

opinion. She even wished me good luck. Time cools enmity,
I suppose. Do you ever talk to her or your brother?"

"No." Sometimes she could barely remember her mother,
except for the storm of disbelieving fury on that day Janna
chose to stay with her father after the marriage cancellation.
"I have a telscribed note from Andy once in a while. He
seems happy on Mars."

"And what about you, Janna, honey?" His forehead creased
in concern. "Are you still happy with your single leo's life?
You're looking tired."

What an invitation to talk, to tell him everything, yet she
found herself just shrugging. "Part of the job. There's a frustrating case right now. And I miss Sid. I suppose I should
find another roommate."

"For the kind of mothering and fussing Sid did, you need
a spouse."

She snorted. "Marriage?"

"Some people find it very enjoy—"

A pound on the door drowned him out. "Bibi, it's me."

"Just a minute, Dad." She hurried to the door and flipped
back the security strip running down the edge of the door.
"Come in but be quiet. I'm talking to my father."

She hurried back to the phone.

He pushed the door closed behind him. "I have the information on Wofford Ceramics."

Wofford! She bent over the phone. "I'm sorry, Dad, the
job calls. I'll talk to you later." Punching off, she whirled to
face Mama. "Let's have it."

He peeled out of his jacket and fished around in a saddlebag
of a thigh pocket on his jumpsuit. "One of the law school
buddies is in the legal department at the Smith plant down
by Wakarusa. I had him ask about Wofford through his corporate contacts." He produced a much-folded sheet of paper
from his pocket, opening it as he dropped onto the couch.

Janna curled up on another section beside him where she
could look over his shoulder. Not that reading the paper

helped much when it was written in Mama's note-taking hieroglyphics.

"Wofford is a fair-size company, incorporated in Texas but with offices in England, Spain, India, Taiwan, Australia, and the Republic of South Africa."

"What does it do?"

"Not much exciting, just buys up local pottery and dishes and other ceramic products at each of its offices to ship to other offices for distribution and sale. However..." He paused to grin at her.

Janna doubled a fist. "I didn't cut off my father to play games. However what?"

"Wofford is owned by Exline, Limited, in England, which actually produces ceramic products, mostly dishes and pottery. Exline, in turn, is a division of L. L. and K., in the RSA. L. L. and K. produces ceramics, too, but more interesting forms, laboratory equipment and ceramic engines for construction equipment."

Janna pursed her lips. "Could Lanour have anything in ceramics worth killing for?"

"It doesn't have to be ceramics. My friend tells me that L. L. and K. remained white-owned for a long time after the union of South Africa became the RSA, but in the last two years it's been bought out and all the personnel replaced with afros. And guess who bought it? Uwezo."

Janna sucked in her lower lip, remembering rumors and speculation she had heard about that corporation being a cover for afro spies. "You mean, our jons could be working for an African government?"

"In which case someone on the Lanour platform must be too."

Janna took a deep breath. "Somehow I don't think this is the kind of results that Vradel, Paget, and Leonard Fontana will be happy to learn about."

# CHAPTER
# NINE

The tape Mama made of his call to Leonard Fontana had not exaggerated the amber of the platform director's eyes. If anything, they looked even yellower firsthand. From where Janna sat beside SCPD director Thomas Paget's desk with Mama and Lieutenant Vradel, the wolf gleam of them stared out of the phone screen at the SCPD director with the intensity of lasers. "Uwezo. Well, son of a bitch. It sure looks like the African corporations have become grown-up competition all of a sudden." He smiled. "Your people have been mighty busy, Director, to trace that corporate chain."

Janna frowned. That smile did not touch his eyes, and if his drawl thickened any more, he would need a matter transmitter to broadcast it. What was the good-old-boy act hiding?

Beside her, Mama pushed his glasses up his nose. "I wonder what happened to his concern about Chenoweth," he murmured. "We tell him it's murder, not just using a corpse, and he has yet to mention or react to that."

True. Why not? Janna leaned forward to see the image better, to catch any nuances of expression.

Director Paget gave Fontana an equally chummy smile. "We encourage our officers to be resourceful and imaginative, Mr. Fontana." In his serpentine-striped jumpsuit and collar-length, smoky-blond hair combed back behind his ears, he looked even more corporate than the man on the screen.

"However you did it, y'all are to be congratulated." Fontana grimaced. "Now I reckon it's up to the home office to see what we can do about recovering our property."

"Does that mean you've identified what was stolen?" Paget asked.

The smile widened fractionally. "I'm afraid I'm not at liberty to say, Director."

Mama suddenly stood. Before Janna could haul him back, he reached out and swiveled the phone screen around to face him. "Excuse me, sir, but I would like to ask Mr. Fontana how he can be so confident that we're dealing with only a corporation. Or does industrial espionage often involve murder?"

Above an evaporating smile the wolf's eyes froze. "What murder? Naturally we investigated John Paul Chenoweth's death. It's important to prevent recurrences of such tragedies. My chief and assistant chief of security both examined the pressure suit and I sat in on the inquiry. Other workers in the crew with him saw the accident, and they testified that his suit caught on the edge of a girder and ripped. No one else was near him. It couldn't have been murder."

"Caught and ripped?" Mama said. Janna started to reach for him, but Paget waved her back. "It's my understanding that pressure suits use kevlar in their fabric. As a law officer, I've had experience with that in body armor. Something thin and very sharp might cause a puncture, but nothing *rips* it."

Fontana hesitated. "Normally, no, but materials do fail now and then."

"That doesn't explain Uwezo's agents hiring someone to steal the hearse before your man died, though," Paget said.

The smile spread across Fontana's face again . . . except to his eyes. "That sure doesn't, does it? I reckon maybe I ought to look into the matter a little further. Thanks for the input. If we learn the names of the two men down there, I'll pass them on so you can swear out warrants."

Then they were staring at a blank screen. Paget turned to nod at Vradel. "We can file it, Hari."

Janna stiffened. The order did not surprise her, but her reaction to it did . . . anger, protest.

Mama yelped, "Close the case! But we haven't solved anything." He frowned. "Are we getting pressure from somewhere in Lanour–Tenning?"

"Maxwell—" Vradel began.

But Paget waved him silent and smiled at Mama. "We *have* solved it. Semi-solved, anyway. We have john doe warrants out for those two afros, and that's all the action we can take at present. The murder isn't in our jurisdiction."

Janna began, "We could check all international flights out of KCI on the twenty-third for—"

Vradel groaned. "Oh, god, not you too."

"I admire dedication," Paget said. "To a point. Each one of us possesses only so much energy, however, and a wise person expends it on productive activity. I don't perceive any feeling of appreciation or cooperation in Mr. Fontana. So the case being on his turf, let his security personnel sweat over it. The weather bureau is predicting a warming trend this weekend, and when that happens, the deeks will be out on the street in force again. Save yourselves for them. They may not appreciate us, either," he said with a thin smile, "but they're on *our* turf." He paused. "You probably missed your day off because of this case. Finish your paperwork today and take tomorrow off."

"But—" Mama began.

Blue eyes narrowed to chilly cobalt chips. "Dismissed, Sergeant Maxwell."

Mama's mouth closed. He followed Janna toward the door.

The dictyper hummed as Janna talked into it, translating her words into amber letters on its screen where she could inspect and edit them, sometimes to a phrase the dictyper suggested, before commanding a print. Next to her Mama silently signed the reports as they fed out of the print slot.

She watched him from the corner of her eye. "Come on. We can't win them all. Paget is right; let the lend-lease leos sweat the case."

He pushed his glasses up his nose. "They're not going to solve it. They don't give a damn about Chenoweth dying, just whatever he smuggled out."

She raised a brow. "You were pretty concerned about that yourself, I recall."

"But I wanted to know who killed Chenoweth too."

Janna sighed. "I guess we'll never know. Don't let yourself worry about it if you want to keep your tick straight."

"Schnauzer Venn's brain training really works on you, bibi," he said bitterly.

Anger flared in her. Nice thanks she got for trying to help. With difficulty she held on to her temper. "Look, once we're out of here tonight, let's just forget the place. Take me to the opera we missed last week."

"It's too late. The company's gone back to Kansas City."

"So . . . let's go to K.C. to see them. Your runabout can't make the distance, but if we don't waste time in leaving, we can make the commuter bus."

Mama sat up straighter. "Go to K.C.?" His eyes gleamed behind his glasses. "I think you have something there. Don't worry about making the bus, though. I'll arrange for a road car and we'll drive."

He hummed under his breath as he returned to the reports.

In fact, he appeared to be humming inwardly the rest of the day, even during debriefing while all around them uniformed officers, command officers, and investigators voiced the usual litany of complaints and frustrations.

Venn cheered everyone on, of course, twitching the schnauzer-dog mustache and bushy eyebrows that earned the psychiatrist his nickname. It was all supposed to help them discharge job-related tension, preventing breakdowns and burnout. "That's good, but not all bad happened today, did it? Don't forget, you see the worst in people, but you may also see the best in them. Any examples of that?"

Leaving the station by way of the garage when debriefing ended, Mama grinned. "What a great cheerleader he must have made in school. Well, what do you think of the car I've arranged for us?"

Janna stared at the bright red D-F Monitor. "That's our duty car. We can't—"

He held his finger to his lips. "It's all arranged with my friend in the motor pool, and perfectly legitimate. Come on, we need to dress and get going. Kansas City Society will be there, real castlerow types, so try to dink up."

Janna rolled her eyes. "In contrast to the drab rags I usually wear, I suppose?" Maybe it had been a big mistake to suggest this excursion.

Much to her surprise, however, she enjoyed the evening. The audience at the New Bartle Auditorium glittered, dinked up indeed ... draped in furs and jewelry, wearing metallic fabrics and iridescent body paints, the latter under transparent thermal-plastic bodysuits. The scents of expensive perfumes and fragrant tobaccos and drugs eddied deliciously around her. Mama's scarlet-and-gold stripes blended in well. She saw now why he encouraged her to dress well and wished she had worn something more than a plain cobalt tabard over a black bodysuit.

Mama's whispered annotations about what was happening and who was doing what to whom made *Volpone* not only understandable but entertaining. Somehow the singing sounded less like screaming when she knew what it meant. Afterward they had caff and a snack at a top dink restaurant in the stockyards, as were a good many other members of the audience, Janna reflected, watching the furs and jewels at the other tables. Mama critiqued the production and singing while they ate.

She raised a brow. "Does all this expertise come from your single year in theater arts at UMKC?"

He shook his head, forehead creased in seriousness. "I may have switched my curriculum to criminal justice, but I've never stopped being interested in the arts. That year just introduced me to everything and whetted my appetite. I can't say that I'd never heard good music before or seen a ballet or classic play—we had television, after all—but I never understood anything about what I was seeing when I bothered to watch it. But here, suddenly it was like gaining sight and hearing after having been blind and deaf. Opera is such *spectacle*, full of costumes and blood and grand loves and foul murder. No one in it ever has *little* problems. Sometimes I've thought, what if life were like opera? My god, how dramatic our jobs would be."

Janna whooped in laughter.

It was after midnight before they left the restaurant. Janna strode beside Mama, admiring the steam of their breath weaving fairy wreaths around their heads. Warmed by food and wine and amusement, she barely felt the night air biting at her face and sinking through the fabric of her long coat. Breathing deeply, she decided she had not felt this contented since Sid married.

Punching the lock combination of the car door, Mama said, "Now to find a hotel."

Contentment evaporated abruptly. Janna stiffened. "Now just a minute, Maxwell!"

He looked around, frowning over the top of his glasses at her. "My god. Loosen, bibi; it's strictly business. That was the only way I could get the car. In the morning we'll drive up to Kansas City International and—"

"The hell we're going to KCI tomorrow!" She snatched at the keys and, capturing them, raced around to the driver's side. "What do you want to do, earn us more days off but without pay?" She punched the lock combination with angry stabs. "It *isn't our case anymore*. Leave it the hell alone!"

Sliding open the door, Janna jumped across the airfoil. "We're going back to Topeka and pray no one finds we took a department car on personal business."

Mama climbed in the passenger side, sighing. "Just when I think you're turning into a genuine human being, you revert to By-the-Book Brill."

She started the car and lifted off with a savage leap that whipped both their necks.

She would have liked to make the drive back in stony silence, but Mama either refused to see her anger or was determined to batter through it.

"How can you just turn your back on this case, bibi?"

Was it worth trying to convince him that she hated giving up as much as he did, that she did not want John Paul Chenoweth's killer to escape responsibility for the act, either? Would he even believe her? As they crossed the county line, she finally answered him. "Pragmatism, Maxwell. I have to, or how am I going to work effectively on the assaults and murders Morello will dump on us tomorrow? Do I slight those victims for the sake of—" The yelp of a siren behind them interrupted her. She glanced in the rear scanner on the dash to see a light rail flashing through the wind-driven snow. "I think we're being hauled down. Damn you, Mama. They've found out about the car."

As the Monitor settled onto its parking rollers, the watch car team approached, one on each side of the car. Janna ran down her window. "Good evening, leos."

The she-lion on her side said, "Both of them together. Once in a while we get lucky."

The voice sounded familiar. "Villalba? I didn't know you'd transferred to Tecumseh division. Isn't it a little cold to be playing games?"

"Not when there's a case of felony ugly like yours. Did you know there's been an Attempt to Locate on you two since six o'clock?"

Janna straightened. "What?"

The leo on Mama's side said, "Every car in the county has been watching for you. You're supposed to call Crimes Against Persons immediately."

That sounded serious. Janna glanced quickly at Mama. He looked as wary as she felt. "Thanks. Mama, we'd better find a telephone."

A thick-walled little fort of an all-night convenience store up the road had one. Lieutenant Susan Drexel, the morning watch commander, came on the screen frowning, her voice crackling in exasperation and relief. "Have you two been taking invisibility lessons from slighs? Vradel says to tell you Fontana called back. There seems to have been a great deal of chatting back and forth today . . . Fontana with his home office, someone in the home office with the director of the State Police in New York, the New York State Police, and Lanour High Muckies with our own director. The conclusion is that while jurisdiction for investigation of the murder belongs to the New York State Police—that being the state where Lanour is incorporated—since no one in that office has had prior experience with the crime in question, platform security is to investigate, but, quote, 'in the presence of an official agency and officers with knowledge of this crime who will act as consultants and lend an appearance of authority to the investigation.' End quote."

"Presence?" Janna stared at the lieutenant, her heart suddenly pounding.

Drexel smiled thinly. "Pack your bags. Frontier has a shuttle leaving from Forbes tomorrow. You and Maxwell are to be on it."

# CHAPTER
# TEN

The shuttle captain was a small, stocky woman with slavic cheekbones. "We're coming up on Lanour," she called over her shoulder. "Do you two want to take a look at it before we start maneuvering for docking?"

Would she! Janna unclipped her seat belt and, following Mama, pulled herself from her chair behind the navigator up along the cockpit to the back of the pilot's seat, where they could peer over Captain Dorrance's shoulder out the front windows.

The copilot grinned up at them. "In some ways we never stop being kids, do we?"

"No, fortunately," Mama replied. "But some of us need to let out the kid even more often."

Janna had no doubt who he meant, but she refused to answer the jibe. It would only sound defensive and waste some of her sight-seeing time.

As a freighter, the shuttle might lack the appointments for passengers that made long flights more comfortable, but it had its advantages, like sitting up with the six members of the crew and being invited forward for a pilot's view of the universe.

And what a view it was! Janna sighed happily. Stars glittered like cracked ice on black velvet, and the Earth filled the sky above them, glowing with the luminous blue of a star sapphire, splashed with brown continents and the white swirls of weather systems. Did colonists, looking down on it during the shuttle flight up to their ship, ever have second thoughts about leaving? As Fontana had told Mama in that first phone conversation, from here the world looked only peaceful and beautiful, a wonder with none of the evils showing.

Even more of a wonder than something like the shuttle really flying. Seeing it on the tarmac outside the Forbes terminal Friday morning, taller than a two-storey house, the upswept and inwardly leaning tips of its delta wings giving it a wicked silhouette, Janna had been hard put to convince her gut what her intellect knew. It looked so *big* for something that expected to take off like an ordinary airplane.

But, of course, the shuttle had lifted without incident and climbed toward space, first on conventional jets, then scrams, and finally, somewhere far above the ground, firing the rockets that kicked them out of the atmosphere. The navigator had given them a running commentary during the forty-five minutes from ground to parking orbit, explaining everything that was happening. Lifting off was the short part. The rest of the two days of the trip were spent stopping at two other platforms and chasing down Lanour's station.

"I don't see the platform," Janna said.

"There." Dorrance pointed.

Then Janna saw it, a small black silhouette floating against the glow of the planet behind it. It looked nothing like a platform, of course, not even like the wheel-shaped Glenn platform the navigator pointed out to them yesterday as they passed within fifty kilometers of it. The Lanour platform bore more resemblance to a cluster of grapes, a mass of bubble shapes clumped together, even though the broad wings of the solar panels spread wide between the shuttle and station blocked so much of the view of it that Janna could make out few details.

"You'd better belt in again," Dorrance said.

Janna and Mama floated back to their seats. Without a

viewport on her own she had to follow their docking progress through what she could glimpse out of the front windows and the muttering of Dorrance and the copilot in response to garble from the radio.

Mama grinned across the aisle at her. "Spaceship communications don't sound any better than police car radios, do they?"

The shuttle shuddered once. Moments later a muted clang reverberated through it. The shuttle crew unclipped their safety belts. Two pulled themselves aft and up to release the overhead hatch between the cabin and cargo bay.

Dorrance grinned at Janna and Mama and adopted the tone of mechanical cheer of an airline attendant. "We are now at the terminal. Will all disembarking passengers please check around their seats for carry-on luggage and personal belongings? We hope you enjoyed your flight, and thank you for flying Frontier."

Grinning back, Janna slung her bag across her back by the shoulder strap and pulled up the ladder after the crewmen.

It brought her into a large circular chamber where she stopped for a moment, drawing a deep breath. She thought she smelled fresh air, but the impression faded almost immediately. Sometime in the past two days she appeared to have caught a cold or an allergy that filled her sinuses so that she could barely smell anything.

Half a dozen men lounged in the zero-gee of the chamber, some floating holding to metal loops on the walls of the chamber, others standing on those same walls as though they were a floor, a foot through the loops to keep them in place. They wore coveralls of a variety of styles and shades—all basically yellow, however, even those with stripes or checks— with a six-sided blue-and-orange plastic badge on the left breast pocket.

"Hey, Zim. Are things starting to thaw out down there yet?" one man asked. His badge read STORES, and under it, BREDE.

"Only New Hampshire, where the rhetoric's starting to heat up," one of the shuttle crew replied.

"You didn't happen to stop at the Glenn this trip, did you? We heard that Taya Hollander claims to be giving up fame and fortune and the cineround to ship out with the Jubilee Company and every hetero jon and ho bibi in Stores is slavering to know if it's true that they're going to be deprived of new views of her skin."

The crewman shrugged. "Sorry. Is there someone to show our passengers here where to go?"

"The other side of the lock." One of the receiving crew pointed up at a heavy door comprising the chamber's ceiling.

Or wall, or floor. Janna found her orientation changing just by turning in midair. She headed in the direction in which he pointed, pulling herself by the rings on the wall. A crewman punched a code on a number pad to one side of the door. The intermeshing teeth across the center parted to let her and Mama through into a second chamber.

"Enjoy your stay. See you on the flight back," the crewman called as the doors behind them clanged together again.

Moments later a second set of doors on the far side of the chamber opened. Janna gulped. She stared up/down a corridor as round as a pipe and, to all appearances, bottomless. Rings of light panels turned it into a sunny yellow hole, true, marked at intervals by arcs of other colors: sky blue, red, light green. Still, the appearance of infinity remained, and Janna clawed across the paneling for the support of one of the railings running lengthwise down the hole. Mama grabbed it right behind her.

"Don't worry, you aren't going to fall," a voice said reassuringly.

Janna tilted back her chin. An attractive oriental woman in an abbreviated body suit and slipper socks with knee-high tops smiled at them from the top of the tube. Her badge read ADMINISTRATION/NAKASHIMA. "Good morning, Sergeant Brill and Sergeant Maxwell. I'm Ginneh Nakashima, Mr. Fontana's secretary. He sends his apologies for not meeting you personally, but this is the beginning of our official day, and he's tied up with some organizational details. I'll show you to your quarters. By the time you're settled, Mr. Fontana should be ready to have you join him in his office. Just follow me."

"Down that?" Mama pointed at bottomlessness beneath/above them.

Sloe eyes warmed in amusement. "Technically it's down, I suppose, since it's pointed toward Earth, though without gravity, up and down are wherever you wish. Think of the corridor as horizontal, but instead of walking, you swim through it."

She gave one tug at the rail she held and sent herself sailing along the corridor, touching the rail after that only to renew her momentum. The movement looked graceful and very much as though the woman and other people Janna saw in the corridor were indeed swimming. Attempting to imitate Nakashima, however, Janna skidded into the wall almost at once and, to add injury to embarrassment, smashed her nose against the panel as her bag overtook the back of her head. Through tears of pain and rockets behind her eyes she heard Mama's voice, anxious.

"Bibi, are you all right?"

She breathed slowly, waiting for her vision to clear. "Aside from my Pekingese profile, you mean?"

Nakashima came pulling back to them. "I'm so sorry. It's my fault. I should have warned you that it's wise to be very careful until your reflexes adjust to weightlessness."

"Or pack a lighter bag." Janna resumed following the secretary but this time contented herself with moving hand-over-hand along the railing. The arcs of color, she soon discovered, marked the edges of hatches.

"For navigation reference this is the *A* or core corridor," Nakashima said. "These hatches lead to the Stage One modules that have become storage space, or passages through to

Stage Two pods where the greenhouses and gymnasium are located. That hatch goes to the gym. It's a gravity drum, if you feel you need to have a real 'down' for a while, or if you want to drain your sinuses. They tend to fill up without gravity."

So she had not caught cold after all. That was some comfort to know, Janna reflected. "The gym helps?"

"Quite a bit. It also stresses your bones to help maintain their calcium. Here's the *C* corridor where your quarters are located. It's also part of Level One, or you can remember it as the spring-green corridor. All the main branches are color-coded."

*C* was one of four corridors joining the core at this point, Janna noted. The green paneling lasted for three meters down the corridor before yellow resumed. Openings off this corridor came in groups of three. They were spaced around the circumference equidistant from each other, and marked the opening of short branches whose far end terminated in lock-type doors, most open at the moment. Nakashima swung into one with signs above and upside down below reading, C-8 VISITORS/OBSERVATION.

Beyond the lock door, Nakashima dived across a vertical shaft into a corridor opening straight ahead. It looked like a real corridor: square, with a carpeted floor and lights on the ceiling. Oval doorways opened off both sides. Nakashima put her feet down and began walking, accompanied by a familiar ripping sound. Velcro on the bottom of the slipper socks?

"Your rooms are here. We've put you in singles across from each other, but if that isn't satisfactory, we can arrange adjoining rooms or a double."

"No, that's fine," Janna said.

Nakashima touched a green button on a panel beside one of the oval doorways. The door split down the middle.

The room inside looked comfortingly familiar, too, except for the lack of furniture . . . just a sleeping bag/hammock stretched across the room above the entrance and some floor-to-ceiling wires with vests attached to the middle. That *was* the furniture, Nakashima explained. The wires were "chairs." She pointed out other features, such as the closet, which instead of hangers on a bar had a series of clear plastic envelopes stretched between swinging upper and lower arms attached back in the corner. "You slip the clothes you want to hang into the envelopes to keep them flat and put everything else in the pockets on either side outside."

She also explained how to use the bathroom with its dishwasher-cabinet shower and stirruped commode.

"There are microfiche books in the shelves beside the closet, and others in the library in Recreation in *D* corridor."

One of the pockets in the closet contained a pair of slipper socks to replace Janna's boots. Across the hall in Mama's room, another pair of slipper socks waited for him. Then, with baggage stowed and slipper socks on, now able to stick to the floor and walk almost normally, they followed Nakashima back toward the *C* corridor in a chorus of ripping sounds.

Administration lay in a pod down the blue *B* corridor, a honeycomb of corridors and offices with carpeting and light panels making a grid pattern on the ceiling as well as the floors, and furniture hanging above everyone like Swords of Damocles. Janna watched queasily as a secretary in an office they passed pushed away from the desk where she had been standing at a computer keyboard and, pulling her feet loose from the carpet, leapt up to the threatening bulk of files above her.

"Jesus." Janna shuddered.

Nakashima smiled. "You'll get used to it. Mr. Fontana is this way." She walked on, stepping from carpet square to carpet square.

Leonard Fontana didn't use a chair, either. He stood at a broad desk whose top tilted like a draftsman's table. Behind him flickered a bank of monitor screens, some showing figures and letters but others clearly connected to surveillance cameras. He had a real ceiling, transparent, with a spectacular view of Earth. No, not transparent, Janna realized moments later. Unless she had completely lost her sense of direction, they were on the upper side of this pod and should be looking at stars or the solar panels. The Earthview must be a projection, on a tape loop, perhaps, because it moved.

Fontana came around the desk in a ripping of velcro, hand extended. "Sergeant Maxwell, we meet again, and you must be Sergeant Brill. This is an honor." He looked older than he had looked on the phone screen, Janna saw. This close, lines showed in his face, though the flesh did not sag. A benefit of weightlessness, no doubt. "I do apologize for not being in Receiving to greet you, but . . . executive problems. It's like being captain of one whopping big ship. I hope you had a pleasant flight and that your quarters are satisfactory."

"Top star," Janna said, trying not to wince. His handshake almost crushed her hand. "A few features in the room are a bit strange, though."

He grinned. "Well, with any luck we can clear up this problem fast and let you get back to more familiar surroundings. That's all Gin. Remind me to find a way to tell you that I appreciate you taking care of our guests for me."

The sloe eyes smiled at him. "Yes, Mr. Fontana." She left in a soft ripping of velcro.

As the halves of the oval door closed behind her, Fontana sobered. "Actually, I think we may have more than one problem and I hope y'all can help me. I don't understand this lapse in Geyer's security that allowed whatever it was to leave in Chenoweth's body . . . and I'll admit to you now, as I couldn't on the phone, that we haven't identified what that something was yet, except that considering the . . . storage space, it probably had to be plans or a formula rather than an object itself. Which means we may never know until a duplicate of our work here turns up in production by Uwezo. But back to Geyer. Somehow the body slipped out without the thorough examination we use on living people leaving. Why? Of course, I don't expect my chief of security to be there personally checking every crate and person that leaves. But Ian Doubrava, my assistant chief, had been there with the body until a disturbance pulled him away to another part of the station. Was that coincidence, or did someone arrange a diversion? And why didn't the officer left examine more than just the clothing and body bag?" He hesitated, pacing in quick, short rips. "I hate to cast suspicion on my own people but . . ."

Janna's gut knotted. Was Fontana about to say what she thought he was? She glanced quickly at Mama and found him frowning slightly. He must think so too.

"But," Fontana went on, talking somewhere past them, "the security measures had to be circumvented by someone who knew the procedures."

Anger and disgust flared in Janna. He was going to ask, damn him!

"So, as you aid Geyer and Doubrava and any of the others in Security, will you keep your eyes open and, without mentioning it to Geyer, pass on to me personally any thoughts you might formulate on who might be guilty? I think that if I'm given several independent opinions, then matches must be considered very good bets."

"Meaning," Mama said slowly, "that you want us to watch your Security personnel, too, including Geyer?"

*You want us to spy for you, like the officers in Internal Affairs spy on us at home*? Janna wanted to add. *You want us to be peeps*?

Fontana's wolf eyes flicked across them. "I want you to keep your eyes open for *anything* suspicious, Sergeants."

If he refused to admit what he wanted, she could not spit in his eyes. Janna pushed down her anger. "Yes, sir."

"Of course," Mama said.

Fontana smiled. "Then I think it's time to meet with Geyer and Doubrava. Oh, but before I forget it, here are your visitor IDs. They entitle you to the same services as regular employees, though they don't admit you to restricted areas. For going to those places you'll need an escort.

He handed each of them one of the six-sided blue-and-orange plastic badges. These read only VISITOR, but in letters brighter and twice as large as those on his badge. Janna exchanged quick glances with Mama. There would be no mistaking them for new personnel.

With the badges clipped in place they followed Fontana out of the office. This time the trip was short, just across the corridor to the pod marked COMMUNICATIONS AND SECURITY.

The officers and clerks in Security stood at their desks, too, uniformed in body-hugging jumpsuits of two-toned cobalt and powder blue with stylish diagonal divisions across trunk and pant legs. Their badge was the same six-sided ID, but in addition to section identification on the badge, Janna saw wrap-strap pockets down the uniform thighs and familiar clips on the hip belt for a baton, K-12 gas minicanister, and needler holster. No one would mistake them for anything but Security.

As in Administration, the files were also hung from the second floor. The center of the room, however, was occupied by a holograph of the station, and surveillance monitors filled an entire wall.

Another smaller bank of screens glowed above the desk in the inner office.

But that was not all that glowed. A woman leaned against the desk there, one of the most stunningly beautiful creatures Janna had ever seen, as tall and lithe as Janna but with fewer angles. Mixed blood, part of it afro, surely, had produced a regal face and nose, a tightly curling cap of chestnut hair, and skin that glowed luminous and tiger-tawny against the blues of her uniform. Glints of gold shone in the dark eyes too.

"Très bueno," Mama breathed.

Fontana smiled at the golden woman. "May I present my

chief of Security, Tabanne Geyer? And my assistant chief, Captain Ian Doubrava."

The man suffered only by comparison with the goddess beside him. Reaching out to shake his hand, Janna took in a trim body, a mane of thick, dark hair, and brilliant turquoise eyes. Real, contact lenses, or cosmetically colored with one of the new tissue dyes? But who cared? A warm, firm grip met hers. "Welcome to Sky City."

Geyer shook, too, but perfunctorily.

A pocket secretary in Fontana's breast pocket murmured, "Five minutes until conference, sir."

"Well." The director looked back and forth between the four of them. "I'll leave you to get busy, then. Good luck." He ripped his slippers free of the carpet and propelled himself out of the room.

Geyer's smile faded abruptly. Janna sucked in her breath. With the smile went all hospitality, leaving only a darkness as deep and cold as the blackness of space.

"I won't waste time with polite lies," Geyer said in a voice edged with steel. "I don't want nor need you here. I may be just a lend-lease leo to you, but I'm perfectly capable of handling a murder investigation. We have several killings a year, none of which has ever gone unsolved while I've been Security chief. You're here only because the home office has panicked over this smuggling." Her mouth twisted wryly. "Apparently, lost personnel can be replaced, but losing a potential product to another corporation is catastrophic. All the company's blessings and your official badges still don't put you in charge here, however. This is *my* turf and *I'll* police it. You just stand around looking pretty." She paused and her voice lowered to a hiss. "That's an order, not a suggestion, leos, because if I find myself falling over you, I promise you'll go back to Earth without waiting for the shuttle."

And wheeling in a rip of velcro, Tabanne Geyer pushed off from the desk and sailed out of the room.

# CHAPTER
# ELEVEN

## Sunday, February 4. 10:00:00 hours.

In the strained silence left by the Security chief's exit, Janna twisted toward Doubrava, but his glance ducked hers to fasten intently on the row of monitors above the desk. Mama did not look at her, either, just stared in the direction in which Geyer had disappeared, his jaw slack, adoration glazing his eyes. Janna's lip curled in disgust. "You're dripping saliva on the carpet." Had he heard a word Geyer said, or had he been only eyes, lost in the woman's golden glow?

Her hostility was understandable, of course. Janna had experienced the same resentment herself, as a watch-car officer seeing investigators out of Capitol taking a case away from the division, as an investigator having to tolerate federal agents using her work to finish wrapping a case and then taking all the credit. Geyer could also be aware that Fontana had asked them to spy on her. This laser blast tactic withered any sympathy Janna might have felt, however. It also raised a question: Could Geyer have more reason than territoriality for wanting them to stand clear? Might Fontana's request be justified after all? On the other hand, considering how highly placed the smuggler had to be, Fontana could be taking advantage of Geyer's natural bitchiness to make an accusation that would divert attention from himself.

Janna caught Doubrava peering at her from the corner of

his eye and gave him a sardonic smile. "It's so nice to feel appreciated."

He regarded her without expression. "Would you like a tour of the platform? I'll find an officer with the time to guide you."

Ah, yes, the classic ploy. Be polite to the invaders, be hospitable, entertain them . . . but keep them out of our hair. Time to push back. "I'd rather see a transcript of the inquiry into John Paul Chenoweth's death."

Doubrava arched a brow. "Brave. But foolish. Chief Geyer means what she says."

Janna bared her teeth at him. "I know how to threaten too. Such as, can Geyer really afford to have it seem to the home office and Director Fontana as if her investigation won't bear scrutiny? I'm too nice a person to bring that up, though. I'm just one professional making a request of another, who also looks like a nice person."

The turquoise eyes measured her. A corner of his mouth twitched before he pulled it back into a sober line. "But what happens to this nice person's skin if I help you . . . since you aren't making return threats?"

Mama shook himself and, sighing, dragged his gaze from the door. "Surely the chief realizes that if we're consultants, we ought to at least look like we're involved in the investigation and be able to answer intelligently when Fontana and other high company officials ask about it."

"Who knows . . . we might even have an idea or two to offer," Janna added.

Doubrava stared at them for a moment, his face still expressionless. "Perhaps you have a point. There is . . . pressure from the home office to produce fast results. I think there's an idle desk in the outer office you can use. This way."

Like Fontana and Geyer, Doubrava pulled his slippers loose, too, and led the way floating ahead of them. Mama copied him. After a minute Janna did so as well but cautiously, keeping handholds close.

The desk stood between the wall of monitors and the station holo. Now she had time to appreciate the detail of the holo, from the sun panels around the docking bay to branching corridors and clusters of globular pods, and small tubes connecting many of the pods to each other on the same level and some on the next higher or lower level. On the middle level some tubes ended blindly, pointed toward podless corridors on the lowest level.

"What are those?" She pointed to the tubes.

Doubrava glanced over at the holo. "Escape tunnels. In case a corridor is breached, no one will be trapped in the pods."

On the other side of her, monitors reached from floor to floor. One at Janna's eye level showed what must be the gymnasium. The camera, equipped with a fish-eye lens, sat in the wall opposite the entrance. The gym spread out beneath it, circular and distorted . . . exercise machines, basketball court, racquetball courts, swimming pool, and track. Other monitors, each with a letter and number designation on the lower left corner of the screen, showed corridors and pod entrances. Those with *F, G, H,* and *I* letter designations all had closed doors.

"This is quite a surveillance system." She worked her slippers into the carpet for stabilization.

Doubrava nodded. "From here we can watch any point in the station, except private rooms and offices and the labs themselves, of course." He said it with pride.

"Which of these do the monitors in Geyer's office duplicate?" Mama asked.

"She can call up any of them she wants."

But Security was not the only area with monitors, Janna remembered. "What about the ones in Fontana's office?"

The turquoise eyes narrowed. "How does that relate to this case?"

She sighed inwardly. Did all the Security people have to

be so damned cat-nerved? She gave Doubrava a shrug. "I don't know that it does. Sorry. Professional curiosity."

He eyed her a moment longer before replying slowly, "A space station is very much like a ship. The director is our captain and likes to know what's going on. So the director can also call up what's on any of these monitors."

"Big Brother is watching."

Doubrava stiffened. "Everyone coming here understands that security takes precedence over privacy. We have a great deal to protect."

Guilt pricked Janna. She grimaced in apology. "I know. Forgive me."

After a moment he nodded stiffly.

"Do you tape—" Mama began.

But Doubrava interrupted. "I'm forgetting why I brought you out here. One minute, please."

He floated up to a file a short way across the room and, after hunting along the shelflike drawer, came back with a stack of printouts and a file folder. He pulled himself down to the carpet. "These are the inquiry transcript and pictures of Chenoweth's pressure suit." Released from his hand, the printout remained hanging in the air by his shoulder while Doubrava opened the folder and handed Janna a number of 2-D photographs and holo plates.

The printout started to drift away. Mama reached out to capture it. Janna sorted through the photographs. Pressure suits had come a long way in refinement since the twentieth-century body armor she remembered seeing with her third-grade class at the space museum in Hutchinson. A huge rent down the side from the collar ring to the left thigh spoiled the graceful lines of this suit, however.

She stared at the rip in disbelief. "How could he have done this, catching it somewhere? Wouldn't he have been more careful?"

"Care isn't always enough. Occasional snagging happens to everyone. I worked in construction crews on several platforms before taking up security work and probably snagged my suit a dozen times during the course of each project. Granted, I never had any damage this bad, but I've seen a few instances of neglected suits literally falling apart."

"But we know this suit didn't just happen to fall apart. It had to be arranged. Why did the killer pick Chenoweth, do you suppose? Just at random?"

Mama frowned. "I'm more puzzled why anyone is even wearing pressure suits. It's my understanding that you build these pods from the outside in, spraying a balloon form with polymers to make the skin, then filling it with air so that the internal construction can be done in the comfort and safety of an atmosphere."

The turquoise eyes flickered. After a moment Doubrava said slowly, "That's how much of this station was built, yes, but it isn't the only method. We're trying something this time that requires a pipe-and-wire framework. Excuse me, but I'd better go back to my assigned job before the boss catches me fraternizing with the enemy. Of course, if you have any questions, don't hesitate to ask me."

With a nod he floated back toward the inner office.

Mama's brows hopped. "Which doesn't necessarily mean he'll answer."

"At least he hasn't offered to bite and claw. Let's see what the inquiry had to say."

Sliding the photographs aside under a clip secured to the desktop, she read the transcript around Mama's shoulder. Blue jumpsuited Security officers came and went from the office, eyeing them curiously and murmuring to other officers but never speaking to Mama or her directly. Solidarity in the face of outsiders, or Geyer had them well under her thumb.

The evidence produced by the inquiry seemed straightforward enough. Eleven members of the construction crew all testified to the same thing, varying only in details. They had been putting together pipe for the framework of a new pod. Chenoweth, wearing a jetbelt, had been hauling reels of the wire used to weave between the pipes for added stability. He passed too close to the free end of one pipe. One crewmember actually saw, or thought he remembered seeing, the suit catch on the pipe end. He testified that he did not react immediately, thinking nothing of it until moments later, when he and everyone heard Chenoweth scream over his suit radio that the suit was ripping. Several people had been close enough on the sun side of him to see the particles of freezing oxygen and water vapor showering outward from his suit. They had started for him, pulling along the frame, or using jetbelts if they wore them, but his jetbelt had continued to operate, too, carrying him away from the frame, and by the time anyone could catch up, Chenoweth was dead.

Very straightforward, except for one small detail, a detail that sent an electric shock through Janna.

*Question, Director Fontana: Mr. Carakostas, identification in the suit indicates it was assigned not to John Paul Chenoweth but to Clell Titus. How did Mr. Chenoweth happen to be wearing Mr. Titus's suit?*

"Son of a bitch," Mama muttered. "Then Chenoweth's death could have been an accident after all, poor devil."

*Response, Crew Chief Carakostas: Chenoweth complained to me that his suit's heating element wasn't functioning properly on checkout. I examined the suit with him, but since we couldn't find the cause of the malfunction immediately, and Clell Titus wasn't on the shift, I advised Chenoweth to borrow Titus's suit and unlocked the locker for him.*

*Question, Assistant Security Chief Doubrava: Did Chenoweth run a checkout on Titus's suit before leaving the locker area?*

*Response, Crew Chief Carakostas: To the best of my knowledge, yes; he was beginning the checkout when I left him for my briefing with the crew chief of the incoming shift.*

*Question, Security Chief Geyer: But you cannot testify that he finished the checkout. He could, in fact, have rushed*

*through the checkout because of the delay caused by the other*
*suit's malfunction and not followed the protocol completely.*

Janna grimaced. "It sounds as though she's trying to set
him up for a charge of negligence, doesn't it?"

"Someone set someone up, that's for certain," Mama said,
"and Chenoweth had the rotten luck to fall into the trap."

Janna frowned at the transcript. "I wonder if we can arrange
to see the suit."

They pulled through the office, back to the inner office.

"Nice of you to tell us that Chenoweth couldn't have been
the intended victim," Janna said.

Doubrava looked around from reading printouts and arched
his brows. "Wouldn't that have been redundant when you
were going to read it in the inquiry transcript?"

"But the transcript doesn't have much detail about the suit
itself, except testimony by Maintenance and Clell Titus that
the suit had passed all safety checks two weeks before, and
the photographs are all of the exterior," Mama said. "Could
we take a look at the suit itself?"

Doubrava considered and sighed, pursing his lips. "I think
Chief Geyer might look on that as going beyond a mere
appearance of involvement."

"What if you want to see it and we just happen to tag
along?" Mama suggested.

"Why should I want to see it?"

Janna did not for a moment believe he could really be that
light-witted, but she said, "Obviously the suit was sabotaged.
It must show some evidence of that."

His mouth thinned. "You might give us credit for thinking
of that already. After your conversation with the director on
Wednesday, Bane—I mean Chief Geyer sent the suit down
to the labs for examination right away."

It must be handy, having the most sophisticated scientific
facilities just down the corridor. "And?"

"And what?"

God! This was like pulling teeth. Fighting to keep exasperation out of her voice, Janna asked, "And what did you find?"

He hesitated before replying, glancing past them toward the door. "A time bomb. Someone had pulled the lining out of the suit and made long cuts along several places in the inner surface, stopping just short of puncturing through, then replacing the lining."

"And waited for the suit to snag." Anger flared in Janna. And waited for a man to die so a plan or formula could go down to a buyer on Earth.

Mama took off his glasses and left them hanging in the air beside him while he rubbed his eyes. "But he couldn't afford to wait too long. The ground contacts arrived in Kansas on Tuesday the sixteenth. The law seminar they were using as cover wouldn't last forever." He pulled out a group of papers shoved haphazardly under a clip on the desk and shuffled them into a neat stack that could be precisely secured before recovering his glasses. "And speaking of time, sabotaging that suit doesn't sound like something that could be done in one minute while the suit storage area happened to be empty."

"Probably not," Doubrava agreed.

"But could it be that easy to take it away and bring it back hours later?"

"Obviously someone managed to."

Irritation pricked Janna. What kind of answer was that? "But why use Titus's suit? Is he the careless kind, someone the killer might feel certain would snag his suit sooner than someone else?"

Doubrava shrugged. "Not to my knowledge." He paused, then added, "Geyer wonders if maybe the smuggler wanted to do double duty, eliminate an accomplice as well as provide transportation for stolen goods."

Janna exchanged quick glances with Mama. Greed among thieves? "You've investigated Titus? What did you find?"

Doubrava shrugged again. "Nothing conclusive."

Not another round of that! "Captain Doubrava—" she began angrily.

Mama pinched her under a shoulder blade. "I think we've taken enough of the captain's time for now, bibi. Let's go learn our way around the station."

"If you'll wait a moment, I'll find you a guide." Pulling loose from the carpet, Doubrava floated toward the door.

"Thank you, but we don't want to tie up any of your personnel. It'll be more fun if we get lost a few times."

Doubrava stopped in the opening and turned back to frown at them, his body taut. "Not necessarily. Unauthorized personnel aren't allowed below Level One and we don't treat trespassers kindly, even those sent by the home office."

Mama spread his hands. "I have no intention of wandering anywhere much but the gym, the cafeteria, and somewhere to get a drink." He paused. "You do have somewhere to drink, don't you?"

"Recreation, pod D-3." Doubrava frowned. "I hope you realize that it isn't general knowledge we're conducting a murder investigation, and certainly no one is to know we've lost any of our research."

"Understood."

Tension visibly loosened in the security officer. "Then enjoy your wanderings, and if you get lost too often, call me." He smiled at Janna. "I meant it about asking me questions. Come back anytime. I'll keep the desk out there for you as long as you're on the station."

Leaving the Security offices, Mama grinned at Janna. "I think you made a conquest. Would that I were so lucky." He sighed.

"Really? I didn't have any idea he was your type." As Mama's eyes rolled behind his glasses, she added, "No, I know who you meant, and you're lucky she hates us. She'd eat you alive. Haven't you been burned bad enough by Lia?"

Looking past her, he sucked in his breath. "Maybe I'm looking for a cure for Lia," he said softly.

Janna regretted having said anything. Hastily she changed the subject. "Are we really going to let ourselves be restricted to sight-seeing?"

His eyes focused back on her, crinkling with his grin. "If they don't want to make us part of this case, we'll just have to be clandestine."

She grinned back. "Let's get on with the tour, then."

# CHAPTER
# TWELVE

### Sunday, February 4. 10:30:00 hours.

Finding their way around the station proved to be no problem. Specific destinations might be difficult to find, but color coding of the corridors and letter/number designations on the pod entrances constantly informed them where they were. No visitor could stray to Level Two by accident, either. Pulling along the *A* corridor past the Level One intersections triggered a recording, a polite feminine voice: "I'm sorry, but you are now entering a restricted portion of the station. Please return to the visitor levels."

"Shall we see what happens next?" Mama asked.

"I don't care to, no." Janna turned back.

She found a wiry man in a Mohawk haircut and the two-toned blue uniform of Security floating behind them. "Next," he said in a conversational tone, "the warning would have been stronger. 'I'm sorry, but you *must* turn back.' Then a holo image fills the corridor, a door with STOP: RESTRICTED AREA printed on it in flashing red letters, and alarms go off in Security. If you still continue, an automatic mechanism leaves you physically incapacitated and we carry you away to recover under confined conditions."

Mama cocked his head. "Physically incapacitated? Interesting. How?"

Mohawk grinned. "That we don't tell. You're welcome to find out by experimentation, however."

"Maybe we ought to look at the gym," Janna said.

The gym intrigued her, a track that sloped perceptibly upward, yet the surface always felt level. The drawback was the open structure of the drum. Working out on the impressive array of exercise machines, a person would see handball and basketball courts sitting vertically left and right and, most unnerving of all, a swimming pool directly overhead.

They peeked into the greenhouses, too, one in another gravity drum, one zero-gee, both jungle gyms of plant racks full of grains and vegetables. A third contained a wildwood growing unrestricted from the core sphere of Earth toward the skin of the bubble . . . except that some plants looked as though their branches and roots could not quite decide in which direction to grow. A little more exploration located the cafeteria.

To her surprise Janna found she could actually taste the food. The spices came through despite her clogged sinuses. "Can you imagine what their spice budget must run each year?"

Mama's eyes glittered behind his glasses. "No doubt it's astronomical." He ducked the drinking bulb of caff she threatened to throw at him.

At other tables around them station personnel stood wolfing down their food and chattering with companions, but not all anchored by slippers in the carpet, Janna noticed. A number, like the man with waist-length braids at the the table next to her, had suction cups dangling from their belts and stabilized themselves by sticking the cups to the underside of the tables. Their legs did not move normally, she realized presently, just trailed along behind them as they sailed across the room. Paralyzed? This would be a good work environment for a paraplegic.

Not everyone chattered, either. Some ate with attention riveted on a six-screen cubical newscanner in the center of the cafeteria that ran stock market quotations and business news.

Mama peered at it. "Lanour is down five more points."

A woman at the same table as the man with braids hissed. "That damn board!"

Janna raised a brow toward them. "I understood it was the proxy fight that's causing the drop."

The couple stiffened, then the man with the braids nodded. "It is because certain members of the board of directors are pressuring stockholders loyal to Crispus Tenning, our president and chairman of the board, into selling their shares." His mouth was grimly set. "It's the only way the board can gain enough proxies to vote old man Tenning out as chairman and pressure him into retiring from the presidency."

Mama leaned closer to Janna. "I wonder which faction sent us up here."

After lunch they drifted over to Recreation, a pod with a cylindrical central corridor whose arrangement of round doorways indicated the rooms must be arrayed like layers of spokes. And judging by the amount of noise and smoke issuing from the doorways as they irised open to admit or discharge people, and by the names written around the circumference—Siriusly Yours, Fluidics Inc., The Quark, and Damnation Alley, among others—the Lanour platform boasted more than *a* place to drink.

"Belithroche?" Mama grinned at the name around one doorway. "I have to see what that is." He tapped the control plate.

Inside they found that the "floors" on the walls to their left and right were long, softly glowing surfaces with a pie-wedge shape and waist-high tables sprouting out of them from small islands of carpet. The bar stretched out at their feet, a double bar, really, with half toward each floor. As a bar, Belithroche seemed brighter, quieter, and cleaner than most, no narcotic smoke, no holo band for music, only something mellowly twentieth-century-sounding. Of course, this was early yet.

Even so, several dozen patrons stood at the tables and bars, slippers settled into the carpet pieces. The patrons wore a

variety of hairstyles and clothes Janna would have expected
to see only in the evening on Earth, more skin than cloth.
Near the doorway a couple leaned over the bar, the woman
in one of the new plastic-film bodysuits, transparent except
for glittering nebula swirls of gold and silver imbedded in it,
her male companion ponytailed and shirtless beneath a tank-
topped jumpsuit. They sipped from drinking bulbs, suction
cups popping and releasing each time they picked up their
drinks, and loudly discussed something they illustrated to
each other by sketching on the bar. The sketching reminded
Janna of Lieutenant Vradel. How very far away he and Topeka
and Earth seemed from here.

The bartender, dressed in a hooded red-and-blue costume
with a web on his chest, floated along the bar toward them.
"Good evening. What can I mix you?" Intensely green eyes
peered out of the hood's eyeholes.

Janna raised a brow. "It's just past twelve hundred hours."

The bartender shrugged. "It's evening to me, and to most
of my customers."

"That's an interesting ensemble," Mama said.

The green eyes crinkled. "Spider-Man, a twentieth century
comic character. Classics are my bob."

"Is that the reason for the Benny Goodman music?"

"You recognize it?" The bartender sounded pleased. "I
don't know if the customers like it but at least they don't
complain, and I figure a boss is entitled to some privileges."

Janna arched her brows. "You own the bar? The company
doesn't?"

The green eyes studied them. "Obviously you're not here
for one of the director's How-To-Run-a-Successful-Station
tours or he would have told you that he talked the home office
into letting groups of the station staff take franchises at a
token cost and work the places in their off time. Anyone with
a yen for the perfect watering hole can buy up a franchise
and design his own. We make our liquor, too, top-dink stuff,
much better than we can import. Try some."

"Is Belithroche something classic too?" Janna asked.

The eyes crinkled again. "Sort of. It's short for Better Living Through Chemistry. My group are all chemists." The eyes swept them again. "What brings you to the Lanour?"

"Death," Mama said.

Janna pinched him. "Mama!"

He ignored her to lean toward the bartender. "We work for the company that makes your pressure suits. Our bosses and your home office sent us up to look at the pressure suit that ruptured."

"Yeah? Excuse me." He moved down the bar to refill the bulbs of the sketching couple, and add a few lines and symbols to what Janna now saw was a chemical diagram, before floating back to them. "That was a hell of a thing about Chenoweth. I thought those suits couldn't rip."

"So did we," Janna said. She might as well follow Mama's lead. "We're wondering about operator error."

The bartender sniffed. "Working for the manufacturer, I suppose you would."

"Did you know Chenoweth well? Or Clell Titus, whose suit he borrowed? Did either of them drink in here?"

"I didn't know either of them personally. We don't get many from Construction in here. They prefer the noise in Damnation Alley and Helen's Half Acre. You might try there, and the other places. Be careful going in The Quark, though. People say it's full of color and charm, but it's run by some very strange ducks."

His snicker followed them out of the bar.

The only similarity between Belithroche and Damnation Alley was the floor plan. A blast of voices and jivaqueme and a cloud of smoke enveloped them at the door. The air scubbers must really earn their way here, Janna reflected. Through the narcotic haze and the pulsing red light from the floors and band holo at the far end, she could see that the place was over half full. Two bartenders worked the double bar, one a woman with her hair pulled into a topknot bound and waxed so that it stood straight up. Her costume consisted of nothing more than ribbons connecting bands at her neck, wrists, ankles, and waist.

Mama sighed, watching the glimpses of flesh between her ribbons as she moved. Personally Janna preferred the male bartender, who wore almost nothing but a huge tattooed or painted eagle. It covered his torso, wings spread out across his shoulders and upper arms, talons reaching down his hips. A moment later she realized with a shock that he had almost nothing else to clothe; his legs stopped in stumps below the hips.

Sailing up the bar toward them, he smiled genially. "What'll you have?"

He had lungs, though, and they matched Vernon Tuckwiller's for making himself heard.

Janna tapped her ID badge and shouted back, "We hear you make top-star liquor. If these are good here, pour us a sample. Your choice."

The bartender grinned. "Two Mutant-makers coming up."

With a name like that, she sipped cautiously from the clear plastic bulb the bartender brought back. To her pleasant surprise the drink, dusky red in this light, slid down smooth and warm, just perceptibly cinnamon in taste. But then the fission came. Heat spread through her body like a shock wave and up her throat to the top of her head with explosive force. She gasped.

Mama tried his drink and arched his brows. "Are you sure you can dispense this without radiation safety gear?"

The bartender's grin broadened. "There's no point in drinking if you can't taste it."

"True." Mama took another sip. "Say, did you know John Paul Chenoweth, the construction worker who died here a couple of weeks ago?"

The eagle's wings rippled across the bartender's shoulders. "Sure. Why?"

"We're here about the suit he was wearing." Janna gave

him the same story Mama had told Spider-Man in Belith-roche. "What can you tell us about Clell Titus?"

Dark eyes went as sharp as the eagle's. "What does that have to do with a suit failure?"

She smiled at him. "We have to learn all we can, like did he always check his gear carefully before and after using it? I take it you're a friend of his?"

The bartender hesitated. "I know him from serving him. Nice jon. Hard worker like almost everyone up here. He drinks and uses a few drugs, and he gambles. Has a temper, sometimes, though he never causes enough trouble to yell for Geyer's Gorillas. I knew Chenoweth a little too. Not that I want to speak ill of the dead, but he was the kind of person I might expect to have an accident. Nice kid, for a temporary, maybe preoccupied with finishing his year out and going home. His wife had a baby just last month, and that's about all he talked about. He was always showing pictures of the kid his wife telscribed up. I never crewed with him—my section is Maintainence, not Construction—but I can tell you from experience that letting yourself get distracted can be fatal." He paused. "If you want information about Titus, why don't you talk to the group at that table over there?"

Following the direction of his pointing finger, they pushed off from the bar and floated toward a table with four men and two women, all remarkably similar in appearance, the men clean-shaven, both men and women with hair cropped within millimeters of their scalps and all wearing bold-patterned bodysuits so thin and tight that they may as well have been nude.

"Evening," Mama said.

The group looked around with broad, toxy grins, grins that quickly faded to polite smiles.

"What can we do for you, visitors?"

Mama's grin never faltered. "We understand you work with Clell Titus. Our company manufactures pressure suits, and in cooperation with Lanour we've been asked to determine the reason for his suit failure."

They stiffened. One woman snarled. Color sprayed across her face at eye level gave her a mask. "In *cooperation* with? As though we didn't know Seever was a subsidiary of Lanour. What are you supposed to do, prove Clell didn't take care of the suit?"

"Not at all," Janna said.

Six pairs of eyes raked her. "Sure," a man in gold-and-black zigzag stripes said. "And I have this piece of alpine meadow property on Venus." He turned his back.

The woman in the painted mask said, "We heard Security sent the suit down to the labs. You look there for the cause of your suit failure." She turned away too.

Janna grimaced at Mama. "Doesn't the outpouring of warmth remind you of home?"

"Let's try another table."

They worked their way through the bar, but most of the response was the same. Those who knew Titus refused to say anything that might throw an unfavorable light on him.

One man insisted, "I've crewed with him off and on since he's been up here, and he's a cautious jon, conscientious about suit maintainence."

"In the accident inquiry he testified that the reason he wasn't on the shift when Chenoweth borrowed his suit was because he had crashed after a week of double-shifting. How did he keep going? Amphetamines and Dreamtime?"

The man flung his head, setting his ponytail rippling. "He knew how to take them. He didn't let them make him careless!"

"He gambled. Did he have debts that could worry him, or problems with relationships? A bad enemy? Anything that might distract him?" Anything that might make him vulnerable to being sucked into industrial espionage and smuggling?

The man's mouth clamped in a thin line. "You go to hell."

Patrons in Helen's Half Acre, whose psychedelic play of

lights left Janna struggling to keep down her lunch, were no more helpful and more political.

"Is Lanour trying to prove worker negligence so it doesn't have to pay off on the Accidental Death clause of Chenoweth's contract?" demanded the bartender, a woman in a feather bikini and cap and wings painted on her back. Birds seemed to be a popular motif. "If you want a place to lay blame, why not ask Lanour why it decided to disregard the safety of its workers and build these new pods from inside out, so they'd have to use pressure suits in the first place, instead of working in an atmosphere?"

Janna raised a brow. "Are you sure the new pod procedure wasn't your director's idea?"

The bartender's curled lip was as good as a spit. "Fontana has his faults but one of them isn't stupidity, and he cares about us, unlike the groundsider toads in the home office, who don't have the slightest idea what it's like up here."

"And what is Clell Titus like? It must be hard card, having someone else die in his suit. How's he taking it?"

"Why don't you ask him?"

Which was about the most polite response they received there. After an hour of trying to draw people out on Titus, they left.

In the corridor outside they clung to a railing for support and breathed deeply to clear their lungs and heads. Janna grimaced. "It really is like home ... 'us' against 'them,' and we're 'them.'"

Mama took off his glasses, blew on the lenses, and resettled them. "Maybe there's another approach to learning about Titus. Lanour must run some kind of security check on anyone it's thinking of sending up here. Let's see if Fontana will let us look at the personnel records." He paused. "If so, we can also take a peek at Geyer's and Fontana's."

"Fontana." Janna pursed her lips. "What could someone with the position and power Fontana has gain by selling off company secrets, anyway?"

Mama shrugged. "I'll admit I don't know right now. Maybe there's an answer in his file."

Janna's stomach was settling back into quiesence, and the narcotic haze was clearing from her head. "An answer I'd like is how the killer was able to sabotage that suit. He couldn't do it on the spot, but surely he would have attracted attention carrying it away and returning it hours later."

They started pulling along the railing toward the pod entrance. Sailing past one doorway, however, a chorus of familiar bleeps and buzzes made Janna look in . . . and stare. Multiple lines of arcade holo games lined both floors in one of the most impressive arrays she had ever seen. "Top-star!" She grinned at a man pushing one pointed end of his ID badge into the token machine inside the door. "You must have every game on the market in here."

The man snorted. "I don't know if *any* of these are what the company sent up anymore. The computer bobs keep breaking into the programming and changing it. One time I found that whole row over there wired together. When your game piece went left or right, it jumped to the next machine. Now it's Deathrace you have to be careful of." He grimaced. "Above 100,000 points they send choppers and planes after you, and after 500,000 points there's a killer satellite to zap you with its laser. You can't see it, just its shadow."

Janna hauled herself tight against the side of the doorway to make way for a couple leaving and three young men entering.

"That's a step up in sophistication from the versions I've played before. It must give you a fat bonus when you escape."

The man snorted. "Except you can't escape. If you avoid the satellite, an alien fleet swoops down and nukes the whole village. And when you're finally hit, the machine gives you a shock that'll straighten your hair right out."

She frowned. "A shock? Someone ought to correct that."

The man smiled wryly. "Admin claims Maintainence tried, and the machine shocked the tech to protect itself, but I think it was just another bob. I think that's how they change the programming, dressing like Maintainence and pretending to service the machines."

The hair lifted on Janna's neck. Maintainence!

The man deftly caught a package of tokens as the machine spit it out. "I understand Fontana is offering amnesty to whoever programmed it if he, or she, will change it back."

But Janna barely heard him. She whirled toward Mama, grabbing the edge of the doorway to keep from careening end over end across the corridor. "Maintainence, Mama!" She dropped her voice so no one in the corridor or arcade would hear. "Service personnel are invisible. That could be how our killer got to the suit."

"Invisible to us maybe, but not—" He pointed into the corridor, at a glass knob bulging unobtrusively between two strips of paneling.

She frowned at the lens. "I wonder if Big Brother has a camera in the EVA prep room. Let's see if Doubrava means it about answering—"

She broke off to stare at a mermaid swimming up behind Mama. It had to be a costume, of course, but it looked uncannily authentic, from the slim young woman's iridescent green tail and the seaweed draped over her breasts to green-in-green eyes and green-gold hair floating fanlike around her head.

The mermaid stopped beside them and hovered, smiling, tail waving slowly to keep her in position. "Are you the people from Seever?"

Mama answered first. "What can we do for you?"

"I think I can help *you*. My name is Jenin LaCoe, and I know a few things about Clell Titus. But"—she glanced around, pushing back her hair to clear her peripheral vision— "I can't talk here." Her voice dropped to a whisper so low, Janna had to read her lips to understand her. "Follow me to the Pie-Eyed-in-the-Sky."

With a flip of her tail the mermaid swam up the corridor

to a door near the far end. Janna glanced at Mama with raised brows. Could this be the break they needed?

"Let's see what she has to say, bibi."

They pulled along the railing after the mermaid.

While following the tail vanishing through the bar's doorway, however, all Janna's nerves jerked taut. The light in the floors shone so dimly that the tables and bar became only shadowy shapes in the darkness. Feeling blind, and with leo-trained reflexes screaming warnings of her vulnerability, she whipped sideways out of the bright circle of the doorway. Mama dived in the opposite direction. The action came automatically, almost without conscious volition, but even as she flattened against the wall to wait for her vision to accommodate, her heightened senses howled more warnings. The loud jivaqueme music sounded wrong. In a moment she recognized why. It echoed as sound should not in an occupied room. Adrenaline rushed icy-hot through her.

In the darkness the mermaid's voice called above the music, "Why don't you come over here?"

"Ten-thirty," Mama's voice replied.

The code not for acknowledgment but for transmissions that failed to conform to regulation. Janna sucked in her breath. He was signaling her that he did not like this either. "Ten-thirty," she echoed. "Signal 14?" Officer in trouble.

"We might as well have some light," another voice said from above Janna, a voice that belonged to neither Mama nor the mermaid.

The room brightened and the music cut off. A man in a bodysuit with black-and-gold zigzag stripes slid down to plant himself in front of the door. Janna drew in a slow breath of recognition. He had been one of the group they first approached in Damnation Alley. Two other men from the group stood at the half of the bar on Mama's side of the doorway, one of them with his hand still on the control buttons of a portable tape player. At a table with the mermaid stood a fourth man, one Janna had never seen before, square-built with short salt-and-pepper hair.

"Thanks, Jenin," he said.

"Always," she replied, and, with a flip of her tail, swam for the door.

As it irised closed behind her and the guard moved back in place, the square man raked first Janna, then Mama, with slate-gray eyes. "I understand you two have been asking a lot of questions about Clell Titus and making accusations by implication. I don't happen to think that's very polite. A person ought to make his accusations face-to-face." He paused. "I'm Clell Titus." And in a silence so absolute that Janna heard her pulse drumming in her ears, he floated toward Mama and her. His voice dropped to a rasp. "Now let's hear what you have to say."

# CHAPTER
# THIRTEEN

## Sunday, February 4. 17:00:00 hours.

Titus had an interesting assortment of friends, Janna reflected, that mermaid and now these three: Zig-zag, a dwarf, and an afroam. She eyed them appraisingly. Zig-zag at the door did not look all that imposing, but of the others, the afroam easily made two of Mama, and despite the shortness of his arms, the dwarf had a powerful set of shoulders. Of course, physical strength might not be all that much of an advantage in weightlessness, but mass should. Calculating the distance to each, Janna ran through all the defensive moves she had ever learned or used, searching for one throw or punch that might work without gravity. All she could think of, however, was a lesson in high school physics: for every action there is an opposite and equal reaction.

"Come on, ask your questions."

The rasping voice brought Janna's attention back to Titus and his granite eyes. His voice echoed in the emptiness. No one must hold a franchise for this space at the moment. Behind the bar, the enclosed shelves sat bare of bottles and drinking bulbs. Trying not to be obvious, she glanced around the room searching for the surveillance camera. Or would it be activated in an ostensibly unused room? Big Brother might *not* be watching here.

Keeping her voice carefully neutral, Janna said, "Your

friends are commendably loyal but a bit oversensitive. We make no accusations."

"Maybe we should," Mama said. "Would a man with a clean conscience feel the need to bring extra muscle and meet in the station equivalent of an alley?"

Janna wanted to strangle him. Damn the man! Was he trying to incite assault? "Mama," she hissed.

"Clear conscience!" Titus snapped. "Are you trying to say I'd deliberately neglect my suit? You're brainbent! My life depends on that suit. Even my wife and kids don't get the coddling that suit does. If anyone mishandled it, Chenoweth did."

Mama said, "Is it normal procedure to use each other's equipment? Aren't there spare suits in case of malfunctions?"

They all stared, then glanced quickly at each other. Zig-zag growled. "Yes, but when Carakostas is in a hellfire hurry—"

"Let them ask our superiors about procedure," the afroam said, interrupting.

Zig-zag bit down on the rest of the sentence.

"But I guess you're lucky he did give Chenoweth that suit, or you would have been in it when it ruptured," Mama said.

For a moment Titus stopped. He stared narrow-eyed at Mama. "You make it sound . . . inevitable."

"Perhaps," Janna said. "We'll know when we've looked over the suit itself."

The dwarf asked, "Are you checking to see if the coolant tubing could have microcracks that caused leakage inside the lining and weakened the fibers in the fabric?"

The others' smirks set off a clang of warning in Janna. Trap question! She glanced quickly toward Mama. How should they answer?

"Leaking coolant? That's preposterous," Mama said.

The group looked disappointed. Janna breathed an inward sigh of relief. Among all the clutter of trivia in that strange brain must be the plans for a pressure suit too.

But the dwarf continued to fix Mama with a gleaming stare. "Why is it preposterous?"

This time Mama did not answer immediately. Janna's mind raced, planning self-defense.

The dwarf floated closer to Mama by one table. "If you really do work for Seever, surely you know why."

Janna tensed. The wall at her back should help her fight.

Mama, however, said coolly, "What do you mean, if we really work for Seever?"

"Because I don't think you do, not after watching you come through that door. You're people who take no chances of being a target when going into dark rooms you don't know. I can think of several professions where that's standard survival technique, but a Seever troubleshooter isn't one of them. Can you answer any questions about how a suit is constructed?"

Janna swore. They were not going to talk themselves out of this. Bracing herself, she said, "The home office sent us to ask questions, not answer them."

Titus floated toward her, hands reaching for the front of her jumpsuit. "You'll answer one. You'll tell us who the hell you really are and why you're here, or I'll wring your groundsider neck."

The threat to lay hands on her triggered icy fury. "Ten-ninety-eight, Mama." The code for riot or mass disturbance. Drawing both knees up, Janna kicked straight out with the soles of her slippers, straight into Titus's gut and groin.

Her back slammed into the wall with the force of her kick, but to her great satisfaction Titus tumbled backward across the room, groaning in agony.

The other three men started for her. Janna made a missile of herself, pushing off from the wall straight at the afroam. At the corner of her vision Mama went for the dwarf. Just before she hit the afroam head-on in the stomach, she saw the dwarf roll aside and Mama rocket past to crash into the tables. Janna and her target flew backward together down the length of the room. She grinned. A hold on him made her fight repertoire useful again. Reaching up, she grabbed both his ears, and pulling him toward her, drove a knee into the afroam's groin.

They hit among the tables, with the afroam landing first, under her, taking most of the shock. Janna left him writhing. Pushing off from the table, she arrowed back toward Titus again, this time tucking and rolling in midair so she would hit him feetfirst.

The dwarf intercepted her with a flying dive. They slammed sideways into the floor. Janna went for his eyes with her fingers and took a fast look around for Mama. He struggled with Zig-zag among the tables on the opposite floor. His glasses were gone. Then a hand grabbed Janna's hair and jerked her head back so hard, she winced in pain. Titus's granite eyes stared down into hers.

"Now I *will* break your neck!"

"You'll do nothing of the kind, Titus!" snapped a whiplash voice. "Back off right now. You, too, Janulis. Hedgecoth, let go of Maxwell."

They obeyed. Titus grinned at Geyer swinging in through the dilated door. "Hell, Chief, I didn't mean it. We were just hazing the groundsiders a little."

"I know what you were doing." Her eyes glinted gold. Never had gold looked so cold, Janna reflected. "We followed the entire incident on the monitors. Now you and your friends get the hell out of here before I throw you in detention for assault."

Titus frowned. "It was self-defense. These bastard groundsiders are trying to blame me for Chenoweth's death."

For a moment Janna had the irritated feeling that Geyer wanted to laugh, but then her mouth compressed into a thin line. "Leave them to me." She glanced from Janna over to Mama, who groped among the tables looking for his glasses. "I promise they won't be bothering you again." Kicking off from the door, she sailed across to Janna. "I don't know if you're deaf or just arrogant, but I'll assume the former and warn you one more time. All inquiries here are conducted through my office, even those ordered by the home office, so if I fall over you again or find you making more trouble, I don't care who you are, *you,* not your assailants, will go into detention."

This time she deserved the look of admiration Mama gave her, Janna reflected. However blistering, the reprimand still gave away nothing of their identity or mission.

"Ian," Geyer barked.

"Yo." Doubrava straightened where he hovered in the doorway with two other officers from Security.

"Leash these two. Find them something safe but productive-looking to the home office to keep them occupied."

Spinning away again, she pushed off from a table and glided out the door past Doubrava.

Across the bar Mama sighed. "Top star." He looked after her until she disappeared, then resumed hunting for his glasses.

Titus whistled. "Sometimes I can believe she actually got the job on ability."

Doubrava's head came around toward him. "I think the chief ordered you to sail, Titus."

The mild tone did not quite mask a flinty edge. The group left hurriedly, towing their still-groaning afroam compatriot.

With a wave of his hand Doubrava dismissed the other officers as well, then hooking a toe on the edge of the door to stabilize himself, he folded his arms and clucked his tongue. "Naughty, naughty. She almost didn't come over here to rescue you, you know . . . but if you'd been hurt, that would have meant trouble for Titus."

"By all means protect the home folk," Janna said.

A corner of his mouth twitched. "Now the question is: Having rescued you, what do we do with you? What will keep you busy but out of trouble?"

Mama floated up off the floor, sighing with a sharp note of frustration. "Do you record from the monitors?"

The turquoise eyes gleamed. "Why?"

"Going through them could keep us occupied for a while. How far back do you have them?"

"Twenty-eight days. Then the tape is reused. What are you interested in?"

"Whoever sabotaged that suit couldn't have done it too long before Chenoweth died. I'd like to see who opened Titus's locker besides Titus and the crew chief. And damn it," Mama added, squinting around him, "I'd like to find my glasses."

Doubrava arched a brow. "I've already seen the tape. It doesn't help, but that makes watching it busywork, I guess, so . . . fine, I'll show it to you. There are your glasses." He pointed toward the far end of the room where light glinted on the lenses and frame, floating toward the ventilators. "I'll catch them for you."

Coming into the Security office, Janna could see through the open door of the inner office to Geyer standing at her desk.

Doubrava glanced toward his superior, then headed for one of the outer office desks. "We'll look at the tape here." He tapped on the computer terminal clamped to the desk and punched in a code. "This turns the monitor into a video screen and accesses the tape files, which are cross-referenced by date and camera. We want to see A-2 on January fifteenth."

"The Monday before Chenoweth died," Mama said.

"Was it a Monday?" Doubrava's fingers played across the keys. "We don't keep track of days by name much. Ah, there."

A picture came up on the screen, a long tube of a room with the camera in the center giving a fish-eye view in both directions and down on a double row of lockers dividing it longitudinally. A deserted room. Numbers in the lower right corner noted the date and time: 01/15/80/00:00:01.

Doubrava touched several more keys. The numbers changed

in a dizzying blur. "We want you occupied but not forever." Soon people appeared—blurs, too—hurtling themselves in and out like frenzied insects. Another touch on the keys froze the picture. The time indicator said: 07:45:47.

"Titus's locker is on the right side of the row, just about here." He touched the upper part of the screen. "Now watch for the orange Maintainence coveralls."

He tapped the terminal keys again. The picture resumed movement but at normal speed.

Janna frowned, watching the men and women climbing into pressure suits. "You can't mean our saboteur is coming *now*. The place is full of people."

But seconds later a figure in baggy orange coveralls swung in through the oval door at the extreme bottom of the screen and sailed up the length of the locker room. Janna leaned forward, squinting at the face. It was bent down, away from the camera, however.

The Maintainence tech stopped at Titus's locker. Without hesitation he punched a combination on the push-button lock. Pulling out the pressure suit except for the helmet, he closed the locker again and started back down the room toward the door with the suit in tow.

"Gutsy bastard. I give him that," Janna said.

Mama grunted. "Smart. What could be less suspicious than walking in and taking the suit in front of a dozen or more witnesses? Can you freeze it again?"

The picture froze. Their suspect tech faced directly toward the camera, but his face was too small for Janna to make out details, other than that he wore a mustache and full beard. "What about enlarging the picture?"

Doubrava grinned. "Big Brother has all the conveniences." His fingers tapped computer keys.

The tech's face spread to fill the screen. More keywork altered contrast, sharpening the picture. For all the good that did. The beard and mustache hid everything but a broad nose and dark eyes. The badge on the coverall read, SMITH.

"I don't suppose you have a Maintainence tech named Smith who looks like that," Mama said.

"Similar, but his whereabouts are accounted for at the time in question. Frustrating, isn't it, all this top-dink equipment, and it doesn't solve anything? We can't even tell how the jon is built inside those coveralls."

"Or even if he's male," Janna said thoughtfully. Broad nose, dark eyes, and possibly female. She glanced toward the inner office.

Geyer had left her desk to hover in the doorway, watching them without expression.

Doubrava followed Janna's line of sight and frowned thoughtfully.

Janna looked back at the screen. The tech had swarthy skin, but if he were Geyer wearing a false beard, the skin tone could have been altered too.

"If the face fur is false, though, I wonder how genuine the eye color is," Mama said.

"Then it could be anyone."

Mama took off his glasses and polished the lenses on the sleeve of his jumpsuit. "Anyone who could gain access to the labs and be thoroughly familiar with security procedures."

Doubrava grinned. "Like me. Or any number of our officers. There are people in Admin with knowledge and privilege, too, like Ginneh Nakashima. She's too small to be Smith, there, but she could have an accomplice."

"You haven't mentioned Fontana," Mama said.

Doubrava's grin faded. "Of course not. Of all the people here, he's the last person to sell the platform out."

"What happened when Chenoweth's body was being shipped out?"

The turquoise eyes narrowed. "This is—" He broke off, glancing over his shoulder toward the inner office again, where Geyer was turning away and returning to her desk, and he shook his head a moment later. "No. It's wickers. She wouldn't, either. The shuttle arrived on the twenty-first. While the receiving crew from Supply was helping the shuttle crew off-load material for us, Officer Zachary Lowe and I collected the body from A-5 where it had been stored. Before we moved it to the docking bay, we checked the bag and clothes for any contraband. I remember debating whether a dead body ought to go through the NMR scanner in sick bay, like living personnel have to do when leaving. Director Geyer and I had not discussed the matter, and she had gone off-duty. Before I could make a decision, Dispatch came on my ear button advising me that Officer Keline Talltrees was requesting a supervisor in corridor *G*. So I headed for Level Two.

"Officer Lowe says that as I left, I told him to do a body-cavity search. I don't remember. At that point corpses had become the farthest thing from my mind. He did not make a thorough search, he admits—he didn't like handling a corpse—but it never occurred to him to look down its throat in any case. And I doubt he could have pried the jaws apart to reach in, even if he thought of it. The body was stiff from being in cold storage. By the time I returned, Officer Lowe had sealed the body in the transport bag and kept watch over it while the shuttle crew loaded it on the shuttle."

"Why did this Officer Talltrees call for you?" Janna asked.

He grimaced. "She had had what appeared to be a false report. A man called from G-8—or what the dispatcher assumed from the voice was a man; he never came in screen range, claiming to be watching the door, through which he purported to see one of the technicians in a neighboring lab going berserk and attacking her coworkers. Officer Talltrees located no disturbance of any kind in G-8, however. She asked Dispatch for the location of the phone from which the complaint had been made but found the lab closed and locked. Personnel in neighboring labs in the pod told her it had been closed for the past eight or ten hours while Dr. Thora Shaw, the single chemist working there, was sleeping. No one else could have opened it. The lab has a biolock, programmed for only Dr. Shaw.

"I helped Talltrees check every pod along *G*, just to be sure the automatic trace hadn't malfunctioned but, after finding nothing, decided that one of the electonics bobs had made the call as a joke and tapped into the lab's phone line to hide his real location. We have a few people here with a warped sense of humor."

Janna remembered the Deathrace game programmed to shock the player.

Doubrava pursed his lis. "Now it's obvious the call was a diversion to pull me away from Chenoweth's body, though I don't know how the person could be certain that would prevent a thorough inspection of the body. Unless you think Lowe is the smuggler or being paid off by the smuggler."

"Maybe the smuggler knew how Officer Lowe would react to searching a dead body," Mama said.

"Knew Lowe." The turquoise eyes went thoughtful and swung from Mama to the monitor screen. "A friend or acquaintance, you're thinking? But it wouldn't necessarily have to be. There could be something revealing in the psychological profile in his personnel file. Looking at those files wouldn't be difficult for someone who can manage access to the research in the labs." Doubrava paused, touching the screen. "I wonder if it could be someone in Maintainence, after all. As Sergeant Brill has observed, service personnel do tend to be invisible, and when seen, who questions their presence?"

But even saying it and clearing the screen with a quick arpeggio across the terminal keys, Doubrava's glance slid sideways toward the inner office, Janna noticed. Could he, like her, be suddenly wondering where Tabanne Geyer had spent her off-duty time the day that Chenoweth's body left?

# CHAPTER
# FOURTEEN

Speaking of the devil.

The golden woman leaned out the door of her office and crooked a finger. "I'd like to see the three of you, please."

Janna detected no anger in Geyer's voice, no steel or acid. It sounded neutral. Still, she found herself glancing around the room, hunting the glint of a lens that would mean Security's chief could use her bank of monitors to watch, and listen to, her own outer office.

Seeing none failed to reassure Janna, nor did the way Geyer rapped the door's control plate once the three of them swam in past her. The door closed, its halves coming together with a sharp hiss.

Geyer spoke with the same abruptness. "I have an apology of sorts to make."

Janna blinked. That she had not expected. A glance sideways at Mama caught him with brows skipping in astonishment too. Doubrava looked more thoughtful than surprised.

"Or maybe *explanation* is a better word." Geyer smiled fleetingly. "I was a bit . . . unfriendly when you arrived. But I had reasons, and not just that even lend-lease leos can be jealous of their territory or that I've worked too hard at this job to appreciate the implication that I'm not competent enough to handle serious trouble."

What about her boss suspecting that she might be party to

the trouble? Janna reflected wryly, or did Geyer *not* know
Fontana wanted them to spy on her?

"Perhaps I should have explained then," Geyer continued,
"but . . . the home office did send you, after all." She floated
back to her desk, where she set her slipper socks in the carpet
and crossed her arms, not a distancing, judgmental gesture,
but as though she were cold. "I had no way of knowing
whether you were here as consultants or to discredit the administration of the station."

Mama asked, "Why is the station caught in the middle of
the attempt to force Crispus Tenning out of the corporation
presidency?"

Geyer's face froze for a moment, then her brows rose. "So
you're retentive too."

"Too?" Janna said. The rest of the remark obviously re-
ferred to their conversation at lunch with the man in the braids.
Geyer must have been monitoring them from the moment
they left Security that morning.

"In addition to being intelligent and persevering and a little
headstrong. I just finished talking to your commanding officer. He assured me no one uses either of you." She studied
Mama speculatively. "Especially not Sergeant Maxwell, who,
I suspect by the lieutenant's undertone of regret, is sometimes
beyond the control of even the department."

Janna blanked her face and said nothing. Mama's chin came
up. He opened his mouth as though to protest but closed it
again without a sound.

Geyer went on. "The platform is Tenning's pet project and
Fontana his fair-haired boy, so, of course, his enemies are
just waiting for the chance to take over and reorganize, if not
shut down the platform altogether. This smuggling and murder could provide the perfect excuse if we have to rely on
outside assistance to find and plug the leak."

And as the person responsible for a security that had failed,
of course Geyer would be one of the first casualties of re-

organization, Janna reflected. Would she now ask them to stay out so she could look good to the home office?

"I'm terrible at the art of timesliding, though," Mama said. "And I want to know who killed Chenoweth."

Geyer nodded. "Since nothing short of detention is going to make you take a vacation, it seems, I have another proposal, one which will hopefully not only solve the case but deprive the board of directors of ammunition against old man Tenning. You heard what the people here call Security. Geyer's Gorillas. They don't like to see my people coming, any more than your city's citizens welcome you. Your citizens would prefer you to foreign troops, however, and right now everyone here sees the home office as villains."

Janna saw where Geyer was headed. Anger flared in her. "You want us to be bad guys!"

Geyer frowned. "You object? It's the same nice lion/mean lion strategy you use. Of course, by encouraging people to cooperate with me means I'll have to take any credit, but which do you want, glory or the killer?"

Deliberately let a lend-lease leo look better than them? Intellectually Janna saw the logic in it. Intellectually. She frowned.

But Mama shrugged. "We might as well, bibi. Titus will be giving us bad publicity, anyway."

He looked at Geyer as he said it. Was he thinking that this way he could be on friendly enough terms to have a chance at becoming friendlier? Well, far be it from her to force safety and sanity on him. Janna sighed and nodded.

Mama's eyes gleamed, though he did manage not to grin from ear to ear.

"As long as playing bad guys lets us keep on poking around, we'd like to look over personnel records," Janna added.

A crease started between Geyer's eyes, then faded as her expression smoothed into studied indifference. "If the director gives you access to the files, I don't see how I can interfere.

You'll find him in his office watching the station on his monitors. Playing spider."

Janna straightened, curiosity perking at the sudden edge in the golden woman's voice. Could there be a conflict over the monitors?

Doubrava started for the door. "Now that each side has made its deal with the Devil, anyone else who has a circadian rhythm that recognizes nineteen hundred hours as past time to eat, follow me to the cafeteria."

Janna followed.

At nineteen hundred hours the cafeteria looked as it had when she and Mama ate lunch there . . . the same stream of people in and out, the same brisk disappearance of food. Was it dedication or the cheerful oranges and yellows decorating the room that stimulated diners to eat and run? The cubical newscanner still ran business news and stock quotations, but on only two faces. Other screens carried more general news, and one had weather.

"Pity. We're missing a blizzard in Colorado," Janna heard someone say sardonically.

The atmosphere had changed, though. Chilled. Conversations broke off as she and Mama floated toward the food line with Doubrava. Side glances followed them. Titus and company had been busy. Obviously the grapevine remained one plant that functioned as efficiently in zero-gee as it did on Earth.

"How early tomorrow can we see Fontana about permission to look at personnel files?" Mama asked.

"Tomorrow?" Doubrava grinned. "We can go over to Admin right after we eat. I'll have the shish kebab," he told the attendant behind the counter, a dwarf woman, and turned to Janna. "It's the best way yet to keep vegetables and meat together and in a manageable form." He caught the tray as the attendant slid it over the counter. "Fontana is rumored to sleep five hours out of forty, but I've never seen evidence of it. Sometimes I think if he does, it must be standing at his desk."

"Playing spider." Janna pointed at the shish kebab, too, when the attendant raised inquiring brows. "That doesn't appear to please Geyer."

Doubrava's smile froze for a just a moment. "You must have misunderstood. Why should we object if the boss wants surveillance capability? Now, there's usually someone in Records twenty-four hours, so once we're authorized to look at the files, we can start anytime you want."

Which closed the subject of the monitors, Janna noted. They must really be a sore point. Why? Encroachment on Security territory?

"How about eating over there?" Doubrava pushed away from the serving line to head toward one of the tables.

Mama imitated him but pushed too hard and almost tangled in the tables overhead. Janna walked, slippers ripping along the carpet, an arm holding the cover on her tray.

As they settled at the table Mama said, "Too bad Chief Geyer couldn't join us."

A group in orange coveralls occupied the table directly overhead. Glancing up at them, Doubrava lowered his voice. "Come on, Maxwell. How can she be seen fraternizing with the enemy?" Then his mouth twitched and the turquoise eyes crinkled at the corners. "She leaves that to me, as official leash-holder and one who is widely known for his charm, general good humor, and undiscriminating—some say taste-less—willingness to keep company with anyone, even groundsiders and corporate High Muckies." He winked at Janna.

She found herself smiling back at him. He did have charm. "If you like to be sociable, how did you ever end up in security work?"

"The uniform." He grinned. "That and a space job are a gold-card lure for flash bibis."

"I can't believe how *fast* it works!" a voice cried.

Janna looked around to see a group of men and women in a rainbow of coveralls sailing noisily into the cafeteria. Snatches of their chatter carried across the room.

"Damn right. If it weren't for having to put up the frame-work..."

"...spraying polymers over a balloon the way we used...?"

"...forced back to spherical structures when the advantage..."

"Have you heard?" a young woman among them called to the group at a table near Janna. The light glittered on a frosty swirl of gold and silver crossing her depilated scalp and diving down her neck under the collar of her green coveralls. "That spider thing finished covering the torus pod on Level Two—a flawless skin in less than twenty-four hours!—and now it's almost done with—"

A companion hissed, tilting his head toward Janna, Mama, and Doubrava. He murmured something. Instantly the group went silent. They turned their heads to stare, frowning, then continued on to the food counter, murmuring in whispers too low to be heard.

Janna grimaced. "Our reputation is established, it would appear." She watched the group edge down the food line. "What's this spider they're talking about?"

Doubrava hesitated. "I don't know the details—that's restricted information—but it's one of the wonders from the labs. I gather it spins a skin over a framework, like a spider wrapping up a fly. The advantage of it over other methods is not only speed but the mostly nonmetallic composition of the skin, which means we can build or expand space stations fast and cheap."

"Nonmetallic," Mama said. "Could it build ships too?"

"Ships?" Doubrava quirked a brow. "I suppose. I never thought—my god!" The turquoise eyes widened, and his voice dropped to a whisper. "If that's what went out of here,

Uwezo could produce a fleet of mining ships and send them out to the asteroids before anyone knew what was happening."

"Giving Uwezo one hell of a mineral monopoly," Mama said thoughtfully. "They have the diamond cartel as a sterling example of what to do with their power too."

Cold slid down Janna's spine.

When they saw Fontana in his office a short time later, she brought up the spider. "Have you considered that the spider might have been what Chenoweth carried out?"

Earth filled the ceiling, a fleece-swirled sapphire, serene and lovely, but across the desk, amber wolf's eyes regarded her with taut watchfulness above an easy smile. "Sure I've thought about the spider, and the implications of losing it. There's also a dozen more gadgets and processes we've been playing with that our rival corporations would give a golden Texas summer to put their paws on. That's why you're here, Sergeant darlin', to help me stop sweating by catching the traitor and sweating out of him what he stole. So, of course, you can look at the personnel files. Anything y'all need, you just ask for. Hear?"

Mama took off his glasses and peered myopically at Fontana while polishing the lenses with loose fabric on the torso of his jumpsuit. "Anything that will keep us occupied and out of your way, that is, isn't that right? Strange. We might just be able to help you, and while we may be here at the insistance of the board, you know we aren't its agents. If you've watched the monitors, you must have seen enough to know that whatever we accomplish isn't likely to help the board much, either. So why are you afraid of us?"

Oh, god. Janna fought an urge to stuff his glasses down his throat. What the hell was he doing . . . accusing Fontana? "Mama," she hissed in warning.

But at the same time she found herself watching the platform director for his response, and from the corner of her eye she saw Doubrava doing the same.

Fontana's face petrified. The wolf's eyes chilled. Then suddenly he smiled, but a different smile from before, a wry twisting of the corners. "It isn't fear, it's resentment, the usual animosity toward one's support group, and I apologize." The drawl had disappeared from his voice. "I shouldn't take it out on you."

*"Usual* animosity?" Janna asked.

His smile became more sardonic. "Usual in isolated and stressful environments like antarctic stations, undersea research labs, submarine crews...and space stations. Wim Freeman, our station psy-in-the-sky, tells me that the stress can erupt as irrationality, like murder or the incident on one oceanographic ship where a dispute between scientists and crew over a freezer used for both soft drinks and specimens resulted in the whole freezer being thrown overboard. More often, though, it becomes hostility focused on one's support group." Pulling his slippers loose, he floated over the desk to come down beside Janna and Mama. "Undersea labs start cursing the crew of their surface ship. Astronauts snarl at ground control. There's some reason to believe that in Russia's Salyut 6 mission way back in 1980, Tyumin and Popov turned off all communication with the ground for two days. Our support group is the home office."

"But you really do have enemies there," Mama said.

Fontana hesitated. "I don't know they're *my* enemies. They disagree with the way I run the platform, true, but that may be more a reflection of their feelings toward Crispus Tenning and the fact that they don't understand the differences between a planetary lab and an orbiting one."

"You've tried explaining?"

Doubrava snorted. "To groundsiders?"

Fontana scowled at him. "Of course I've explained, numerous times, but we disturb them. They come here on occasional visits expecting to find a weightless duplicate of one of their groundside labs, and instead they find a spherical orientation—file cabinets and tables on the ceiling—and over thirty percent of the personnel paraplegic, amputees, or affected by some other physical condition or disease that is considered limiting. Actually, it's only limiting in a gravity field, but—I'm sorry . . . I tend to climb on a soapbox when it comes to defending my recruiting policies. Visiting executives meet other personnel who look like skinhead trippers or who dress as birds or fish, all qualified people but highly individual, and they find a thousand-odd people free-running according to their personal circadian rhythms. I'm sure it looks like chaos. They instinctively want to 'restore' what they perceive as 'order,' never understanding that they're really trying to impose the rhythms of Earth and never understanding that those rhythms are inappropriate to a place where up/down and day/night have lost real meaning and become merely terms of convenience. But who knows? In their place I might feel the same."

Fontana's eyes did not match his tolerant tone, Janna noticed. A hard light made them look more lupine than ever. He obviously had stronger feelings about the home office than he chose to admit. Could it give him a motive for smuggling and murder?

"Shall I call Records and tell them you're coming over now?" Fontana asked.

Janna opened her mouth to agree, but Mama spoke first. "It's been a long day for us. I think I'd like to make use of your local recreational facilities this evening and wait until tomorrow to start on the files."

For a moment Janna stared at him in astonishment—what, Mama quitting on this case before midnight?—but the surprise faded when she noticed that his eyes had focused past Fontana and on the monitors behind the director's desk. Tabanne Geyer's golden glow dominated the center of a screen tuned to Recreation's central corridor. She hung with a toe hooked under a railing to stabilize herself for a conversation with another woman in a dress whose voluminous sleeves and skirts turned its wearer into a billowing cloud of chiffon.

Janna murmured to Mama, too low for Doubrava to hear. "Don't you think you ought to rein in your hormones? She's one of our suspects, remember."

He just grinned and whispered back. "That's why I want to observe her closely."

She hissed in exasperation. "You're impossible. But I should expect that by this time. Will you try to be careful, at least?"

He sobered for a moment. "Always, bibi. Good day, Mr. Fontana." With another grin and a wave he sailed out.

Janna followed with Doubrava. He cocked a brow at her. "You seem to have been abandoned. May I have the pleasure of your company?"

She glanced sideways at him . . . the pleasant face, turquoise eyes, and charming smile. She smiled back. "Why not?" With a little bit of the local liquor in him, he might be persuaded to talk about Geyer and Fontana, and about the conflict between them. "Lead on."

# CHAPTER
# FIFTEEN

<u>Sunday, February 4. 20:30:00 hours.</u>

A young man danced naked in the center of the Quark. He used a pole with two loops on it to anchor himself, sometimes hooking both feet through them so that he stood out at a ninety-degree angle from the pole, sometimes putting a hand and foot through them. In that attitude he alternated the direction in which his head pointed. Janna watched in fascination. Up and down became meaningless, Fontana had said. She saw what he meant. The dancer appeared equally comfortable, whatever direction he faced.

Fontana had spoken of people here developing a spherical orientation too. The tables on the ceiling were evidence of that, but Doubrava's quarters, where they had gone for him to change out of his uniform, were an even more graphic example. While he vanished beyond a divider made of a set of shelves and a floor-to-ceiling fish tank, Janna had stared around at the suite. Any resemblance to her room ended at the shape of the door and the construction of the closet, which could be seen distortedly through the fish tank. Doubrava had decorated as though every surface were a wall, or perhaps a ceiling. Cloud murals covered what corresponded to the floor and ceiling in her room, reflected in endless progression by mirrored walls, so that she and countless ever-more-distant images of her floated in an infinity of sky. Even the oval door appeared suspended in midair.

"I'm surprised you didn't decorate with starfields," she had called.

Doubrava came around the fish tank sheathed in a shimmering bodysuit whose color matched his eyes. "I tried that for a while, but space is so dark, and it can cause agoraphobia in a person here and there, killing her amorous mood."

A young woman replaced the male dancer on the pole. Janna looked around for Mama, as she had watched for him when they went into Fluidics Inc. on their first stop of the evening. As nearly as she could tell in the pulsing light by looking through a holographic molecular diagram that filled the room, he did not appear to be there. If Geyer had consented to his company, they must have gone somewhere else. Not surprisingly. From the snatches of conversation Janna caught above the wail of experimental afroasian compositions for the flute, sitar, and drum, Janna gathered that like the Belithroche and Fluidics Inc., The Quark catered to the scientific staff. The surprise was that Doubrava came here.

Or was it? Around and above her, the discussions on chemistry and physics, accompanied by illustrations scribbled on the tabletops, alternated with groups who seemed on the verge of a public orgy . . . like the pair at the next table, dressed mostly in spray-on glitter and clinging together as if determined to disprove that two solids could not occupy the same space simultaneously.

But if scientists did not appear much different than the good citizens at home, their club decor was unique. Janna eyed the holographic molecule, struggling to remember her college chemistry and identify it. "I'd have expected a place called The Quark to go for subatomic subjects."

Doubrava shrugged. "I don't know whether quantum physics is hard to illustrate or that they think chemistry gives them more chance to attempt humor."

Janna blinked. "Humor?"

"Like using an ethanol molecule or part of a sex hormone. Or a terrible pun. One time, I remember, they had a hydrocarbon with flowers instead of a spheres representing the different atoms."

She frowned. That was a pun? Oh. Flowercarbon. Janna groaned. "And you continue to come here?"

Doubrava grinned. "Between masochism and my determination to acquire higher education through osmosis—" He broke off, face blanking and head tilting. Janna identified the attitude instantly . . . someone listening to his radio. She arched a brow. Was he such a rock jock that he wore his ear button even while off-duty?

"You can't stand to be out of touch?" she asked.

Absently he replied, "Not permitted to be. The curse of being a supervisor. Sometimes I think I might as well have a radio permanently implant—" He listened intently for a moment, then pulled loose from the carpet under the table and pushed for the door. "Come on."

She kicked off to follow him. "Is it serious?"

But he did not reply, and a glimpse at the inward look in his eyes as she caught up with him told her he heard nothing but the voice murmuring in his ear.

In the core corridor Doubrava stilled the warning voice by pushing one end of his ID badge into a slot in the wall and looking straight into the r.r. plate above it until the voice invited him to proceed.

As always, the corridor stretched away to the vanishing point beneath them, but Janna discovered that it continued to do so even as they neared the Level Two corridors. The station must be expanding downward as well as adding to Level Two. Construction's green coveralls predominated among the colors worn by the people she could see farther down. The construction must also be very recent. She could not recall any Level Three monitors in Security.

Doubrava swung into a corridor with navy-blue paneling at the junction. Whatever the problem was, its location became immediately obvious. A crowd of people clustered at the entrances to the fourth group of pods, almost completely blocking the corridor . . . like a clot in a blood vessel, Janna mused. Past the second group of entrances, she began to hear yelling, which grew louder and more distinct every meter closer to the crowd.

Doubrava burrowed through the clot using elbows and knees. "Security. Let me past. Bendure, Ourada," he barked at two officers hovering in the hatchway. "What the hell do you think you are, spectators? Clear this corridor."

The officers flushed. "Lieutenant Paretsky wanted us to stand by in case she and Trent needed more backup."

"Backup? Guess whose back will be up if she comes and finds that human long-jam. I'll help Paretsky and Trent. You send these people sailing." Doubrava propelled himself past them through the hatchway.

Janna debated whether to offer her help but quickly decided it would be inconsistent with her bad-guy role and probably would be resented. She followed Doubrava.

A honeycomb of small labs filled the pod. The yelling did, too, accompanied by the crash of glass. "No! I won't let her have it! It's *my* project!"

It was a male voice. A female voice screamed as more glass shattered.

The noise led them straight to the source, a lab on an upper level of the pod, where the glittering splinters of glass swirled through the air like flies. A bulb beaker hurled out the door past a petite, olive-skinned female officer and a husky, blond male to smash against the opposite wall, adding more shards to the air. The woman's voice screamed again inside the lab.

"Please, Dr. Chelle," the female officer said. She pulled herself up the doorway and peered in from the top. "No one is taking the project away from you. Your year here is up, and it's merely being turned over to someone else to continue."

"I'm being robbed! I applied for permanent status, but you bastards won't take me; you're just taking my project and giving it to this bitch!"

"Dr. Chelle, you know that no one owns a project. They all belong to—" Another bulb beaker was hurled out the door, narrowly missing Paretsky as she pulled back. Blood spotted her face where the swarming splinters had nicked her.

"It's *mine*!" shrieked the man in the lab. "If I can't stay to finish it and can't take it back with me, no one can have it."

Doubrava cautiously warded off glass with his arms as he slid up beside Paretsky. "Who's in there with him?"

Paretsky glanced around. "Dr. Mara Xidas. Apparently he hadn't yet learned that his application for permanent assignment had been turned down, and when Dr. Xidas asked him to brief her on the project, he went berserk. I can't get anything coherent out of Dr. Xidas, but from the sound of her she's still alive."

Janna brushed at splinters floating toward her. If this was an example of Dr. Chelle's temperament, she could see why he had been turned down.

"We need a vaccuum," Doubrava said.

Paretsky nodded. "I've sent for it, and for the sleeper."

More glass smashed inside the lab. Shards of it shot out to join those already in the corridor. "It's a damn plot," Chelle shouted. "I'm not some damn cripple or misfit, so you're stealing my project and throwing me out!"

"Where the hell is that sleeper?" the blond officer growled.

Janna had never heard of a sleeper. "Don't you use K-12?"

"Too much risk of it getting into the ventilation system," Doubrava said. "We don't want the whole station curled into whimpering balls of fear."

"A needler, then?"

"Do *you* want to stand in that doorway long enough to brace yourself so the recoil won't deflect the needle?"

"My god," a voice said behind them.

Janna turned to see Geyer waving away glass splinters. She had changed from her uniform into exercise shorts and tank top. Sweat darkened the chestnut hair at her temples and across her golden forehead. Mama floated along behind her in shorts and tank top too. Borrowed? They did not seem something he would have thought to bring. Sweat tracks streaked his face and bare scalp. Janna arched a brow. Were he and Geyer spending a romantic evening together in the gym?

More flying glassware snapped her attention back to the situation inside the lab. Dr. Xidas screamed again.

This time the blond officer managed to reach out and catch the beaker as it shot out the door. He grinned triumphantly.

Geyer frowned. Her voice managed to sound warm and soothing, however. "Dr. Chelle, this is Chief Geyer from Security. You know this is no way to solve your problem. Let me call Director Fontana and Doctor Freeman down here and let's all sit down and discuss your complaint like intelligent, civilized people."

"You people aren't civilized! You're goddamn thieves. I don't think you're even human anymore!"

"Oh, come now, Doctor. It's understandable that you're upset, but—"

"You're damn right I'm upset! Take a year contract, Fontana said. Work my own hours on any project I wanted. If I did well, I could stay and be a permanent part of the most exciting research team in the solar system. But he *lied* to me! I've done well. My critters will grow fast and fat and provide all the protein you want. But he won't let me stay!"

Janna heard more movement behind her, and through the pod maze came two more officers, both with large backpacks. The hose attached to one identified it as a vacuum. The other, with wires leading to what looked like a bullhorn the officer held, had to be the sleeper.

Geyer motioned them both forward. "Are you sure? Let's ask the director about it. But first, may I have someone clean up this air so we can breathe without inhaling glass?"

"No!" More glass shattered. Dr. Xidas shrieked as though she were being murdered. "Talking's just more tricks!"

Geyer nodded to the officer with the sleeper.

The officer dived through the airborne glass to the door. Stopping himself by catching the edge with his free hand, he pointed the bullhorn into the room and pulled the trigger. From the far side of the corridor Janna pulled herself into a position where she could see into the lab. A lean, balding man with his eyes white-rimmed and face colored purple with fury came arrowing toward the doorway with a broken beaker. He went slack, as suddenly as if a switch had been snapped off.

Momentum carried his body on, however, where the blond officer caught him. Then the officer with the vacuum went to work.

Altogether a neat, professional job. Janna nodded to Geyer. "I'm impressed."

"Me too," Mama said. But he was looking at Geyer, not the officer with the sleeper.

Geyer smiled thinly. "And to think we're only lend-lease leos."

All of them but the blond officer edged into the lab past the officer with the vacuum.

Dr. Xidas, a corpulent woman with close-cropped salt-and-pepper hair, floated in a sea of shattered glass and fragmented cultures, also unconscious but apparently unharmed except for numerous nicks on her face and surprisingly slim, long-fingered hands. A medical team appeared with a stretcher to take both her and Chelle to sick bay. The officer with the sleeper unhitched the backpack to reach the control for deactivation.

Janna eyed the sleeper. "How does it work?"

The officer looked toward Geyer.

"Sound waves," she said. "It induces a narcoleptic state."

Mama's eyes gleamed. "Is that what's in the core corridor?"

Geyer looked around the lab. "We need to get someone in here to clean up and see what can be salvaged."

Which probably meant it was, Janna decided.

Mama sighed. "We could use something like that at home."

"It has its drawbacks," Doubrava said.

"Which are?"

He grimaced. "As you saw, it doesn't have all that fine a focus, and . . . the effect tends to persist. Dr. Xidas will be going to sleep on us every time she's excited for the next few weeks. Very inconvenient." He turned toward Janna. "Shall we finish our drink?"

She nodded. For a moment she considered asking Mama to join them, but one glance at him showed her that was pointless. Mama had eyes only for Geyer.

Coming out of the pod, Janna glanced on up the corridor, a sunny-bright tube carrying people in a rainbow of coveralls. "I don't suppose you could entertain me with a tour of this part of the station?"

Doubrava hesitated, then shook his head with a smile. "Sorry. But you can see the new pod if you like."

It lay toward the end of the corridor. Reaching it, Janna studied the four open hatchways. "Which one?"

He spread his hands. "Any of them. It's a torus, a doughnut shape circling the corridor. It'll give us more room when the interior is finished than a cluster of three globes does."

"This spider thing will cover any shape?"

"That's what I understand."

Janna pulled herself through one hatchway. There was little to see, however. To her disappointment and surprise, it had no active construction, no crews, and no work lights. The only illumination came from the corridor, and that showed her nothing more than radial girders stretching outward into cavernous darkness.

Doubrava floated up behind her. "It's just a shell so far, I'm afraid. On the other hand, there's no spy eye in here, either."

He was almost breathing in her ear. Janna grinned inwardly and moved out along a girder hand-over-hand. Not so fast, jon. "I'm a little surprised there's no work crew. I had the impression that every section runs twenty-four hours. Or is Construction busy on exteriors on Level Three?"

"Who cares?" Doubrava swung past her and, with the faint light shimmering on his bodysuit, launched away from the girder to the next one, spun around it, and arrowed back in a maneuver any gymnast on Earth would have envied. "Until they start on this interior, we have a top-star playground." Grinning, he pushed away from the girder and hung in midair, holding out his hands. "Come space dancing with me, Brill."

The grin pulled her like a magnet. Reaching out, she took his hands. In a moment she found herself wrapped in his arms, the two of them spinning off through the air into darkness. The circles of light marking two of the hatchways shrank to peepholes.

"Are you sure Geyer intended you to keep this tight a leash?" Janna asked a little breathlessly.

The breath from his laughter tickled her ear. "She said anything that would keep you occupied. "Duck!"

A girder brushed by the top of her head.

"Maybe we ought to go back to The Quark."

But she did not really want to. Exhilaration bubbled up through her, and a warm pleasure that she suspected had to be attributed to Doubrava's nearness. The danger of the girders only added spice to their flight.

Doubrava began, "If we go anywhere, I'd much rather—" He broke off and let go of her with one hand to snag another girder and halt them. "No, I guess Paretsky can take care of that one without me."

His radio again. Thinking back to the incident they had just left, Janna frowned thoughtfully. "Does Geyer wear her button all the time too?"

She felt him nod. "Of course."

"And you both answer interesting or difficult calls even when you're not on duty?"

"Like this evening? Usually."

"Did Geyer come around when you and Officer Talltrees

were checking that false report the day Chenoweth's body left?"

He stiffened against her in the dark. "There was no need for her to."

"But wasn't that the kind of incident where you would expect her to check on what was happening and how you were doing?"

Slowly he replied, "Yes," and she heard the soft intake of his breath. "I remember being a little surprised at the time that she didn't appear, but I never thought any more about it. That's strange. I wonder why she didn't come."

Janna smiled grimly. Why, indeed.

# CHAPTER
# SIXTEEN

## Monday, February 5. 7:30:00 hours.

The scent of honeysuckle filled Records. Janna breathed deeply, surprised but pleased. A young amerind woman at a desk on the ceiling looked down at her with sooty-dark eyes. "You're the other one. Back there." She pointed toward a lattice divider partitioning off one side of the room. "I've shown the . . . gentleman how to access the files Mr. Fontana said to let you see."

Now Janna understood why she smelled honeysuckle. The vine and its small yellow-and-white flowers covered the slim plastic lathes of the lattice.

"That's a nice touch," Janna said.

"Mr. Fontana suggested plants to naturalize the environment, and vines don't seem to care which direction is up." The clerk returned to her terminal.

Dismissed, Janna thought with a grimace.

On the far side of the honeysuckle Mama stood at a terminal too. His jumpsuit, crossing-guard orange with a chain of large black diamonds down the side, augmented the lighting. Looking around from the screen at her, he grinned. "Vradel would never believe this, me beating you to work. Is your circadian rhythm slipping you off the clock already, or did Doubrava just keep you awake too late?"

She raised her brows. "You're sun and bells this morning."

"I had a good night's sleep."

The emphasis on the pronoun and the faintly superior tone invited a comeback. Janna bared her teeth. "I'm not surprised after the way Geyer put you through your paces in the gym. Quite a game of anything-you-can-do-I-can-do-better."

Mama shrugged. "She had to seem like she was trying to make me look bad so onlookers wouldn't think she was sympathetic to the home-office devil. How do you know about it?"

For a moment Janna considered saying that she had overheard conversation on the topic in the cafeteria, but for all their fights and differences, she and Mama did not lie to one another. "I saw it. After the incident in the lab Doubrava and I wondered where Geyer spent the day the body left. He suggested we look through the surveillance tapes of the day, and we went back to Security, only we happened to glance at the monitors and see you in the gym."

Well, maybe she lied a little, but only about *how* they found Geyer and him in the gym.

As they'd hovered together at the monitor wall Doubrava had said, "While we're at it, maybe we ought to take a look at what she's doing now too." He punched keys on a panel in the middle of the monitors. "That holo isn't just decorative. Every ID badge has a transponder built into it. By calling up the badge name, we can locate it in the holo. See, there the chief is."

A light had pulsed in the pod labeled GYM in small, glowing letters.

Turning to the monitor bank, they'd checked the gym and found Geyer and Mama on the track. The golden woman ran like a deer. As they continued to watch, Geyer had moved on to the racquetball courts where she played with demonic accuracy and speed.

Thinking back to watching the game, Janna raised a brow at Mama. "She's very athletic, isn't she?"

"Very." Mama smiled at the computer screen. "She reminds

me a little of you, and in more ways than that. Her job is her life too."

Janna almost said, "I know," but bit the words off unsaid. Somehow she could not quite bring herself to admit to him that they had not stopped watching when Geyer and Mama had left the gym.

Doubrava's brows had arched. "They're staying together? Pairing up with a stranger isn't at all like Bane; she takes a long time to accept people. Shall we keep surveillance and see where they go?"

It had felt more like peeping than surveillance to Janna, perhaps because her own partner was one of the subjects, though Doubrava's attitude stilled some of her misgivings. He'd watched not with the avid curiosity of the voyeur but with the dispassionate remoteness of someone observing an ant colony.

He turned the sound on. Geyer said, "Come in here. I want to talk."

She had taken Mama into the junglelike greenhouse. It had no footpaths, just hand lines. Geyer led the way along one, from one monitor to another, through a red blaze of Virginia creepers into a tangle of sunflowers, vine-cloaked saplings, and feathery ferns.

To Janna's surprise Mama had followed, and without choking or sneezing . . . Mama, who was allergic to everything green or furry. Those new allergy treatments must really be working.

In the middle of the wildwood Geyer had hooked one knee around the hand line and turned back to Mama with arms crossed. "You stuck with me. I'm impressed. Tell me, what do you hope to prove by becoming my shadow?"

From the angle of the camera, suspended high above them, Mama's expression could not be seen, but his voice had sounded earnest. "What makes you think I want to prove anything but what good company I am? You're a very attractive woman."

"One of the most beautiful you've ever met, no doubt." Bitterness hardened the rich voice. "The curse of my life."

Janna had stared, startled. The pause before Mama spoke indicated that he, too, had been caught by surprise. "Most women wouldn't think so."

She'd hissed. "They haven't been me. I've worked long and hard to get where I am. I'm damn well qualified. Yet when Fontana floats his little executive tours through the station, showing off his masterpiece, if the corporate muckies are men, nine times out of ten, when they have questions about Security, it's quite obvious that they assume Doubrava really runs the section, covering for the flash bibi who was made chief probably as a reward for sexual virtuosity!" Her eyes had flashed. "Sometimes I really hate men."

Doubrava had switched off the sound, but the image of Geyer's face remained . . . tight-lipped and bitter.

That image came back to Janna now as she settled her feet into the carpet beside Mama and frowned at the Personnel computer. "What does Geyer's personnel file have to say?"

"I'm looking at Nakashima's right now. Interesting family. They make handcrafted furniture. She also has a brother on Mars and one who died on Mercury in Project Sunbath. Nakashima herself is also interesting. She's picked up a master's degree in botany by correspondence while working up here as Fontana's secretary."

Janna peered around his shoulder. "Anything to suggest that she might be involved in our—Mama, they monitor calls too!"

On the screen had come a list headed CALLS AND TELSCRIBED LETTERS. Most of the entries consisted of only a date, time, and name, but one near the beginning read: "10/15/75:23:37:02: Call to Rose Nakashima Wakabayashi terminated by Communications for breach of security. Employee warned. No further action."

"And censor them." Mama grimaced. The action loosened

his glasses, and he pushed them back tight on his nose. "Fontana wasn't kidding about tight security."

Janna pursed her lips thoughtfully. "Those calls are probably taped, too, which would make it hard for our smuggler to communicate with the ground contacts. Maybe the messages went by shuttle?"

Mama considered. "Possibly, but it would be more efficient to call or telscribe using a code."

"I wonder who Geyer calls and writes to groundside."

He stiffened. "Bibi, I told you, too much of her life is tied up in this job for her to act against it."

That was a defensive tone if Janna had ever heard one. She eyed him speculatively. "You sound like you're losing objectivity, partner."

He glanced sideways at her. "I wonder how objective *you* are." He punched keys. "Remember what you keep saying: Look at *all* the evidence and find the person all of it fits, not look for evidence against a particular suspect. But aren't you doing exactly that with Geyer?"

Now she stiffened. "I—" Was she? Janna wondered uncomfortably. "We know it has to be someone high up. Geyer is just one possibility. Fontana is another. Let's look at his file first, then."

It came up on the screen almost before she finished speaking.

For a while she and Mama read in silence. Janna sucked in her lip. Geyer's life might center around her job, but the facts printed on the screen added up to the station *being* Leonard Makepeace Fontana's life. Born in 2025, he had worked for Lanour since graduating from Texas A&M with a master's in business, starting in a sales position for a subsidiary company, Citadel Pharmaceuticals. Within two years, however, he had transferred to Seever Astrotechnologies and gone to work in their Houston office. From the names and titles listed as friends for a Lanour security check, he apparently spent his leisure time chumming with NASA scientists and space center personnel, though along the way he also acquired a pilot's license and a BS in psychology. In '53 he won an award for suggestions on modification of the Seever pressure suit.

"So he knows pressure suits," Mama said.

Janna nodded. A strike against him.

In '54 he wrote to Crispus Tenning with suggestions for a space station that Lanour was rumored to be thinking of building. The letter must have impressed Tenning, because within a month Fontana had been transferred to the newly formed subsidiary, Lanour Aerospace, and began a rocket-driven ascension up the corporate ladder. Straight toward platform director.

A psychological evaluation by the station psychologist described Fontana as ambitious, dedicated, and a workaholic.

"I can see why he might be resented," Janna said, "but it looks like the station project is as much his baby as old man Tenning's. I'd think harming it would be the equivalent of cutting out his own heart."

"Unless he's certain he's about to lose the station, bibi, then it's sweet revenge. Selling off the work here to competitors will cripple Lanour, maybe fatally."

She ran a hand through her hair. Could Fontana be certain of the proxy fight outcome so far ahead of time? "Who has he called and written?"

The list looked unpromising. Except for a handful of other people, none contacted more than one or twice a year, he talked only to Crispus Tenning—on a scrambled signal—and his wife and children in Beaumont, Texas.

Mama polished his glasses on his jumpsuit. "His wife would be a perfect cover for messages."

"We'll have to see if we can talk our way into a look at the tapes of their conversations. All right, now let's see Geyer's file."

Mama readjusted his glasses. "How about Doubrava?"

Janna straightened with a jerk that threatened to tear her slippers loose from the carpet. "Doubrava!"

Behind Mama's glasses, his eyes watched her keenly. "You're not excluding him, are you, bibi? Remember objectivity. After all, he knows both construction and station security."

Her jaw tightened. "There is a small matter, though, of being up near the docking bay with witnesses at the same time someone was calling a disturbance in from Level Two."

"An accomplice. Titus, maybe. He isn't quite what he seems, bibi."

Janna eyed him. "I take it you've already had a look at his file."

Mama nodded. His fingers moved over the keyboard.

The file that came up on the screen seemed unremarkable at first. Doubrava had washed out of shuttle pilot training but promptly applied for orbital construction work, and after ten years of that, working on various NASA and private space stations, including the Lanour platform, had applied and been accepted for a Security position on the Lanour platform. In the course of it all he had run through five one-year marriage contracts.

Mama arched a brow at Janna. "He has as much trouble maintaining relationships as I do."

Janna sniffed, then the security check sent her eyebrows climbing. "He's rich?"

According to investigation by Lanour's operatives, Doubrava had made a fortune speculating in the stock market and continued to accumulate credit. All the investments were made for him by a Denver librarian named Adresina Petree, whom Doubrava had met and had an affair with while on vacation in Greece in '69. He called her once or twice a week.

"Interesting, isn't it?" Mama said.

"Except that he was speculating successfully for a year before he switched to security work, and each of the stock

transactions has been verified as genuine." Anger still smoldered in her. Why, she could not quite decide. Doubrava
meant nothing to her beyond good company and a pleasant
sexual partner. Did he? "It's perfectly possible there's nothing
more involved than a friendship between two people who
found something more practical than sex in each other."

"But he works when he doesn't have to."

"Maybe it's for the job, not the credit. Look at his record.
Every job he's tried for or held has put him up here. The
psychological evaluation characterizes him as seeing space
work as romantic in nature and attractive to women. But if
we can see those call tapes, we'll find out what he and his
librarian friend talk about. Now, are you going to call up
Geyer's file or do I ask the clerk to come in here and show
me how to do it?"

With what seemed to Janna like great reluctance, Mama
typed in the Security chief's name.

Janna leaned around him to read the file as it rolled up the
screen. "Tabanne Uzuri Geyer. Born San Francisco, '38. She
doesn't look forty-two, does she?"

Mama just grunted in reply.

Janna read on silently.

Geyer's father was a captain in the San Francisco PD . . .
the source of her interest in security work, no doubt. She had
graduated from Stanford in '56 with degrees in criminal justice and psychology, picked up a pilot's license, then attended
the Fangman Academy in Abilene, Texas, in '56.

Janna's brows hopped. The Fangman Academy trained
bodyguards, some of the best in the world.

After Fangman's, Geyer had joined Personal Security Services, working out of first the San Francisco office, then
Houston, where she had studied electronics and egonomics
in her spare time.

"Versatile woman," Mama murmured.

"I thought of joining PSS once," Janna said. "Wearing
fancy clothes and hanging on the arm of some rich and pow-

erful man while he went about his business or played in Las Vegas and Monaco sounded like a dream job."

Mama rolled an eye in her direction. "What stopped you?"

She shrugged. "I guess it didn't fit in with some light-witted idea I had back then of ridding the world of bad guys."

In Houston, Geyer had met Thomas Hogan Holle, Lanour's vice-president in charge of marketing. In '70 he hired her away from PSS to be one of his full-time bodyguards, but when the Lanour platform activated in '73, Geyer had trans-ferred to station Security.

Mama tapped the entry on the screen. "That looks like someone else wanting a particular job above all else. It had to mean a big salary cut."

Her salary would have gone up again, though. By '74 she was assistant chief, and a year later she had moved into command of Security. Still, the job could not pay what being bodyguard for Holle had, Janna reflected. Something about it mattered more than financial rewards, and more than per-sonal relationships or a family. Geyer had never married, not even for a one-year contract.

"You see?" Mama said. "Her life centers on this job, like yours does on your job. She has a trust, and she won't betray it any more than you'd sell out your badge."

"What if she were about to lose the job?" Janna could not forget Geyer's bitter comment on how corporate executives perceived her ability. "Doesn't that give her the same moti-vation as Fontana to strike back at Lanour?"

The psychological evaluation described her as single-mind-edly loyal to friends and superiors she respected, but also reserved and suspicious, slow to accept new people into her circle. A security check turned up a membership in the Af-rican Heritage Association. Janna pointed that out to Mama.

He shrugged it off. "Not everyone in the AHA is radical, bibi. Several members of my family have joined, too, and you won't find more conservative, patriotic people. They even still vote Republican."

But his confidence faltered when they reached the call list. Geyer made few, just to her parents, sister, and a couple of women identified as former colleagues in PSS. The pattern of calls to one of them, however, a Raine DeBrabander, had suddenly gone from twice a month to twice a week starting around Christmas.

Mama swore softly and stared at the screen, cheeks sucked in. After a long while he sighed. "We need to see those tapes, bibi. Maybe they have nothing useful on them. After all, someone here must have looked at them as soon they knew about the smuggling and no arrests came of it. Still . . ."

"Still," Janna echoed, "the lack of arrests could have something to do with which of our chief suspects did the reviewing."

Mama kneaded the back of his neck, as though it ached. "I think maybe as soon as we've gone over the files for Titus and some of his friends, we might ask about the call tapes."

If nothing else, Janna reflected, the reaction to their request ought to tell them something useful.

# CHAPTER
# SEVENTEEN

<u>**Monday, February 5. 12:45:00 hours.**</u>

Geyer was not in Security when they arrived at the office after lunch, only Doubrava, who was hanging upside down at the monitor wall, slippers sunk in the carpet of the ceiling/floor. Like some exotic blue-furred, turquoise-eyed bat, Janna thought suddenly, and bit her lip to keep from giggling.

"You want to see the call tapes?" He paused with fingers on the buttons of the panel controlling the station holo. "Of course. Does that mean you found something useful in the personnel records this morning?"

Janna searched his tone for sharp edges or anxiety but heard none, only the same dispassionate curiosity he had shown watching Geyer on the monitors the night before. "Not that I can discuss right now. Where's your boss?"

"I'll look in a minute." His fingers played across the panel. In the holo, light flashed in a pod on Level One.

"It's in C-9," said a burly officer at a desk by the holo.

Doubrava's fingers moved again. The flashing pod swelled, replacing the station holo and turning transparent. Now the light flashed in a room in the middle of the pod.

"C-9-55, to be specific." Doubrava grinned down at Janna. "Big Brother is also useful for finding certain lost items. Dickerson," he said to the burly officer, "call Stoer and tell him where to find his badge, but since this is the second time he's mislaid it in two weeks, suggest that after this he try:

one, drinking a little less so he can retain the memory of his
revels; two, taming the passion within himself long enough
to undress neatly instead of shedding clothing indiscrimi-
nately; and three, picking up carefully after himself when
leaving."

With a grin the officer turned to the phone built into his
desktop and punched in numbers.

Doubrava tapped keys on the wall panel, restoring the
normal holo of the station. "I hope you find the tapes more
useful than we did. We've had two people doing nothing for
the past week but reviewing them, and they've found nothing,
not even after running the tapes through a computer cryp-
toanalysis program. Our killer is obviously *very* good at en-
coding. Where would you like to start? We have thousands
of hours of tapes, indexed by date and person."

"With midnight the morning of Saturday the twentieth and
going through Monday the twenty-second," Mama said.

Doubrava raised a brow. "Why just those three days?"

Again, though Janna listened closely, she heard no special
emphasis, nothing but normal curiosity. "Because we can be
certain our killer made a call or telscribed a letter to the ground
contact sometime during them. Uwezo's agents didn't know
the date and manner of delivery when they hired the slighs
on Friday, but they had all that information by Monday night."

Doubrava arched his brows and smiled. "I wish we'd thought
of that. Of course, you realize that you'll still have hundreds
of tapes to watch. Half the station calls friends and family
groundside during the weekend period. But having given you
fair warning of eyestrain to come, follow me."

He pulled loose from the floor overhead and sailed toward
the door.

They met Geyer coming in. She smiled at Mama. "Hi, leo.
How are you this afternoon? And where are you all going?"
She glanced up toward Doubrava as she asked.

"Communications," Doubrava replied, and explained why,
including the time-limit reasoning Janna had given him.

Geyer stiffened. It was difficult to tell in eyes as dark as the Security chief's, but Janna thought her eyes blazed for just a moment before her face set in an expression of reproof. "And you'd load our visiting firemen with the tedium of checking those calls? Absolutely not. Put our own people on it."

Doubrava blinked. "But they *want*—"

"I said put our own people on it, Captain!" Pushing off from the doorway, she sailed across the office through the middle of the holo toward her own office. In that doorway she paused to look back. "I don't mean to shut you out of the case, Mama. In a couple of minutes I'll show you the operation of the surveillance cameras and you can help me by watching Titus and his friends." She vanished inside her office.

Janna eyed the door speculatively. "Doubrava, did you ever go through the surveillance tapes to see where she was when Chenoweth's body left?"

He glanced toward the office door. "She's probably popped because we wasted so much time looking through the whole month's tapes. Let me talk to her. I'm sure I can fix things."

"You didn't find her, did you?" Janna said.

He hesitated. "There are no cameras in personal quarters."

"Or in the labs."

Doubrava stiffened. The turquoise eyes narrowed. "She's got nothing to hide! I'll be right back."

Not quite. He remained in Geyer's office for nearly fifteen minutes. Janna would have given a great deal to know what was being said, but he had closed the door behind him going in.

After waiting for several minutes, Mama strolled along the monitor wall in a slow series of velcro rips, studying the screens. "Those executives groundside are light-witted to want to replace Fontana. He has to be doing something right. Look at this place. It's as busy as an ant colony before winter, but no one looks unhappy."

But they did look very earnest, driven by some inner passion as they pulled and kicked along the corridors past the surveillance cameras. "I wonder where Titus is in all that."

Mama grinned. "Let's find out." He caught the burly officer's eye. "Officer Dickerson, since Chief Geyer seems to be occupied, will you help us find Clell Titus?"

The officer glanced toward the closed door. Through it came the sound of Geyer's voice, the words unintelligible but the tone furious.

"She may be occupied for a while yet too." The officer pulled his way over to them. "Operation of the locater is really quite simple."

And it was, once he showed them how.

"What if we want to track Titus back earlier?" Janna asked.

"Then you have to use a computer terminal, but that isn't difficult, either."

Janna wished she had paper to write down the codes, but at least by tapping on the microcorder in her pocket, she had vocal instructions that would hopefully recall the key combinations he pressed.

After the officer returned to his own desk, she and Mama practiced, first by finding Titus on the holo. The signal from his badge transponder flashed outside the Level Three corridors.

"Let's see what he was doing before he went out to work," Janna said.

Mama pursed his lips. "About eight hundred hours he would have been in the locker room. We can backtrack him from there."

At eight hundred hours Titus and the rest of the construction crews were leaving in pressure suits for the air lock. Janna backed up the tape to watch him come into the locker room with the dwarf and afroam that had been with him in the empty bar. Talking and laughing, they floated up the row, stopping at another locker, where Titus started to punch the combination before the afroam said sharply, "Clell, what the hell are you doing?"

Titus started and pushed away from the locker, glancing up toward the camera. "I was only going to borrow some boosters from Kirchmeier. Do either of you have any extra?"

The dwarf said, "I don't work boosted. It's a good way to end up snagged and ripped open like Chenoweth."

Shrugging, Titus went on to his own locker and climbed into his pressure suit.

Janna switched to the camera in the core corridor at a time just before Titus entered the locker room. From there they traced him back to breakfast with the two other men and the mermaid, now minus her tail. To Janna's disappointment the conversation contained nothing incriminating, just chatter about the torus frame they were finishing and somewhat worried speculation on the Lanour proxy fight. Janna was following Titus out of the empty bar where he left them yesterday, when the door of Geyer's office hissed open. Doubrava sailed out.

Nodding at them, he headed for the door. "Let's go."

Janna cleared the computer and followed him. "You must be very persuasive."

He grinned over his shoulder. "Just remember that Security takes the credit if this finds our killer. Agreed?"

Janna could not believe that a question of credit was enough by itself to change Geyer's mind, but at this point, how he managed it mattered less to her than that he had, giving Mama and her a chance to see the call tapes. She nodded agreement.

Like every other section in the station except the visitor's quarters, Communications used the ceiling as well as the floor. As in the bars, those occupied the position of walls in relationship to the door. A long communications console with stations on both sides stretched the length of the wall/floor to the left. And here, too, where dividers semipartitioned the right-hand floor, flowers covered them. Yellow roses this time. Fontana's preference?

Everyone in the room looked around as the door divided. Most nodded greetings to Doubrava. He spoke to a dark-eyed, asian-looking young man, and in five minutes the technician had them installed at an empty station on the console with a stack of tapes and a thick file folder.

Mama quirked a brow at the folder. "You mean people still write?"

Doubrava grinned. "Not much. From here, calling doesn't cost that much more than telscribing. These, however, are transcripts and translations of the calls." He slipped the first tape into the console slot.

The calls began almost immediately after midnight, and as the images of both caller and callee appeared on the split screen, Janna understood the need for translations. Of the handful of calls by scientific and computer personnel, Janna could understand only the Australians'. The others to Japan and Taiwan hit her ears as unintelligible singsong.

Janna read the translation instead, grimacing at the syntax. It must be the output of a dictyper. Computer translations might be faster and less work than human ones, but they remained gratingly literal.

"Quite an international staff," Mama commented.

"Lanour is a multinational, but even if it weren't, I think Fontana would hire qualified personnel wherever he could find them."

For the most part the calls were tedious, recitations of personal activities unrelated to the the callers' jobs and gossip about people Janna did not know. Still, she studied every word, hunting a pattern that might be a code. If it were there, though, it was too subtle for her. Mama apparently detected nothing, either. He only shrugged when she lifted her brows at him.

Activity died down after that, until about three, when two

calls went to Egypt and Israel, both from computer bobs who obviously had no interest in anything beyond programming.

At four and five the calls were to Germany, England, and Ireland, as boring as the earlier calls, though Communications had temporarily interrupted one to Germany.

As the callee's half of the screen went blank, a flat voice said, "Security breech."

The caller switched to furious English, face reddening. "What the hell do you mean, security breech? What the hell is secret about the torus design of the new pods?"

"The design employs a new and experimental process. In the future it would be safest to avoid mention of all details concerning construction and work routine."

"Then what the hell is it I am permitted to talk about?" the caller snarled in frustration.

The Communications technician replied only, "You may resume your call."

It resumed with the caller railing against the strictness of Security and the clique-ishness of the permanent staff. The end of his assignment to the station could not come soon enough. He did not know why, Janna read in the translation, so many people seemed eager to live here permanently.

Activity stopped until noon, but then the calls became an avalanche raining on the U.S., Canada, and Mexico. They came so fast, they must have tied up almost every one of the station's frequencies. Janna watched what seemed very much like the hundreds of calls Doubrava warned them about. But at least she could understand all but those to Quebec. And familiar faces appeared.

Titus . . . talking to his wife, children, and co-husband in Maryland. Listening, rather. He let them do most of the talking. The co-husband asked, "Are you still finding adventure enough up there, Clell?"

On his half of the screen, Titus grinned. "Have you ever known me to stick with another job this long? I expect it to get even better too."

Janna frowned at the transcript. "Can we read anything special into that?"

"Not offhand, bibi, but put the transcript aside to go over again later."

Several calls later Geyer's regal face appeared on the screen. The older woman on the other half the screen, although thinner and darker than Geyer, bore enough physical similarities that she had to be a close relative.

"Hi, Mom."

Mama leaned toward the screen, but his interest had to be Geyer, certainly not the conversation . . . hello, how are you, what have you been doing? Watching, though, the exchange resonated in Janna, and after a few minutes she identified the reason. The Security chief's smile and noncommittal replies that skipped the specifics of her job sounded just like Janna's conversations with her father. She felt a sudden involuntary kinship with the golden woman and swore. Sisterly feelings toward a suspect were the last thing she needed.

"Mama, what do you think?"

He frowned at the transcript, then shook his head. "I don't think so; not this call, anyway."

How could she trust Mama's judgment, or her own, now, for that matter? She set the transcript aside for closer reading later.

Fontana made two calls, one to his daughter at Texas A&M, the other to his wife in Beaumont.

As the second started, Doubrava grinned. "Dig in your slippers, children. The fun begins."

On the callee's half of the screen a slim, tanned woman with two-toned green hair and Egyptian eye makeup exercised in the nude beside a swimming pool.

"Hello, Len." Mercedes Fontana's rich voice echoed slightly. She stopped jumping jacks long enough to peer toward the screen. "You look tired, honey. Is the job runnin' you or has some sweet young companion been interferin' with your sleep?"

The wolf's eyes crinkled at the corners. "I don't have time for that much involvement. Sex has to wait for the few minutes here and there when I have nothing better to do."

The woman laughed, a rich, sensuously animal sound. "Lord, don't I know that. My space man. You don't even care that I take my pleasures elsewhere, do you?" She came over to turn the phone and stretch out on a chaise the screen now faced, arching her browned body.

"As long as you don't bring them home while Drew's still living there."

She sat up, tossing her green-striped hair. "I'm lustful, not improprietous." She lay back again, smiling. "We play down in Port Arthur. Let me tell you about the last time."

"Don't you have any respect for my Communications and Security people who have to monitor this call?" But the corner of Fontana's mouth twitched.

"They go through this every time," Doubrava said. "It's like a ritual."

"Len, honey, they deserve some break from the domestic drivel they're forced to hear most of the time. Y'all listenin' close now?"

The next five minutes left Janna staring at Fontana's wife in shocked admiration. What stamina and imagination! "Isn't it still illegal to say things like that over the air?"

"No, but I'm surprised the tape doesn't melt," Mama said.

"Interesting" was Fontana's only comment, however. "Can you find paper and a pencil and take down a list of errands I need to have you run for me?"

She sighed. "Don't I always? Mercedes Fontana, maturing Girl Friday, that's me."

Janna stiffened. "Mama! This might be it."

Doubrava blinked. "It's just pick up this and talk to that person. Be sure the dog has his shots. That kind of thing."

"But does the request for errands always follow the porno?"

The turquoise eyes went thoughtful. "You think the list could be code?"

"What better code, and what better timing for it than when everyone is still salivating from the latest chapter of Lady Fontana's Lover?" Mama said. "Exactly what time of day did Chenoweth die?"

Doubrava sucked in his lower lip. "Eleven hundred thirty hours. But . . . I still can't believe Fontana would sell out. Why don't you just put that transcript aside with Geyer's and go on?"

Nothing else looked as promising as Fontana's call, however.

"Anyone interested in eating?" Doubrava asked.

Janna looked up at a wall chronometer to see with surprise that it was past eighteen hundred hours. They had been working without a break all afternoon!

"Can we have something brought in?" Mama asked. "I'd like to get through as many of these today as possible."

Doubrava had Communications call the cafeteria. Janna and Mama moved on to Sunday's tapes.

Fontana made two more calls, but in both cases, there was no transcript, and both halves of the screen showed only static behind the date and time.

"Scrambled calls to Crispus Tenning and the home office," Doubrava explained.

Doubrava called his librarian friend in Denver.

"Interesting woman," he said as the tape started. "There, I thought she was just a vacation playmate, but when these two jons at the next table started arguing about stocks and bonds and the money they were losing, she said, 'I don't know what's so difficult about the stock market. It just takes a wide range of reading and a little commonsense calculation. I'll bet that I could invest a few thousand credits and triple it in six months.' Construction carried heavy hazard pay in those days, so I had plenty of extra credit and I said, 'Apple, you're on.' She *quadrupled* it in *three* months."

On the screen Doubrava and a dark-haired woman with a quiet, madonna-type beauty exchanged a few introductory pleasantries, some sexual innuendos, and then settled into a spirited but interminable and detailed discussion of Doubrava's portfolio.

Janna yawned.

"Stocks would make a good code too," Doubrava said.

Mama peered over the top of his glasses at the assistant chief. "You're not a professional confessor, are you?"

Doubrava grinned. "If you're going to make everyone in the station suspects, you can't leave me out."

Stocks *would* make a good code, Janna reflected, and after a minute, she laid the transcript with the pile of other possibles.

Geyer made her twice-weekly call to her former PSS colleague.

"Men are sons of bitches," she spat.

The bitterness raised the hair on Janna's neck.

Raine DeBrabander, who, like Geyer, looked like someone who should be modeling or should be the darling of the castlerow set, raised golden brows. "What has who done to you this week to get you this fused?"

Abruptly Geyer's face shuttered. She shrugged. "Nothing in particular, I guess. Sometimes I think other people aren't really people to men, just pieces in a game." She paused. "You know what certain members and would-be members of Lanour's board of directors are trying to do; tell me, do you think they deserve anything that happens to them?"

Janna caught her breath and glanced quickly at Mama. He was biting his lip.

DeBrabander leaned toward her screen. "Does Tenning have some dirty tricks he's planning to pull to keep power?"

Geyer's jaw tightened. "I don't think he's even going to attempt a fight. I think he wants his enemies to believe he's resisting, but at the last minute he'll just walk away and let the company go to hell."

"And you and the station with it? That bastard! After all the loyalty you've given him."

Geyer frowned. "I don't blame him. It's the board's fault. The consequences are theirs. If they weren't so—" She broke off, breathing deeply, and when she resumed, it was in a light tone, encouraging girl chatter.

But Janna stood with a chill in her spine and knots in her gut. "She's dirty." Somehow, though, the knowledge failed to bring her the satisfaction that the nearing solution of a case usually did. "The instructions to the agents are in her conversation with her mother somewhere, and now she's trying to justify her actions to herself."

"I won't believe that," Doubrava said.

"The only other explanation I can think of is almost as bad," Janna said. "She knows about the murder and is trying to justify *inaction.*"

The turquoise eyes bored into her. "I won't believe that, either."

Watching the two women on the screen gossiping about their old agency, Mama sighed heavily. "In any case, I suppose we ought to talk to her."

Doubrava drew in a deep breath. "Why don't we pull all her call tapes for the past couple of months and study them first?"

Mama's mouth thinned. "Don't you think she deserves to be confronted directly, so she can defend herself?"

Doubrava frowned at Mama, then at the screen until the end of the call, then nodded with obvious reluctance. He tapped his ear. Janna watched his throat move as he subvocalized. He listened, spoke again, then shook his head at Mama. "She's left the office for the night and is in the Rec pod. Let me go after her. I'll meet you back in Security in fifteen minutes."

Janna watched him sail out of Communications, then turned back to Mama, who stood frowning at the console screen, rubbing the back of his neck. "I'm sorry, Mama." She meant it.

"It isn't right yet, bibi. For a moment there I thought we

had it, but..." His shoulders moved irritably. "If someone had murdered some of the board of directors, we'd have motive galore. There would be reason for everyone looking guilty. They all stand to lose if Tenning does. I can't believe in any of our suspects smuggling just to hurt Lanour, though, despite Geyer's conversation. No, there's something more, something we're not seeing, a piece missing, and this won't make sense until we have that piece."

# CHAPTER
# EIGHTEEN

**Monday, February 5. 20:00:00 hours.**

Janna looked around Communications but did not see the young asian who had been on duty when she and Mama came in, nor anyone who looked familiar, for that matter. Not surprisingly. Even with the station's free-running schedule, the shift must have changed hours ago. Pulling her slippers loose from the carpet, Janna jumped up to the nearest desk to return the tapes and transcript folder.

The thin young woman there started violently, head jerking around from her computer terminal as Janna braked by grabbing a lidded wire basket screwed to the desktop.

"Sorry," Janna apologized. She slipped the tapes and folder in the basket and closed the lid to keep them from drifing away. "I didn't mean to frighten you."

A glittering swirl of nebulas surrounded the clerk's eyes, matched by metallic bronze tipping on her hair. She grimaced sheepishly. "It isn't your fault. I just can't get used to the idea that people hurtling down from the ceiling aren't falling. Sometimes I wonder how I let myself be talked into working up here. Thank god it's only a year." She peered past Janna up to where Mama drifted along the console, peeking over the technicians' shoulders. "You're the troubleshooters from Seever, aren't you? Have you found out yet what made that pressure suit rupture?"

Janna arched a brow. Did some station personnel still be-

lieve that story? Temporaries must not be on the grapevine.
"Not definitely, though we hope to complete our investigation
soon. It was a tragic accident."

"Tragedy is in the eyes of the beholder."

Janna recognized the jolt in her head. Internal reality had
just stumbled over an inconsistency. The leo in her pounced
on it. Casually she asked, "I take it you knew Mr. Chenoweth
and weren't overly fond of him?" she asked casually.

The nebulas around the clerk's eyes sprung into sharp relief
as she flushed. "I'm sorry; that was a snide thing to say,
especially when I didn't know him, not personally. Of course
his death is tragic. He has that new baby and I'm sure his
wife will miss him. On the other hand, I've heard plenty
*about* him." She leaned toward Janna, lowering her voice.
"Not to speak ill of the dead, but it's toads like him who give
us temporaries a bad reputation! He carried around a whole
pocketful of 2-Ds of the baby, but just for coup bait. You
know . . . he'd be all toxy with liquor and talking about how
lonely he was without his dear wife and child, and the next
thing you knew, he was trying to drag you off to his hammock
to 'comfort' him . . . and bouncing you off the walls if you
refused. I heard that once he even tried it on our chief of
Security when she was out of uniform and he was too drunk
to read her badge. She bounced *him* off the walls! He didn't
know how to keep his mouth shut when he was sober, either.
We had to interrupt or terminate several of his calls for security
breeches."

Electricity crawled under Janna's skin, raising the hair all
over her body. Inconsistency, indeed. This was a very different Chenoweth than everyone else talked about. "Mama,"
she called, and sucked in a slow breath before quirking a
brow at the clerk. "What kinds of security breeches?"

The clerk shrugged. "I'm not on the console. I just log the
calls for the personnel records."

Mama appeared not to have heard Janna. He continued to

hover behind one of the console techs, intent on something on a screen.

"Mama," Janna repeated in a sharper tone, and smiled at the clerk. "Do you remember the date of the last time he committed a breech? Distress or anger over being reprimanded could make a man careless."

The nebulas drew toward each other. "I don't remember an incident near his accident. He didn't always call when I was on duty, of course."

"Of course. Mama!" What the hell was so engrossing up there? Janna kept smiling. "Could I see his calls for the week before he died, then?"

"Certainly." The clerk held out her hand.

Janna blinked at it.

"I need to see your authorization from Director Fontana or Chief Geyer."

Damn! Bluff time.

Mama finally responded, drifting down from the console. "You wanted me, bibi?"

What *had* he seen? His eyes glittered in excitement behind his glasses. Janna forced herself to concentrate on the clerk, however. "My authorization? Ms."—she peered at the clerk's badge—"Ms. Kling, we've been in here most of the day reviewing call tapes. Obviously we're authorized."

The clerk hesitated, then tapped the keys of her terminal. From where she stood Janna could not see the monitor, but moments later the clerk's smile became apologetic. "I'm sorry, but Captain Doubrava pulled the tapes earlier. I can page him and ask for authorization for the new ones, though."

"What tapes?" Mama asked.

Switching to Spanish, Janna explain hurriedly.

To her astonishment and irritation, however, Mama showed no interest in the information. His eyes slid away, upward, focusing on the communications console. In English he said, "We don't need to look at any more tapes, bibi. I'm not sure what you thought they could tell us, anyway. Come on. We have an appointment with Chief Geyer in Security." And pushing off from the desk, he sailed across the room and out the door.

Damn the man! Janna followed sputtering. "Maxwell, what the hell is the matter with you? Don't you understand? There's a direct contradiction in how Chenoweth has been described to us. If Chenoweth isn't the sad innocent we've been led to believe—"

"It doesn't make a bit of difference," Mama tossed back over his shoulder. "He died in Titus's suit, not his own. No one could have known he would be wearing it, unless you want to postulate that someone sabotaged his suit so he would be forced to wear Titus's also-sabotaged suit." He used a corridor railing to catch himself so he could turn. "Forget Chenoweth, bibi."

Anger flared in her. Was the bastard blind? Or had whatever he had seen on the console sent him blue-skying?

Fuming, Janna almost missed the words he mouthed soundlessly before turning away again: *Big Brother*.

Anger chilled instantly to caution. Her neck prickled with the feel of the cameras focused on her, and through it, watching eyes and listening ears ... Geyer's or Fontana's. For the benefit of the cameras she continued to scowl for another minute, however, then sighed as she jerked on a railing and sent herself sailing after Mama. "Maybe you're right."

They swung through the door into Security. A hispanic officer stood at a desk just inside. Mama gave her his most disarming smile. "We're supposed to meet with Chief Geyer. Shall we wait in her office?"

The officer glanced around long enough to identify them, then nodded and returned to the sheaf of printouts clipped to her desktop.

They sailed across the office, through the middle of the station holo, and into the inner office.

"About Chenoweth..." Janna began.

"Later, bibi." He headed for the desk. "Watch for Geyer."

"What are you—" she began, and broke off, because it was obvious what he was doing.

Settling his slippers into the carpet, Mama quickly typed on the keyboard below the row of monitor screens. Communications, the reception area outside Fontana's office, the cafeteria, and two corridor scenes came up on the screens.

Janna raised her brows. "When did you learn how to work that?"

"Watching Geyer when I came back here last night after leaving you in Fontana's office."

"What do you hope to see?"

He turned on the sound for the cafeteria. "Maybe how fast the grapevine works. A message came in while I was watching the console in Communications. Crispus Tenning is on his way up for a visit."

Tenning! Coming here? For the second time that evening she felt a jolt inside her head. "This close to the stockholder's meeting, or am I wrong in assuming it's sometime in the next couple of days?"

"You're not wrong; it's tomorrow."

She sucked in her breath. "Then Geyer was right. He *is* walking away without a fight."

In the cafeteria the P.A. came on. At the sound of Tenning's name the clatter of utensils and the roar of multiple simultaneous conversations died instantly. The announcement of the visit fell into the silence of a vacuum. Despite the distortion of the fish-eye focus, Janna had no trouble reading expressions. Behind the service counter and at the tables, personnel stiffened as they listened. Faces drew taut. One young woman started to cry. Several other people crossed themselves.

Janna watched grimly. "I'm surprised he has the guts to come here to say good-bye, though."

"That isn't all that's surprising." Mama pointed at one table where men and women in green coveralls were whooping and hugging each other in unbridled delight.

His fingers raced across the keyboard in letter/number combinations. One after another, the screens switched to other cameras. The same mixture of grim and gleeful faces repeated everywhere. And if the station looked like an ant colony before, it seemed even more so now . . . a galvanized colony. Personnel hurtled along the branch corridors and dived by the dozens down the core corridor, stopping barely long enough to shove their badges into the security slot and let the computer read their retinal patterns.

Janna shook her head. "I wonder what kind of rumors have been circulating. Even a major reorganization shouldn't affect everyone, but they act like they need to squeeze in as much time on their projects as possible." She grinned. "Do you suppose there'll be a mass repeat of the Chelle incident, with the station's entire scientific staff barricading themselves in their labs and refusing to be evicted?"

Mama did not appear to hear her. He leaned across the desk toward one of the monitors, staring intently. "What the hell."

Janna backstroked toward the door to check the outer office. All the officers there had left their normal tasks and were floating in a cluster by the monitor wall, anchoring themselves by holding to the edges of the desks while they watched the screens and talked among themselves in low, rapid voices. Janna kicked off from the door to return to the desk and see what had surprised Mama so much.

The screen of interest showed her nothing unusual at first, just the Level One intersect and the personnel traffic out of the branch corridors and up and down the core. The bustle had thinned a bit but without any lessening of the hurry. Then she noticed the panel colors in the branches and read the signs at the core intersect. Her eyes dropped to the lettering on the bottom of the screen. A-L2. Level Two!

Janna's head jolted one more time. Why were so many people heading for Level Three? And Maintainence and scientific personnel among them? There was nothing down there but corridors and a few pods in the process of—

The thought broke off abruptly as details of the scene sank in, and this time her mind did not jolt. The leo in her reared back, roaring. "Mama," she said slowly, "why do you suppose there's a security barrier instead of just a cautionary warning for a construction area?"

He looked around. The light from the panels in the wall behind him reflected off his scalp but left his face in silhouette, unreadable. "Good question, bibi. Here's a brother to it. Why is talking about construction details of this station a security breech?"

Mama had to be thinking of the German whose tape they had seen that afternoon, and maybe Chenoweth too. What else of a restricted nature could he know about? But the sideleap of reasoning that connected the two just now in that gleaming chocolate head defeated her understanding. There was nothing to do but play straight man for him. "They're using an experimental building process."

Mama snorted. "The Construction crews can see the results, but how much could they know about *how* the spider works, and *why?* No, bibi, there has to be another reason."

A stab of his finger deactivated the row of monitors. He shoved away from the desk toward the wall where he could see the main office. Janna looked out too. The room was deserted except for the hispanic officer. She floated with a toe hooked under the drawer handle on a desk, staring dreamily at the station holo in the middle of the room.

Janna heard Mama's breath catch. "That's it!" he whispered. "Jan, describe that holo. What do you see?"

She stared at him. He was obviously quite serious, but . . . "What do you mean? It's a three-dimensional reproduction of the station."

The wall had no carpet or handholds. Without a stabilizing grip on anything Mama rose slowly toward the ceiling. "How do we know?"

Half a dozen thoughts collided in her head.

Drifting in midair, he continued. "Most of us see only the inside, and not all of that. Even the shuttle pilots can't see much. Remember how wide the solar panels are? Construction is the only group who knows the whole, true form of the station, and they aren't allowed to talk about it."

From the scramble of chaos seeking order, thought coalesced into coherence, into understanding. Janna sucked in her breath. "Level Three."

Mama nodded. The action made his whole body bob gently. "John Paul Chenoweth, who tended to talk too much and was in Construction, died suddenly and violently."

Janna let her breath out again. "You're blue-skying. The trap was set for Titus." Still . . . Something nudged Janna, something she had heard or seen, something that almost made a connection. She groped mentally, scrambling after the half-seen thought, and cursed as it slithered out of her grasp.

"Maybe," Mama said.

The nudge came again. Janna focused all her attention on Mama, waiting for him to continue.

"I can't help but wonder why the crew chief gave Chenoweth Titus's suit instead of using one of the spares that are supposed to replace malfunctioning suits."

Another nudge, sharper this time. Janna bit her lip. Mama's concern bothered her, too, now that he mentioned it, but it was not *the* thing. "Maybe we should invite Carakostas in for a chat too?"

Which reminded her . . . where were Doubrava and Geyer? They should have been here long ago. She peered around the door to check the office again.

"Actions speak louder than words, bibi." Mama frog-kicked and drove back for the desk, where he grabbed the edge to push his feet down into the carpet. Then he reached for the keyboard of the computer fastened to the slightly slanting top.

Janna grinned. Of course. That was much better than asking

someone what they had done. "January twentieth." She sailed back from the door to edge in beside him. "About eight hundred hours."

The tape of the locker room at eight hundred hours showed the room filled with the crew going on duty. A pleasant-looking man in his late twenties stood at Titus's locker pulling on a pressure suit.

"Back it up, Mama."

The tape blurred. The timer jumped to fifteen minutes earlier. Slowed and sent forward again, the tape played for several minutes before Chenoweth entered the locker room. Laughing and joking with other men and women in the crew, he propelled himself down the line . . . straight to Titus's locker. Without hesitation he punched the combination, pulled open the door, and lifted out the pressure suit.

The breath stuck in Janna's chest. "Mama, are you sure we have the right day?"

But the date appeared on the screen next to the time: 01/20/80.

Chenoweth slid into the suit. Still joking with the people on either side of him, he kicked off from the closed locker to sail toward the corridor door.

No thoughts collided this time. No readjustment of reality jolted Janna's mind. The memory that had eluded capture before lay down and rolled over before her . . . Titus coming into the locker room and going straight to one locker before prompting by his companions sent him on to the one she and Mama had been told was "his," the one Chenoweth had just now opened.

Her eyes met Mama's. In them she read the same conclusions she had just reached. With icy anger seeping through her she voiced their thoughts. "We've been skinned. It's all been a lie . . . the trouble with Chenoweth's suit, substituting Titus's. Even the hearing was a fake. Chenoweth *was* the intended victim."

Mama's jaw set grimly. "And everyone here has conspired to keep us from finding that out."

Including Geyer, he meant. Janna sensed that without asking. Or maybe especially Geyer. Chenoweth's behavior on that one occasion would not have given her any great fondness for him. "I wonder if we're dealing with two crimes here, after all, a murder and a smuggler who is making good use of the death." Though toady behavior by itself hardly constituted much of a motive for murder.

"Except that the smuggler knew about the death before it happened," Mama reminded her.

There *was* that—which left them with a problem. "Why should an entire station want to protect a smuggler and a murderer?"

"An interesting question, but I had hoped you'd never ask it," Geyer's voice said.

They snapped around. Janna grabbed the desk for stabilization.

Geyer floated with one hand gripping the edge of the doorway, her face grim.

Doubrava hovered behind her, grinning. "They're good."

Her mouth thinned. "I'm glad you find it amusing, Ian. Use Castaneda to help you take them to detention."

"Detention!" Janna hissed.

The dark eyes flicked over her. "I'm too busy to play games any longer. This way I can be sure of where you are and what you're doing without wasting manpower watching you."

She pulled aside.

Doubrava and the hispanic officer came in through the door past her. Doubrava held out a wrap strap to Janna with an apologetic smile. "I'm sorry it has to be this way. Turn around, please."

"And if I don't?"

"We'll use force," Geyer said simply.

Angrily Janna turned, crossing her wrists behind her back.

The wrap strap circled them, slick and slightly warm on her skin.

The hispanic officer wrapped Mama.

Strapped wrists handicapped movement in zero-gee more than on the ground, but the officers solved the propulsion problem by taking their captives' arms and towing them ... out of the inner office and up through a door in the ceiling into a vertical corridor beyond. The door was transparent, as were all the doors opening into the corridor. It gave the detention section a deceptively open, unprisonlike appearance. The transparency was to make visual supervision easier, Janna knew, and judging by the badge slot and r.r. plate by the outer door, the push-button locks by the others, and the near invisible reinforcement of monofilament mesh that Janna could see inside the material of the doors themselves, the plastic was surely one of the super-impact varieties, as strong as any iron plating.

"It's too bad you're so dedicated to your job," Doubrava said. "This could have been a very pleasant visit."

"It's too bad you want to protect a murderer," Janna countered.

Doubrava hesitated only a moment before shrugging. "The greatest good for the greatest number of people. I'll put you in number five. Maxwell can be across the corridor in six where you can wave at each other."

Janna set her jaw. Once she went in that cell, she might never learn who the murderer was. The problem was how to stop them from putting her in. Or was it? These people might be good at their jobs here, but no lend-lease leo had the time on the street she did.

Mama pursed his lips. "We can be like Ike Garman and his friends, remember, bibi?"

So he had been thinking along the same line she was. Janna bit back a grin. "I remember, Mama."

The deek had come home from his first prison term educated in an entire repertoire of vicious tricks to help him

overpower careless officers even when strapped. He had passed
on his knowledge to his best friends. She and Mama had not
been careless, but they wore bruises for weeks as mementos
of bringing in members of that rat pack.

"Each delivering a message to the other side of the corridor," Mama said.

Doubrava and the other officer let go of their prisoners to
punch the door combinations.

As the doors slid open Janna hissed, "Now, Mama!"

She drew up her legs and kicked out against the wall. It
drove her not into Doubrava, but across the corridor and
headfirst into the spine of the hispanic officer, hurling both
of them into the detention cell. Mama arrowed for Doubrava.

Once in the confines of the cell, Janna had six walls to
use, but one was enough. Her elbow drove into the hispanic
officer's throat, and while the woman writhed choking and
gasping, Janna backed up to the floating form and quickly
searched her for the wrap-strap polarizer. Seconds later Janna
stripped off the strap.

She eyed Castaneda's uniform but decided against taking
it. Too small. Janna relieved the officer of her ear button,
however, and traded badges.

Eventually Geyer would know to trace her by Castaneda's
badge, but in the meantime it ought to buy some freedom.
So would the radio.

She swung out of the cell to find Mama in the corridor
carrying Doubrava's badge and ear button. Her conscience
twinged. "I hope you didn't hurt him seriously."

Mama settled his glasses straight and worked the radio into
his ear. "He'll be fine, I promise."

"Then what now? Visit Fontana? I can't think of anyone
else everyone would want to protect. Or maybe we'd do better
to hole up until Tenning arrives and tell him what we know."

Mama frowned. "I wonder if it's Fontana they're protecting. This station has something very odd going on and, just
like the murder and the smuggling have to be parts of the

same crime, it and the cover-up and keeping us running in circles after this suspect, the other has to be part of everything else too."

"You mean what's on Level Three."

He nodded. "So I think that somehow we'd better find a way to have a look down there."

# CHAPTER
# NINETEEN

<u>**Monday, February 5. 21:10:00 hours.**</u>

Visit Level Three. Janna sucked in her lower lip. "That isn't going to be easy."

Mama shrugged and grinned. "What are two security barriers?"

"Three." She pointed down the corridor at the closed door to the Security office. Beside it, the smoky eye of the r.r. plate mocked them above the badge slot. "That has to be unlocked from this side, too, and then there's the office to cross without being caught."

Something thudded behind Janna. She glanced around to see the hispanic officer gripping the molding of the cell door with one hand and, between coughs, pounding on the plastic with the other.

"That's a problem too," Janna added. "She might make enough noise to attract attention, and sooner or later Geyer is going to wonder why Doubrava's been gone so long. She'll come looking for him."

Mama's teeth gleamed. "Then we'd better leave." He swung into cell five and emerged a moment later towing a wrap-strapped and limp Doubrava by the collar.

Conscience stabbed Janna again. She reached out to touch the darkening patch of a bruise on his temple and frowned accusingly at Mama. "I thought you said you didn't hurt him seriously."

Mama's nostrils flared. "Don't make me the villain. You aren't wasting any concern on her, I notice." He pointed at the officer in cell six.

Doubrava rolled his head, groaning.

"See, he'll be fine." Mama towed him on down to the door. "Watch the office, bibi."

Janna grabbed a handrail at one end of the door for stabilization and peered over the edge of the opening into the room below. It remained empty. She frowned. They needed it that way; still . . . where had everyone gone? The radio in her ear crackled occasionally, indicating activation, but remained otherwise silent. "It's clear."

Pushing Doubrava's badge into the slot, Mama held the security officer by the hair, then lightly slapped his face. Doubrava moaned again. His eyelids fluttered. Quickly Mama turned him to face the retinal reading plate.

Doubrava blinked a couple of times, mumbling. His eyes opened wide. A second later he stiffened, and his eyes snapped tightly shut, but too late. The door hissed aside.

Janna grabbed the edge to keep it open. Doubrava drew a sharp breath, but before he could yell, Mama wrapped a long hand over his mouth and hauled him back toward cell five.

Doubrava struggled, twisting and kicking. With his wrists strapped, however, it accomplished nothing. Mama shoved him in the cell. As the door slid shut behind him Doubrava kicked his way back to it to hover inside with his lips forming words robbed of sound by the plastic barrier. *What do you think you're doing? There's nowhere here to run.*

"Room enough, Captain." Mama blew him a kiss. "Let's go, bibi."

The office below remained empty. Geyer's door was open, but only someone in the doorway itself could see up into the detention section. Keeping high, then, probably gave them the best chance to stay out of sight.

"Stay close to the ceiling," she whispered over her shoulder.

Mama grinned. "I've sneaked through a lot of rooms, but never on the ceiling before."

She stared at him a moment, then grinned back as the mental image struck her. With a last glance toward the chief's door Janna slid through the detention door. Toes digging into the carpet strips and fingers gripping carpet nap and frames of the light panels, she held herself close to the ceiling as she pulled toward the nearest of the file cabinets.

Mama followed.

With the hiss of the detention door closing after him, Janna suddenly felt very vulnerable. If anyone should come in and look up, they had no retreat, no escape. The corridor exit looked a kilometer away.

Heart pounding, she worked cautiously from one file around behind the next, keeping the metal bulk between her and Geyer's door.

The radio broke silence, simultaneously hissing in her ear and from the speaker on the communications panel outside Geyer's office. "Stech nineteen. Edward Zabokrtsky hasn't reported to the cafeteria with the other temporaries. Please locate."

Locate! Janna's heart lurched. Damn! Releasing the edge of the light panel frame she gripped, she kicked off from the file beside her and dived across the room.

"Stech nineteen," the radio repeated.

"Aurora, get that!" Geyer called from her office.

"Nineteen. Hey, wake up, muchacha!"

Janna arched in the air, reaching for a file cabinet passing above her. Her fingers met the metal . . . and slipped.

"Castaneda!"

Swearing silently, Janna clawed at the cabinet. Nails scraping on the metal, she hauled herself up and behind it.

Geyer's head came out of the office door, scowling. "Castaneda, why the hell—?" She broke off, looking around, then up.

Janna dug fingers into the file, slipper toes into the rim of a light panel. Her breath froze in her chest. Would Geyer notice the single eye peering around the file? Was Mama out of sight? She dared not move enough to look for him.

Then that became unimportant. Her heart slammed into her ribs. Geyer was staring at the detention door. "Ian?" With frown deepening, she gathered, obviously to push off to the door.

"Hey, nineteen, is anyone there?" the radio pleaded.

Geyer hesitated, then turned for the radio. She hit the transmit button. "Nineteen here. Locating Zabokrtsky now."

A kick sent her gliding across the room to the holo controls on the monitor wall.

Janna shrank back farther behind the file cabinet until she could no longer see any of the golden woman, only the holo.

Moments later light flashed in a Level One pod. With a blink the enlarged pod replaced the station for a moment. Then the holo returned to normal. Could Geyer really read it that fast? Janna eased back to where she could see again.

Geyer had returned to the communications panel. "Stech. Subject is in C-7-41."

All the while she talked, however, Geyer frowned up at the detention door. Janna braced herself, doubling her legs so her slipper soles brushed against the side of the file. Sure enough, as soon as she punched off the radio, Geyer kicked upward.

The moment Geyer's badge and retinal pattern opened the door and she disappeared through it, Janna shoved off, rocketing for the corridor door.

Mama came right behind and above her.

She resumed breathing again only after they had put a turn of corridor between them and Security's door. Mama's sigh echoed hers.

She did not relax, however. Any second now Geyer would be back at the holo controls, using the transponders to find them. "We'll need to dump these badges, Mama."

"I don't know if that's wise, bibi. We might attract more

attention if we're not wearing any. Why not just go off the map?"

Janna grinned. Unlike many of her fellow leos, when the constant display of her whereabouts occasionally became an annoyance rather than an aid, she had resisted the urge to deactivate her transponders. But now she could finally indulge herself.

Part or all of the blue border must be a photocell to energize the transponder, but where was the transponder itself? Without pausing in movement toward the pod entrance, Janna pinched the badge between thumb and fingers. It thickened faintly in the acute angle of one end.

Just ahead lay the pod door. Mama pointed. "We'll use that."

Traffic continued to be heavy through the corridor beyond. Janna unclipped Castaneda's badge and, holding it behind her, transponder end out, planted her feet in the narrow strip of carpet just outside the door. Mama handed her Doubrava's badge.

"Hold them a little farther away from you and one about fifteen centimeters above the other, bibi."

Smiling at people passing in the corridor, she adjusted the badges' position. At the corner of her vision inside the pod, Mama tapped the control plate.

The heavy doors hissed together, meeting with a reverberating clang that to Janna's horrified ears sounded loud enough to be audible from one end of the station to the other. She fought not to cringe or bolt for cover. Instead she made her eyes wide and turned to stare at the doors along with surprised passers-by. "I wonder how that happened."

The doors hissed open again. Janna snatched up the badges as they floated free. Between her fingers the transponder ends felt thinner.

"Sorry," Mama was saying to an irritated-looking man on the inside. "I hit the controls by accident." Palming Doubrava's badge as Janna slipped it to him, he muttered, "Let's get out of here, bibi."

They joined the traffic resuming its flow along the corridor.

The radio button in Janna's ear carried a stream of chatter between officers rounding up temporaries who had not obeyed an apparent earlier order over the P.A. to report to the cafeteria. She frowned. What the hell were they doing? The big problem, however, was still reaching Level Three. "Have we thought of a way through the security barriers yet?"

A brow rose above the top of his glasses. "Since forcibly using someone else the way we did Doubrava is probably impractical with this many witnesses, maybe we can slip through with a group . . . pretend to put our badges in the slot but keep so close behind someone else that we use their clearance."

It was worth a try.

The corridor opened into the core corridor. Janna looked around quickly for a suitable group.

"There," Mama muttered. "Coming out of the red corridor."

She saw them, three men and two women in vari-colored coveralls. Scientific personnel, probably. Pushing off, she sailed across the corridor after Mama and caught at a railing to fall in behind the scientists.

Geyer's voice cut through the other traffic on the radio, as cold and sharp as a knife blade. "All officers Level One and above, code one thousand."

Janna had no idea what that meant, but the two familiar descriptions that followed let her take an educated guess. "The hunt is on, Mama."

Mama slipped off his glasses and shoved them into a thigh pocket. "Maybe we'd better go down with different groups. They may not recognize us as readily if we're separated."

"Will you be all right without your glasses?"

"I'm not blind. I can see form and color." He squinted noticeably, however.

The scientists unclipped their badges for the security check. Janna started to fall back, then froze, her heart lurching. A blue uniform appeared in her peripheral vision, shooting downward past them. The officer dragged herself to a halt opposite the badge slot and r.r. plate and began looking over the traffic passing her.

"Mama, Security," Janna hissed in warning, and casually reversed direction.

A glance behind her found Mama doing the same. He fell in behind an upbound couple in yellow coveralls. The glance also spotted the Security officer looking her direction.

"Bertroud nineteen," the radio murmured. "I have a possible on that code one thousand, checkpoint Alpha."

Adrenaline pumped its fiery, cold rush through Janna. They were reaching the Level One corridor branches again. She used the railing to swing into the nearest of them.

"Mama. Tag me."

He followed the sound of her voice.

"Code one thousand into *D*."

Janna swore. They had to get out of the corridor. Only, where to go? Those damn cameras were everywhere.

Blue flashed among the coveralls ahead. Janna swore again.

Mama caught at her sleeve. "This way."

They were in the pod before she recognized it as Recreation, and that it appeared deserted. "We're a duck shoot in here," she protested.

But he pushed her toward a door. "Go. Fast."

She found herself in a rest room, mirrors with a cabinet and water-pistol faucets and hot-air dryers beneath her feet, stalls overhead. Had there been rest rooms on the monitors? She could not remember. No lens gleamed in here that she could see, though.

Mama opened the front of his jumpsuit with a rip of velcro.

She stared at him skeptically. "Do you think you become invisible without clothes?"

"Maybe by switching clothes we will. It'll help change our appearance."

Janna stripped too.

"Nineteen, they're not visible in the corridor. They must have ducked into one of the pods."

She had to roll up a cuff on the sleeves and legs of Mama's jumpsuit, but otherwise it did not appear obviously too large, just made her look even thinner and more angular. The bright color, and the sash wound around hair darkened by wetting it down and skinning it back, turned her complexion muddy. In the mirrors she looked very much indeed like a different person.

Geyer's voice said, "Available officers, search *D* pod by pod. Are you listening, leos? You might as well surrender: there's nowhere for you to go."

The irregular green-and-brown pattern of her suit's jungle camouflage pattern changed Mama too. Suddenly he might have been almost any middle-class businessman, albeit a bald one.

Janna grinned at him. "You look positively Establishment."

"I feel drab." He rolled up the sleeves to the elbow to disguise the fact that they ended short of his wrists. The knee-high tops of the slipper socks disguised the mid-shin end of the pant legs.

She cocked a brow. "What's the matter? Do you have a sneaking fear of being ordinary?"

He snorted, but Janna had been reading body language too long to listen to that instead of noticing the microscopic stiffening of his body. Could she have accidentally struck a nerve?

But there was no time now to puzzle on Mama's psyche. She grimaced down at Doubrava's badge on her pocket. The lettering seemed printed in neon. "I wish we had a way to disguise these. If any of Geyer's Gorillas catch sight of them, we're lion meat."

"We'll go down singly, each with a different group. Realistically only one of us needs to make it."

Janna sucked in a long breath. "You make it sound like a suicide mission."

"Who knows." He squinted gravely at her. "A man's been murdered in the course of whatever is going on here, remember."

She remembered. In her ear, officers searching pod D-1 reported their progress to Geyer. Cold bit into her spine. "Try to avoid being number two, okay?"

He grinned. "I didn't know you cared." Then he sobered. "Believe me, if I knew a way around the gauntlet, I'd take it, but we're stuck with that single corridor down."

Around? Did she really hear thunder, or was it all in her head? "Mama!" She grabbed his arm. "There *is* a way around! Maybe. The escape tunnels."

He stared at her, eyes glittering. "Good thinking."

"Except . . . I'm not sure where the tunnels to Level Two are." Janna closed her eyes, straining to picture the station holo. The general shape etched itself clearly on the inside of her eyelids . . . solar panels, corridors, pods. The tunnels, however, shifted, attaching first to this pod, then that.

She hissed in exasperation at herself. A leo should be able to remember details.

"There's one from D-9," Mama said. "We're in D-3."

Janna jerked her eyes open to stare at him.

He shrugged. "Good eidetic memory. Now we just have to locate the entrance to the tunnel from this pod to D-6. As an emergency exit, it ought to be conspicuously marked."

"Still searching D-1. Negative," the radio murmured.

"Also commencing search of D-2," Doubrava's voice said.

Janna set her jaw. "We'd better find that hatch fast. They'll be in this pod any minute." Not to mention the fact that Geyer was probably watching all the monitors for this corridor.

Mama hit the door's control plate and, putting on his glasses, peered out. "It's in Helen's Half Acre."

She edged in the opening above him. Sure enough, an exit

sign glowed red above the entrance to the bar. "Cross your fingers that no one locked up, Mama."

They dived into the corridor and, with one hard pull at a railing, sent themselves rocketing toward the exit sign. Mama rapped the door plate.

To Janna's relief the opening dilated. They swung through into the darkness beyond.

As the door irised closed after them, an electronic signal beeped shrilly in Janna's ear. Geyer's voice snapped, "Code one thousand in D-3, just entering Helen's Half Acre."

Janna swore silently and swam hard for the exit sign that was visible at the far end of the bar. Her searching hands found no door beneath it, however, only a rough, raised, cone-shaped surface. "Damn it, Mama, where the hell is the hatch?" she hissed.

She felt him groping beside her in the darkness. "This is the volcano diorama, remember? It probably—yes, it's hinged."

The surface swung out like a door. Behind it, a dim light came on, showing them a round hatch with a wheel in the center. Janna wanted to whoop. At least there was no complicated system for opening it; it just dogged, like hatches on seagoing ships.

Mama spun the wheel. The bars withdrew smoothly. "Go on, bibi," he whispered as he pulled the door open.

She dived in. And choked. The air lay stale, dead, and cold with the lifeless chill of space. She kicked hurriedly for the far end, following a trail of small lights along the right-hand wall. Behind her, the door clanged shut after Mama.

"They're using the escape tunnel to D-6," the radio hissed.

The line of lights stopped. Janna groped for the door and found a wheellike object on the outside of the other door. Spinning it, however, she could only think: What if they came out into a room full of people?

"What light-wit told them about the tunnels?" Geyer demanded.

Doubrava did not answer, Janna noticed.

The door opened into a short branch corridor. Beyond lay a grid of corridors minus floors and ceilings, canyons with door-pierced cliffs that reached from the top of the pod to its bottom. Janna had followed Doubrava through identical canyons on the way to his quarters. This must be another personnel quarters pod.

"They're in D-6," the radio snapped. "Doubrava, put a guard on the entrance to the other tunnel and the pod door."

"Ten-four."

"Hebrera, bring up the sleeper."

Janna swore bitterly. "Mama, I don't think we're going to make it. We don't even know where the other tunnel is."

He bared his teeth. "Let's ask directions." Unlike the main corridors, the pod had no activity. The only person Janna saw was a young woman in orange-checked overalls coming out of a door up the clifflike wall from them. "Excuse me," Mama called up to her. "Will you come with us to the D-6/D-9 escape tunnel right away? It's very important."

She swooped down to glance at their badges. "Sure. What's happening?"

"No time to explain. We have to hurry."

Swimming rapidly, the Maintainence tech led the way down an intersecting canyon across the pod.

"Ian, damn it, hurry."

"We're almost there."

Three blue uniforms shot around a far corner. Ahead, Janna spotted the red glow of a sign and a circular hatch in the bulkhead.

Mama hurled past the Maintainence tech toward it. "Stay here," he told her, and spun the door wheel.

Janna slid by her too. "There are three more officers coming up the corridor. Go tell them the situation is under control, will you?"

Blinking in curiosity and puzzlement, the tech turned away.

Mama jerked open the tunnel door, and the two of them plunged into more chilly, dark, and stale air.

"You think we can find the down tunnel before the Gorillas head us off?" Janna panted.

His breath hissed beside her. "It's at the point where they could build the shortest possible tunnel, so it'll be on the bottom of the pod, and—"

"Any available officer, guard the D-9/D-12 tunnel."

"And since Geyer apparently hasn't guessed where we're headed," he resumed, "we may just be able to stay ahead of her, despite her monitors."

The guide lights stopped. They burst out of the far end of the tunnel and into more staff quarters and dived down through deserted canyon corridors. Blue flashed above them near the entrance end of the pod. They slid into a cross-canyon out of the officer's sight.

"There," Mama whispered.

The tunnel entrance lay directly below them.

"Doubrava, twenty-one nineteen."

Janna exchanged frowns with Mama. If Geyer was using the Ten Signals, she wanted Doubrava to call the office. Because she had orders she would not risk giving over the radio where their quarry could hear. "We'd better hurry."

No one interfered as they opened the tunnel, however. On the chance that Geyer had somehow managed to lose track of them on her monitors, they dogged the hatch behind them.

The other end of the tunnel opened into a corridor in a laboratory pod. A young oriental woman blinked in surprise at them but, after reading their badges, nodded a greeting. They smiled back and swam past her toward the pod entrance.

Janna listened to the radio. Geyer was ordering all officers but those in D-9 back to other work. She raised a brow at Mama. Could they really have managed to escape? "Where does your eidetic memory tell you the nearest tunnel to Level Three is?"

"The pod below this one, but, bibi"—his forehead

creased—"on the holo, that tunnel and the other one both end blind. If we're wrong about construction down there, we could open the far end and find ourselves breathing vacuum."

Janna's gut knotted. She sucked in a long, slow breath, debating. Should they risk it? With Geyer shaken off their tails, maybe they could go back to the core corridor. Only, traffic to Level Three had been much lighter on the monitors than that to Level Two. It would be more difficult to slip through with someone else. "Vacuum won't kill us instantly. We can just shut the hatch again."

"If we let pressure equalize first . . . and if the rush of air leaving the tunnel hasn't carried us out with it."

She bit her lip. "What do you think?"

"I'm thinking of a number. Is it odd or even?"

She stared. "What?"

"Am I thinking of an odd or even number?"

"What the hell does that have to do with—even." What a hell of a time to be playing games!

"Right. We go."

"I see, a decision based on cool logic." She shivered.

They left the pod cautiously, checking the corridor in both directions. No two-toned blue uniforms appeared among the thinning traffic, however. No one looked their way at all. On the radio, officers in D-9 reported a negative search of the pod. Using deliberate haste, Janna and Mama dropped down into the pod entrance on the bottom of the corridor. Signs inside guided them to the tunnel.

Janna undogged the hatch and swung it open without hesitation, but once inside, following Mama and the guide lights through the suffocating air and darkness, her gut knotted. Did they dare open the far hatch?

She felt Mama hesitate ahead. In her mind's eye his hands froze on the wheel. "Odd or even, bibi?" he asked softly.

Jesus. She swallowed. "Odd."

Metal slid against metal as he turned the wheel. "Find somewhere to anchor yourself."

Her fingers wrapped tightly around the tubing carrying the guide-light wires. She held her breath.

Mama swing open the door.

Light and warmth and fresh air flooded in.

The flood of relief left Janna limp. Shakily she released the tubing and pulled herself out of the tunnel.

"Welcome to Level Three," Geyer's voice said above them.

Janna looked up. A dozen blue uniforms hovered against the bulkhead there, one with the bullhorn-shaped sleeper pointed straight at Mama and her. It was the pod that made her stare, however. Though she had not known quite what to expect, it had not been this, the canyon corridors of living quarters. "Will you tell us what the hell's going on?"

"That's restricted information," Geyer said.

"She doesn't need to tell us, bibi," Mama said. "I think the answer is obvious now. It's a revolution."

# CHAPTER
# TWENTY

<u>**Monday, February 5. 22:50:00 hours.**</u>

Revolution! Janna stared at Mama.

"That's absurd," Geyer said coolly, and tapped her ear. "Nineteen, tell Fontana I have them."

Absurd? Above Janna, the stiffening of several other officers belied that.

Mama said, "Is it? We have a space station actively recruiting personnel to whom Earth and gravity are frustrating and limiting, and picking very carefully, very selectively, over the temporary staff members who apply for permanent assignment. The permanent staff talk about people on Earth as though speaking of another species, and all have knowledge in secondary disciplines, either biological or technological. Your greenhouses are bursting with home-grown food. You're pushing your biologists to develop sources of protein. Level Three construction has restricted access. All construction is censored from calls and mail, construction that turns out to be, at least partially, living quarters. Add to that the company president whose pet project in this station is just walking away from a proxy fight that will lose him control of the company and the station. Except that he's coming here for a visit first, and that news not only generates a great deal of activity but leads to the temporary staff being put in custody. For deportation?"

Geyer's eyes narrowed. "You're quite a creative thinker,

just as Lieutenant Vradel warned me. Maybe dangerously creative. Brainbent."

Janna watched the others, particularly Doubrava, who hovered slightly behind and above his chief, grinning in delight. Mama might be brainbent, she reflected, but he was not wrong. When she added up his list, she reached the same conclusion. "Tenning isn't walking away at all, at least not from anything he cares about. You've reached the point of self-sufficiency, and he's joining you for the declaration of independence."

"And no doubt bringing along families of permanent personnel," Mama added. "That's who these quarters are for."

"They're both very good, Bane," Doubrava said. "Why not tell them? What harm can it do?"

She spun to look up at him. "Harm! You're a fine one to talk about harm." She turned back to Janna and Mama. "Let's go."

An officer with a Mohawk haircut, the same officer they met at the security point below Level One that first day, gestured with the sleeper toward a circle of light at the bottom of the canyon.

Janna remained clinging to the door of the escape tunnel, staring past the sleeper toward Geyer and Doubrava. "No wonder all of you seemed guilty. You are. There's one who's guiltier than the rest, though . . . a killer."

Doubrava looked back unflinchingly, but Geyer's mouth clamped in a grim line. "I said, let's go. Keep the sleeper on them, Hebrera."

Janna swam ahead of the officer with the sleeper, down through the pod—another torus, she saw—and into the Level Three corridor. They reached the core corridor minutes later. Personnel there took one look at the sleeper and flattened against the side of the shaft, leaving a broad path for prisoners and captors all the way to Level One, where Geyer motioned them into the blue *B* corridor.

"Attention," the P.A. said. "Estimated time of shuttle arrival: fifteen minutes."

The Security officers grinned in excitement. "It'll be over soon."

"Just beginning, actually," Geyer said with a thin smile.

"Nineteen, Chief," Janna's ear button murmured. "Director requests you bring the leos to his office."

"You come, too, Ian," Geyer said. "The rest of you go back to your stations. There'll just be two of us with you, leos, but don't try anything or, by god, I swear I'll break your damn necks."

Janna believed her.

The four of them left the corridor at the Administration pod.

Fontana waited for them in his office, a questioning light in the amber wolf's eyes. Earth shone across the ceiling in majestic, dazzling beauty.

Geyer sighed. "They reached Level Three, and I'm afraid they've figured some of it out."

Fontana shrugged. "No matter. They'll be on one of the shuttles soon and out of our way."

"On a shuttle? To Earth?" Janna asked in surprise.

Fontana looked surprised in turn. "Of course. You're going back along with the temporary staff who declined our invitation to stay, or whom we haven't chosen to invite along."

"Along?" Mama said. "You're leaving orbit?"

Doubrava grinned. "They're *very* good."

Geyer frowned but Fontana nodded. "They are. Yes, sergeant, we're leaving orbit. Part of the construction is a drive system we've developed. We're going to set up our factory and mining operations out where the resources are, the asteroid belt. This station was planned with the intention of expanding it from a research facility to include a factory/colony, but the board of directors refused to let us move on to that phase. Too much too fast, they said. Too expensive. Not cost-effective."

"So you and Tenning expanded secretly," Mama said.

He nodded. "Unfortunately, certain board members became suspicious of where some of the corporation funds were being spent, and a showdown became inevitable. Crispus decided we'd better pick up our marbles and leave the game."

Ginneh Nakashima stuck her head in through the door. "Mr. Tenning's shuttle is docking, Mr. Fontana."

Fontana grinned. "The hour of liberation is at hand."

Anger boiled up through Janna. "It's a wonderful game to you, isn't it? No harm done?"

Fontana's grin faded. "I've tried to keep it to a minimum."

"Murder is an acceptable minimum?"

The wolf's eyes narrowed. "That was accidental. It wouldn't have happened if I'd known ahead of time that that was how D—how the spider plans were to be smuggled out."

Cold sank into Janna's spine. In changing the sentence, Fontana had glanced quickly, almost imperceptibly, toward Ian Doubrava.

Doubrava? She stared into the turquoise eyes, her stomach jerking into a tight knot, followed by a flood of ice and fire. "You?" Her voice rasped. *"You* killed Chenoweth?"

The brilliant eyes met hers calmly, devoid of guilt or remorse. "He found out more about Level Three than temporaries are supposed to know. With his mouth it was just a matter of time before he said something in front of the wrong people and gave everything away. Besides, he wasn't much of a loss. A very unpleasant toad and insulting toward my commanding officer."

The anger burned deeper in Janna, anger against Doubrava's cold-bloodedness, anger at herself for not seeing what he was: a sociopath.

Mama's eyes narrowed. "You were part of the station plans and were still spying for Uwezo?"

"I'd found out about the plans, of course, but I wasn't part of them until Bane found the secret cameras I'd planted in the labs and the director, here, persuaded me to join The

Cause. By that time I'd already told Uwezo about the spider. I stalled as long as I could, but I had to deliver it, with the smuggling looking genuine and no convenient leaks in security, to keep the bright, ambitious people who run Uwezo from getting suspicious and using their other sources in Lanour to poke around. The Lanour account that I funneled all my credit into to help with the construction here isn't so obscure that they couldn't find it and learn what we're up to."

Then the long calls about stock were a code, after all, Janna reflected angrily. How like the arrogance of a sociopath to risk suggesting that to her and Mama, sure that they would never take him seriously or break the code if they *did* suspect him. But how had Uwezo paid him? The security check on him would have found any unaccountable source of income.

A moment later the answer came to her. Of course. The stock portfolio. No doubt the first payment had been barter goods, such as jewelry or precious metals, to redeem for credit and start the portfolio. After that Uwezo could use its spies in other corporations to learn tips they passed on to their librarian agent, who then helped Doubrava grow rich on perfectly legitimate investments Uwezo's name could not be linked to. The African multinational had to be congratulated for setting up its agent so far ahead of time and for finding such a good agent, too . . . witty and charming and unable to look guilty because he lacked any conscience to make him feel guilt.

Janna said, "So you believe that the end justifies the means when it concerns your station colony, Mr. Fontana?"

Fontana grimaced. "Believe me, neither Chief Geyer nor I suspected how Doubrava intended to smuggle the plans out. We were shocked and enraged when you told us Chenoweth had been murdered. Up to then we thought the only trickery had been the planting of that false report tape in the phone lines with a timer, so he would have an excuse for leaving

Officer Lowe alone to fumble the exit examination of the body."

"Yet you still did nothing after you'd learned about him?"

"What *could* I do? Legally I'm an accomplice and as guilty as he is." Fontana glanced at Doubrava, who studied the image of Earth on the ceiling, ignoring the conversation. "It's better he come with us, anyway, where he can't do any more harm."

"Just betray you, just as he's betrayed Uwezo, if it's to his own benefit," Janna said flatly. "Sociopaths are like that."

Doubrava pulled his gaze away from the ceiling to smile at her. "Sociopaths burn out. Dr. Freeman says that's happening to me, that I want to come in and join the human race. It's how Mr. Fontana recruited me, by offering me a home."

Janna ignored him to keep frowning at Fontana. "And this is the kind of person you want in your colony?"

Fontana sighed. "Sometimes there's no choice. I'll be responsible for him, Sergeant. If he kills again, we'll deal with it."

Nakashima looked in again. "Mr. Tenning is disembarking."

Relief swept the director's face. "I'll go right up to meet him. Chief Geyer, will you see our guests safely aboard the shuttle? I've had their luggage packed and sent up to the loading area." He smiled at Mama and Janna. "Sergeant Maxwell, Sergeant Brill, I'm sorry y'all had to be dragged into this. Have a pleasant flight back. Oh, Sergeant Maxwell, we're shipping Lanour our research results and all the catalysts and drugs we've produced, a two-year supply of some, but I'd be mighty grateful if you'd see these other items are delivered groundside." From a compartment in his desk he brought out a shoebox-size carton and handed it to Mama.

Then he pushed off around them, out of the office.

"Let's go too," Geyer said.

Doubrava smiled. "Good-bye. I'm sorry about how things

ended, because it's really been a pleasure to meet you." He held out his hand.

Janna ignored it and sailed past him for the door.

In the core corridor they swam upward past a stream of men, women, and children coming down, eyes wide in awe. She ignored them, too, as well as the dazed-looking temporary staff who pulled themselves into the shuttle with her.

Geyer saw them to their seats and belted in. "I—I wish I could say it's been a pleasure, too, but I won't lie. But I hope you'll believe me when I say I regret that we didn't meet under other circumstances. I do admire you both, despite the trouble you've caused me. You didn't let yourselves be intimidated or sidetracked. You're the kind of officers my father would have been proud to work with." She smiled at Mama. "Perhaps we'll meet again someday."

Mama sighed as the golden woman disappeared up through the hatch. "If Providence is kind . . ."

"They're getting away with murder, Mama," Janna said bitterly.

He turned his head to peer through his glasses at her. "Does that really upset you so much, or is it that you liked him and he betrayed you by not being what you thought he was?"

"Don't be a light-wit, Maxwell!" But the remark stung.

As though sensing that, he smiled. "Let's face it, bibi, we're both unlucky in love. We still have each other, though." He patted her hand.

She grimaced. "Is that supposed to be a consolation?"

"Casting off," a voice said from the top of the cabin.

As the shuttle slid away from the station, Janna stared out the port at it, a bubbly black silhouette floating against the blue-and-white glory of Earth.

Anger hissed through Janna. "It isn't right, Mama."

"Maybe not, but . . . don't we often ignore some crimes, like the slighs jacking that hearse, to go after bigger ones?"

She jerked around to glare at him. "My god. This isn't

anything like letting the slighs go. What bigger crime can we possibly go after than a killer?"

"Well." His eyes glittered. "I just took a peek into this carton, and there's a bunch of envelopes just about the size to hold an octodensity minidisk, each addressed to a different corporation. I don't recognize all the names, but they're international, and the ones I do know are involved in aerospace."

She stared at him. Her breath caught. "The spider?"

He grinned. "I wouldn't be surprised, and maybe plans for the propulsion system too. Uwezo will have only a couple of weeks start on them, and no drive. Now, if some corporation sets up a monopoly out there, it won't be by default." His grin broadened, teeth gleaming in the darkness of his face. "I think we're about to see a race, bibi, first for platform space, because I doubt the spider will work in a gravity field, and then to the asteroids, and we get to fire the starting gun. All the colonial moratoriums and exit-tax extortion of Senators Early's and Thayers's campaigns will collapse. Maybe the spider can even make colony ships affordable to slighs. I can see a host of applications for spider-woven products Earthside too. How about for low-income housing modules? In the long run everyone will benefit." He paused. "Is that a reasonable trade for one murderer?"

Janna debated, staring out the port at the shrinking station. "No."

"Yet you accuse *me* of clinging to idealism." Mama shook his head. "Admit it, bibi; deep down you, too, still think you can save the world from itself."

"It isn't justice," Janna continued firmly, "but I don't know what I can do about it." She sighed bitterly. "So I'll live with it."

Mama cleared his throat. "Speaking of living with . . . it occurs to me that I still have a housing problem facing me when we land. Now, you have an empty bed you let me use the other night—"

"What!" She stiffened so abruptly, she strained at the seat belt holding her. "No! Do you see me wearing a sign that says 'stupid'? I'd be over the brainbow in a week!"

"How about just until I find another place, then? I'm a top-star cook."

"I'm more concerned about your housekee—" she began, but broke off as she glanced out the window. The space station had shrunk to a knobby dot. Watching it vanish into the glowing blue of its Earth backdrop, she reflected that a man could have worse faults than Mama's. "All right. I'm probably wickers. I'm sure I'll regret this for years to come, but . . . you can stay at my place until you find an apartment."

He grinned.

"*Just* until you find another place."

"Absolutely."

"You have to promise me you won't go around straightening things all the time."

"Word of honor, bibi."

*And I have this seaside property on Mercury I'll let you have cheap,* Janna thought wryly. What the hell, though. She could take it for a while. Partners had to stick together.